I prefer Jessie but I am one of many; I am a mother, a daughter, a lover and a friend.

Simply put, I am just Jess, no more no less.

I write this not only to prove to myself I can do it, but for my sons.

No matter what the journey brings or provides you, if you want to be something or do something, you are the only one that can give you your future.

THE SECRETS OF WILDERFORT CASTLE

JESSICA JAYNE WEBB

THE SECRETS OF WILDERFORT CASTLE

Vanguard Press

A CIP catalogue record for this title is
available from the British Library.

ISBN 978 1 80016 352 2

*Vanguard Press is an imprint of
Pegasus Elliot MacKenzie Publishers Ltd.*
www.pegasuspublishers.com

First Published in 2022

**Vanguard Press
Sheraton House Castle Park
Cambridge England**

Printed & Bound in Great Britain

Acknowledgements

It has taken much encouragement through the years to finally have this on published paper. I would like to acknowledge everyone who has helped me on my way, with proofreading, ideas, and giving up their time in this venture. There are too many to name (apart from some of the ones below), but you know who you are and I appreciate you!

Just some to name: Frank, Willow, Mum and Dad, Phillipa Wilson, Ellie, Adam, James, Celia, Kate Spencer, my lecturer for English literature who first started me on this journey six years ago.

I love you all, know how special you are, know how special you are to me.

Introduction

Agatha was a child of three when her Aunt Natalie took her in. Her father was long out of the picture, presumed dead, and her mother had passed through circumstances unknown to her.

Agatha had been dropped at the Wilderfort estate by the police, where her Aunt Natalie waited with open arms, loving her like her own. Her aunt was a wild, charismatic woman with many admirers who worked for her. She was always smiling and made Agatha's childhood a happy one.

Aunt Natalie used to tell amazing bedtime stories weaving tales of lost treasure and hidden trap doors, daring escapes, wars of worlds, and guardians of magic.

Aunt Natalie would say to Agatha as a child that magic would bring them out of her, the imagination coming from their love and link together. Aunt Natalie would laugh and say it felt supernatural, grinning, and winking at her.

At night, the memory of Aunt Natalie's tales would trouble Agatha. Sometimes nightmares would wake her sweating, with tears running down her face. Aunt Natalie would come to calm her, she would tuck her back into bed, with the promise of no more stories, but was only told by Agatha the next night that she wanted more.

In her youth, Agatha rejected the idea of taking over the estate and wanted to experience life, a scenario her aunt was not happy with. They fought many times over this notion until the day came. Agatha ran — she ran to start her own life and make her own way she wanted the life she chose. But it wouldn't last. It never does.

Chapter 1
From the present to the past

Agatha, a young adult of seventeen, was told to sit down in the kitchen as she had visitors. She was a slender girl with a slight tan, quite tall for her age and with beautiful long, thick auburn hair tied back in a loose plait with a ribbon. Looking around, she felt nervous, not sure if she was in trouble. It was when the police had walked in, she knew something had happened.

The police sat with her at the table. The kitchen staff offered tea and biscuits. Agatha, still in her maid uniform, sat sullen, knowing the news was bad. "We need to cut to the chase, Miss Wilderfort, it's about your aunt…"

Her head shot up. She looked from one to the other as the news of Aunt Natalie's passing was shared. The angry tears rolled down her face, as she was informed of what happened. Agatha swallowing hard, knowing what would lay ahead of her and the gravity of never seeing her aunt again.

Pollyanna, a younger maid, hugged her as Agatha wept. "Oh Agatha, I'm so sorry, I'm so very sorry." Pollyanna sat down next to her rubbing her back. The police stood. They offered their apologies and condolences in the typical awkward fashion of those in their shoes, walking backwards as they left through the way they had come. Agatha watched them exit the house through the servants' entrance visible from the kitchen. As soon as they were out of sight, Agatha stood and went out of the room. She left Pollyanna standing, stared after her.

Agatha cried the most of that day, more than she had when her mother had passed.

Her employers were graceful about her leaving as Agatha had packed up her life, with her trunk and bags in tow. Her employers hired a carriage for her journey to the station.

From the window of the carriage, Agatha waved goodbye to her friends, fellow staff, and her life in one of the many fancy, Victorian houses that littered the streets of London.

Her journey began with retracing the steps she had taken as a young adult, racing away from a life she did not want to live. The life her aunt lived alone, cut off from the world.

Being the last of the family line and now the sole carer of the Wilderfort estate, her rightful position was set out for her as the keeper of Wilderfort castle. Regret in leaving the life she had paved was bittersweet. She would not step foot in London again for many years to come.

It was not long before Agatha after years of absence stood on the driveway of the dilapidated estate. She looked up at the remains of the castle before her. Her trunk had been lost in transit and Agatha was left with only her carry-on luggage. She felt out of place, and alone, the exact feeling she escaped when she had run away those few years before.

Waving goodbye to the carriage as the taxi ambled away, she still held the paperwork from the lawyer's office. Not moving, she took in the five-storey castle with leadlight windows reminiscent of the cathedral ruins that had previously embodied the grounds. Her mind careened to what next, what she needed to do, and how she was to do it.

As she stepped forward, Agatha fumbled for the keys in her travel coat. Moving towards the steps, she fought the brambles that camouflaged the front entrance.

"Oh my God, you are already fighting with me, you stupid, stupid house." Agatha was frustrated, but thankful her coat had not been torn, and faced her next obstacle — the giant oak doors that loomed over her, with bulky iron fastenings dull and rusty from age.

"How did you survive here alone?" Agatha remarked forlornly, the feeling of wind stirring behind her. She felt the temperature drop as she forced the lock and pushed the heavy doors inwards. Panic enveloped her, she whimpered and Her voice was drowned out through the rush of wind as the heavy doors opened wider. A storm was brewing with strange purple-hued clouds that were billowing closer to the castle. No one could have heard her scream even on a still day. That feeling chilled her. the hairs on the back of her neck rose.

Closing the heavy oak doors was an effort as the winds were rising with the storm. Agatha turned, panting, and was greeted with layers of dust and a vast dark hallway. Her footprints were clearly seen even in the darkness that closed in behind the doors. She looked down and a second set of marks were just visible on the floor.

"Must have been the people that took Aunt Natalie away," Agatha stated out loud. Sadness washed over her as she stared at the floor. She rubbed her arm in a nervous stance. She broke out of her reverie and looked up to the broken chandeliers, over to the holey floor, to ceiling drapes and the eerie light shining through them. A low creeping feeling of dread had risen inside her as realisation hit.

"Well, you finally got me back here, Aunt Natalie. What now?"

Chapter 2
The Castle

It was the smell that woke Agatha out of her rough sleep, the smell of old and mustiness. She was sleeping in her childhood room, the only one that seemed familiar. Agatha had been at the Castle a week; during the day, she would walk through the empty rooms where she relived her memories of the past.

Agatha was avoiding the inevitable, knowing the papers the lawyer had given spelled out the restoration of the Castle as part of her takeover. Agatha knew her aunt had been eccentric, but this!

Restoring a heap of old curtains, forgotten rooms and piles of rock that looked like they needed to be shipped away and dumped rather than repaired!

In the kitchen, Agatha ate the last of the stale bread and drank the last of the black tea when booming echoed through the Castle.

She spilt the tea down her front as the chair fell back from her standing.

Agatha rushed to the giant oak doors. Opening them, she found a man was standing there. He offered his hand to her.

"Good morning, madam, I am Lord Caspian." He took a glance at her attire, pulled his hand away and coughed. "My apologies, I am looking for the new owner of Wilderfort."

Agatha blinked, a bad feeling had stirred in her. "I am she, Caspian." Disdain was already building in her for this impertinent man.

"*Lord* Caspian, my dear," he corrected her as he looked her over again with a smirk on his face. "My apologies, I mistook you for the maid."

Agatha's mind screamed, *Argh, you hateful man!*

She smiled her sweetest smile and pushed down the desire to slam the door in his face.

Looking past him, she could see the carriage he had come in, a black shiny carriage which had a smart blue hue as the light shone on it. A tall man had been standing next to it. His driver, she presumed.

His beady black eyes seemed piercing and had given her the chills when they locked eyes. Breaking away Agatha looked back at Caspian, whom she felt was an overdressed idiot in a tan suit with tails, a blue shirt and matching hat.

Agatha sighed. "What can I do for you Caspian?"

Anger flared briefly on his face. He corrected her again. "*Lord* Caspian, my dear." He pushed past her through the doors and pulled out his handkerchief to cover his nose and mouth as he looked around the entranceway. "Found any treasures or secret passages yet, miss, um, what was your name? I didn't catch it,"

16

Lord Caspian said with the persona of someone talking to their shoes as they picked the crap off with a stick.

"My name is Miss Wilderfort, Mr. Caspian, and yes, I am the new owner of the estate."

Anger flared in Agatha at his manner. She looked at her nails to reflect his disdain, picking out the dirt from underneath them, an attempt to regain her composure of a woman required for her new station of class which she had inherited.

"I do not like your tone or manner in which you are speaking, Caspian." Agatha attempted to temper her anger towards him. "If you don't like *my* manners, then you can walk back the way you came, Mr. Caspian."

An aura of shock flared over Lord Caspian. Obviously not used to being spoken to in this manner, calming as quickly as he flared, he politely bowed his head toward her, looked her dead in the eyes and replied, "Miss Wilderfort, I apologize for my behaviour. I honestly thought you were the maid."

Liar! screamed through Agatha's mind, making her heart race with anger, although she kept silent and showed only a small change in manner.

Lord Caspian continued with a smirk that indicated he knew the effect he created, teasing her and testing her boundaries

"Please, Miss Wilderfort, let me start again, I am Lord Caspian, Lord of the Wilderfort township. I came to make myself known to you, and offer help wherever you need it, while you settle in." He held out his hand again.

Not wanting to cause enemies, Agatha sighed and took his hand and instantly regretted it, as he pulled her close to him, she nearly lost her balance. He was so quick she didn't realise what had happened until she registered how bad his breath was. Unsuccessful in pulling her hand back, Agatha said, "Lord Caspian, let go of my hand. I may interpret this as a threat." Her eyes viciously glared at him and he grinned, loosening his grip.

Agatha pulled her hand away and stepped back, rubbing her hand, and pointed him to the front door. "I think this is your cue to leave, Lord Caspian." She spat his name out so angrily Agatha could feel her body shake in saying his name.

He politely bowed. "Now I have made myself known, Miss Wilderfort, please know I wish for our introduction to be of a positive one. I can help if you wish to restore this castle, although it would probably be better to destroy it, something I can also help with." He smiled at her.

"I need nothing from you, Caspian. Get out." Speaking through gritted teeth, Agatha calmly walked to the doors, pointing her hand outside and motioning him to leave.

As Caspian walked towards them, he walked so closely to her she could smell death on him. It fills her nostrils, and she turned away. Caspian side-stepped closer to her. He was sniffing her.

"Oh, what are you doing? Get out of my house, get out!" She screams at him and pushes him through the door leaving no time for his reply. Agatha slammed the doors, breathing heavily and shaking. Even though the doors were thick, she could hear him laughing.

"Agatha," he said, in a high trilling voice taunting her. "I do look forward to seeing you again. With no man with you, you will have difficulty in hiring staff. I can be of use to you, you know. You are so very alone out here, so far from town."

Hoping for calm, Agatha went to the window and carefully peeked through the curtain. She watched Lord Caspian enter his carriage assisted by the footman.

He was an unusual man, sickly thin with a top hat elongating him even further, his eyes as dark as night. As he looked around, Agatha felt him stare at her with those horrifying black eyes. No white could be seen but she felt the glare. Agatha couldn't take it and moved to hide her face in the wall next to the window.

Agatha knew he was right. She needed a male counterpart, living as she did alone in her new position was questionable at best for her young age and for her new status, Agatha needed one fast if she was to keep a low profile, she didn't want to become any more of a centre stage for gossip than she may already have become.

Partnership in any form with that man seemed a dangerous agreement, one Agatha did not wish to encourage. She knew she had the strength to do this alone but the contrast from living the life of a servant to then becoming a Lady of a castle overnight was a huge obstacle; not only did she feel out of her depth, but also lost within her new role.

Chapter 3
The New Crew

"It's time," Agatha remarked to the empty room after drinking enough water to sink a ship.

After spending the remainder of the morning hiding in her bedroom, Agatha had built up the courage to venture downstairs, into the kitchen.

"It's time," Agatha remarked again. She placed the cup in the sink and put her jacket on.

Grabbing her lawyer's notes and money clasp, she paused, she needed another friend here quickly pulling some paper out of one of the kitchen drawers Agatha writes a quick letter.

'*Dearest Pollyanna,*

I'm sorry I haven't written sooner, it's been overwhelming coming to terms with what I must do here, I know you have employment, and you are happy there, but could you be happy with me, here?

I need a friend, and I also need a housekeeper who I can trust. I have enclosed some money; this can be for your travel if you decide to join me.

I hope you come.

Much love

Agatha.

Folding the letter into a spare envelope from the drawer along with a few pound notes, Agatha filled in the remaining details, picked up her things and walked out the Castle, deeply breathing the fresh air around her. She listed her needs from the town out loud. "Castle history or maps, clothing, shoes, food order and delivery, building crew…" She stopped mid-list.

"What am I doing? Why did you leave me with so much, Auntie?" Agatha looked out at the overgrown fields on either side of the driveway.

"I can't do this alone. I'm not like you." Tears welled up as she coughed and took deep gulping breaths to stop the tears falling. "I can do this, I can do this, I can do this." Agatha willed herself to move and walked the rest of the way to the town, reciting the list to keep her mind busy.

As she began to see the houses start to thicken, it was not long until she could clearly see the township in the distance.

On the outskirts of the town, it was a mixture of stares or smiles from the townsfolk, creating mixed feelings for Agatha, who already felt awkward but knew she needed food badly.

Among the many other items on the list.

Moving towards the apothecary clearly signposted, 'Maybelle's Apothecary' with a caged bird outside, Agatha stopped and smiled at the tiny yellow bird.

When she went inside the shop, the staff were wary of her but served her with the teas she needed as that nightly purple storm really made for poor sleep.

Walking out of the shop she looked up and was hit with glaring!

The staring-while-not-staring scenario was replayed with three-quarters of the passers-by as Agatha made her way further into town.

One gentleman, by the quick look Agatha gave him, walked out of his shop with his white shirt and armbands, greased and shiny hair.

He leaned against the doorway of his barbershop watching her with an intense interest, making her very nervous indeed.

Agatha did what she only knew she could do. She walked ahead and kept walking, acting as if the world was a wonderful place.

She furrowed her forehead and was captivated by every small detail of the town, except those on the faces of the townsfolk.

Agatha had had enough and looked for a new shop to hide in by diving into the first door that opened. It was fortunate that this particular shop was one she needed to check her first item off her list. A bookstore — she had hopes for the castle history and plans, and some relief in the shop keeper being nice in nature, unlike what she had met outside.

Bookshelves were overflowing. Some books were sitting on top of shelves, some books propped against the shelves and some even looked as though they were holding the shelves up.

Distracted and amazed by the vast collection of books crammed into every opportunistic place throughout the shop, Agatha walked straight into a young man.

"Oh! I'm so sorry!" Agatha blushed.

She looked over his tidy fitted style of dress, the way his hair flicked at the left side while parting to the right, his tall lean body.

He gave the impression of knowing how good he looked but Agatha also felt he was still down to earth and humbled by his surroundings.

With a grin on his face the young scholar introduced himself. "Good afternoon, you must be the newcomer, Miss Wilderfort." He offered his hand to her.

Agatha, blushing, took his hand and he kissed it. "My name is Charles, Madam. Charles Ignacio." He dropped her hand and bowed, making Agatha giggle.

"How do you do, Miss Wilderfort? What brings you here to my end of the world?" Charles grinned all the while looking straight at her, encapsulating her.

"Ah! Yes, I am she. So, I gather this is the right place for property history and plans." Agatha tried to maintain calm, but her heart was racing. She went to move further into the shop past Charles and nearly tripped on a book on the floor. Charles reached across to steady her, which again enflamed her cheeks and neck as she looked up at him, so very close now.

Clearing her throat and stepping back with a bashful smile on her face, Agatha shook her head to gather her thoughts,

"I know a lot about your estate, Miss Wilderfort, and your family history. I can explain it if you like."

Smiling, Agatha replied, "Thank you, Charles but unfortunately, I'm not here for my family history, although that would be a great future conversation. I am here to source the property plans."

Charles beckoned Agatha towards the back of the shop. "You do realise your family began this township." Agatha grinned as Charles began offloading some of his knowledge to Agatha.

"There was a great fight between Lord Caspian and your great-great-great grandfather."

Agatha stopped. "Charles, that would make Caspian over two hundred years old. That's not possible."

Charles stopped and looked at Agatha. He frowned a bit but smiled and kept talking, ignoring the question entirely. "Your ancestors were guardians, Agatha," Charles glances over to look at her before turning back to count the bookshelves.

"I really appreciate your history lesson, Charles, but I have a lot to get done today and I really need to get to my next stop."

Charles stopped abruptly, turned and looked at Agatha. She stepped back and walked into a bookshelf. Charles moved towards her and reached his hand past the back of her neck. Agatha gasped then heard the sound of paper scraping off the bookshelf.

Charles pulled off the scroll, cheekily grinning at Agatha briefly. "Here you are, floor plans of the castle and outlying grounds of the estate. May I ask what you need them for?"

"Well," Agatha hesitated a bit. "I have been given the task of restoring the castle. It's part of today's errands to find a restoration crew and a male counterpart..." She trailed off with the last comment and looked at the floor.

Charles grinned. "Well, why didn't you say so? I know just the crew that could help, a lovely lot, plus they used to work for your aunt."

The last comment made Agatha's head shoot up. "Can you take me to them, Charles?"

He nodded. "They are a burly bunch, but I'm sure we can manoeuvre through their introductions without a hitch. They are on the other side of town."

They looked at each other. Agatha stared at his eyes, taking in the depth of the greys with blues, and black topped with silvery flecks — so unusual.

Once she realised how long she had stared at him for, Agatha blushed and looked away. Charles cleared his throat and took Agatha's hand, moving towards the front of the shop collecting a book at the end of the row. "Some history for you as well, Miss Wilderfort."

Charles wiggled the book and the scroll towards Agatha.

A bigger pile of books resembling a mountain, became clearer for Agatha, moving through to the front of the shop, a curious gap became visible in the mountain, as Charles pulled her closer to it. It showed a small old man in giant glasses with huge eyes behind them. He smiled in a shy manner, looking down somewhere below the mountain of books encircling him. The top of his shirt was tired and worn, and he wore a holey cardigan, the seams barely holding the threadbare panels together.

"All right if we use this, my main man." Charles enthusiastically spoke to the shopkeeper, who leaned forward and whispered to Charles, Charles took a sideways glance at Agatha then straightened up quickly.

"Oh, Charles, I also need to post this letter."

Agatha holds it out to him, he collects the note observing the address. "This is Helgam Agatha, he can do this for you," Charles places the letter onto the books in front of Helgam, Agatha leans closer and places some coins on top of the letter.

"Right, miss, if you would kindly follow me, we shall start knocking items off your list, shall we?" Charles put his elbow out for Agatha. She looked back at the shopkeeper, who smiled again and waved to them both as they left.

"Should we not have paid for the map and book, Charles?" Agatha commented in a worried tone.

"Oh, don't worry, we will bring it back once we are done. Helgam is good like that."

Agatha smiled. "What an unusual name, Helgam. Where are you from, Helgam?"

Before Agatha could finish her sentence, Charles motioned her to the front door. "We best be off, Miss Wilderfort. Bye, Helgy! Ha, ha!"

Agatha, looking one more time at the bookkeeper, saw him roll his huge eyes at the nickname Charles used for him. Then he bent down and was gone from sight.

Shutting the door behind them, Charles smiled and offered his arm again to Agatha. She hesitated slightly before sliding her hand through his arm.

They walked down the cobbled street past waist-height open windows with smells of freshly baked bread wafting through the openings. "Oh, that smells amazing, Charles. I need to stop to stock up on supplies. Do you know somewhere we could go?"

Agatha turned toward him, and he smiled. "Nothing like a delectable detour, Miss Wilderfort."

"Please call me Agatha, Charles. I'm still getting used to the new way of conversing with everyone." Charles stopped and turned towards her. "I was a maid before this, Charles." Agatha smiled sheepishly.

"We all start off somewhere, Agatha." Charles turned towards a street filled to the brim of market stalls and criers. Closest to them was the local newspaper boy with his stack of papers selling them for a shilling each, one of which Agatha acquired and paid the boy.

"Why thankie, miss, welcome to town." He smiled a grubby smile and then yelled, "Get your rags right 'ere, folks! Only a shilling, just a shillin'!"

The two moved forward into the hustle and bustle of the market where Agatha ordered food for her to last a few weeks, visiting various stallholders, the last being a woman with a large wagon nearly empty of bread, jars of jams and pickles, fruit and so many other items Agatha lost count of the variety. As she selected many of the items, the lady smiled at her.

"Oi, miss, you that Wilderfort lady, right?"

Shocked by the recognition of who she was, Agatha replied, "Ah, yes, I suppose I am. Is it that obvious?"

"Aye, miss, you have a heavy load to carry. I can drop it off for a small price to the castle if you don't mind waiting until the market has finished."

"That would be lovely, thank you! How much do I owe you?"

Charles stepped forward. "I'm sure this is on your way. Perhaps as Miss Agatha has bought so much of your produce, you would cause favour and be happy with two shilling." The lady looked somewhat downtrodden in thinking she could have got a bargain.

"All right, mister. Two shillin', it is."

Walking away, Agatha was so happy to have Charles with her. She would never have stumbled across the market easily. *Maybe he could be my counterpart in*

guiding me through all this mess Aunt Natalie has left.
Agatha looked at Charles thoughtfully. He smiled. back.

"Charles, are you in need of a position?"

He stopped walking, tilting his head sideways. "What manner of position are you meaning, Agatha?"

"Well, I… thought perhaps you could or well… I could hire you as such to help me with the restorations and putting things in order at the castle. I have no male counterpart and if you are willing…" Her voice trailed off as she looked at him. Her stomach was filled with knots of nerves as she tried to tell him.

"Are you meaning are you asking for me to be your guardian, Agatha?" Charles looked at her with a slight smile on his face.

Agatha looks him over properly. *Smartly dressed,* she thought to herself. *Tidy, clean hair, good manners, no, great manners. I think he would be good with my challenge.*

"Why yes, in a manner of speaking. Would that be something you might consider, Charles?"

"If I didn't know any better, Agatha, I'd say you like my company, as I do with you. I would more than consider getting to know you more and working closely with you." Charles brushed his hand over hers.

Agatha blushed. *Oh, God, maybe I was wrong. I think I'm feeling with my heart not my head.* Agatha quietly panicked at his response.

Charles smiled. "I'm going to enjoy working with you, Miss Agatha."

Bright red now, Agatha looked to the ground. *Stay on the job, Agatha.* She looked up at him again. *Gosh he really is handsome, though.* Agatha's insides turned to butterflies and the heat went down her neck and onto her chest.

Charles encourages Agatha on. "Shall we keep walking, Agatha? We still have a few things on your list."

Moving again, Agatha concentrated on the nearby houses with doors half the size of the average townsfolk which were jotted throughout the edges of the pathway. Some painted and fresh looking, some dilapidated, and the remainder bare cracking and in a very poor state, thus showing the financial standing of the residences as they walked through.

The second bout of publicity with Charles by her side eased the tension that oozed off the local townsfolk.

Women weren't supposed walk alone, especially at her age and social standing.

The couple turned another corner and were walking towards a flower girl wearing a pretty overcoat and a very old and worn but tidy-looking bonnet, carrying a basket full of flowers. Agatha couldn't help but stop to smell them. She picked up the first one, a rare, blue-edged rose, and smiled at the girl before putting it back in the basket. Charles stepped forward to the flower girl. He bought a single yellow carnation and gestured to put it behind Agatha's ear.

A very personal gesture, which was watched by the townsfolk in the area.

Agatha held her breath as he moved closer to her to complete the task. Blushing again, Agatha swore he could hear her heart pounding as he shortened the stem and slid the flower behind her ear.

"You can breathe, you know, Agatha. I don't bite." Charles said with a low voice and a wry smile, he moves away from her, standing and looking.

Gathering her thoughts, Agatha smiled. "That's so lovely of you, Charles. I don't know what to say. I mean, we just met and I just hired you, ha, um, I love the flower…" She trailed off but could see his disappointment.

"Unfortunately, you are correct, Miss Wilderfort. If we are to work together and go and hire your restoration crew, I should probably be more formal in my approach to our, err, relationship." Charles was crestfallen. He rubbed his face and smiled.

"But it does look so pretty on you."

Agatha blushed although Charles was no longer offering his arm to her. He walked forward and turned back. "Follow me, Miss Wilderfort. Your men are not far from here."

Agatha walked behind Charles for the rest of the duration, her heart aching for her mistake and her mind fighting with her conscience all the way.

Turning a few more corners, they delved deeper into the heart of what now looked to be the industrial district, no longer a couple arm-in-arm but strangers walking one in front of the other.

"Ahh, here we are, Miss Wilderfort." Charles motioned Agatha into a factory entrance to the left of the street. Half a dozen men, with one twice his height and girth, were on what seemed like a tea break. The larger of the group was settled on an upturned barrel with a serviette tucked into his shirt at the neck and another barrel next to him holding a rather fine bone china teapot, sandwiches and a delicate-looking matching teacup filled with a liquid that resembled tea, which he daintily lifted to drink from. He even lifted his very thick pinkie finger.

An unusual sight for a man covered in orange dust and dirt.

"Not used to seeing a man of my class sipping tea, I gather," the bulky man politely remarked in a gravelly voice a slight accent could be heard.

'*Is that an Irish accent*?' Agatha thought to herself.

She gazed upon the new additions to the group. Agatha was quite shocked at the grubby giant, his age unknown due to the lines of brick and clay dust seeping into his pores on his face — he looked to be sixty.

"To which of you do I owe this pleasure, Mr. Ignacio? Am I to presume you have brought me the lovely Miss Wilderfort, niece to the aunt we were all so fond of?"

Agatha was surprised he knew who she was. He pointed over to someone who Agatha recognised to be the newspaper boy, scuttling off down the road.

"You know the town is rife with gossip. You see that young boy over there — he is one of my little bird's. He tells me all sorts of gossip, for a price, of course. It's good to stay informed, especially in these parts. Don't you think, Miss Wilderfort?" Crackling through the clay and dust was a broad smile, the creases on his skin now making him look in his eighties, a line of sweat visibly running down his cheek showing his true skin tone against the brick dust.

"My name is Caelan, as most around here call me. I knew your Aunt Natalie well. I'm guessing your visit to us is not a social one,"

Agatha smiled. "So lovely to meet you, Caelan, you are right, of course. It's the Castle, it's in need of repair…" She trailed off, looking hopefully at Caelan.

Caelan stood up and towered over the two. He clapped Charles on the back, which nearly sent him flying forward. Caelan chuckled with his gravelly, deep-throated chuckle.

He looked over the top of Agatha and Charles and bellowed orders to the rest of the group.

"Right lads, gear ready we are off to Wilderfort."

Caelan turned back and looked down to Agatha and spoke in a softer tone with a smile from ear to ear. "When would you like us to start, miss?"

Chapter 4
The Request

With early starts and late finishes, Caelan and his crew made their way slowly from room to room within the castle.

The six am starts for Agatha were already taking their toll as the storms with that eerie purple hue seemed to always make their way to Wilderfort every evening. After restless nights and long days, she was starting to look a bit gaunt. Charles was also feeling the weight of the long days, although swanning in two or so hours later than the others, he too put in the work. Caelan, Agatha, and Charles argued over the way each room should be restored, with Charles making notes and compiling information. His folder for the castle was already becoming quite significant and they had only done a quarter of the first floor. With five storeys to go, it was going to be a long time before it would look like they had made some headway.

Any furniture that was to be kept was put within the largest room, which they had dubbed the ballroom. It had floor-to-ceiling mirrors, or at least they thought it did. The ceiling was so high it got lost in the darkness above.

Two weeks into the clearance, Agatha, Charles and Caelan were working in one of the many great dining halls they had found. Caelan was on a ladder dismantling an old and very broken chandelier.

Caelan stopped halfway and looked down at Charles. "I've got it, I know what we need." Charles, baffled, glanced at Agatha, who had stopped sweeping up parts of the chandelier that had broken.

"What do we need, Caelan?" Agatha said in a very tired voice, half thinking about how far away lunch was where she could sit down.

Caelan finished unclipping the chandelier and carefully walked down the ladder. He continues, "A good jig and a deep drink, love. That's what we need. Get out of your work gear and you can let your hair down a bit."

Caelan winked at Charles. The two weeks that they had all been at the castle, the attraction between Charles and Agatha was painfully obvious. Charles looked hopeful towards Agatha. "I think he might be right, Agatha. It's been two weeks of solid work. I think a drink would do us all some good."

Agatha looked from one to another. "Well, I guess. I mean, a good excuse would be... well... It is my birthday!"

Caelan, now free of the chandelier, slapped his leg. "Well, my dear, we cannot pass on this occasion to celebrate then. Well, well, well, you kept that one quiet. I better go tell the boys!"

He stomped off with spring in his step but no sooner does he reach the door of the ballroom, a young woman enters, looking rather nervously around, she spots Agatha as Agatha spots her. "Oh, Pollyanna you came!".

Agatha squeals in delight drops her broom and races towards Pollyanna. "Well, I couldn't miss you Birthday Aggie'. Pollyanna opens her arms out and embraces Agatha.

"Why Agatha you are head to toe in filth, this place needs a lot of work!" Agatha chuckled in response squeezing Pollyanna more.

"Miss, if you keep squeezing me, I will be plum out of breath!"

Pulling away Agatha quickly introduces Caelan and Charles.

"It's a pleasure to meet you miss Pollyanna, you have come just in time, we were talking of going to the pub for a drink to celebrate." Caelan draws Pollyanna away for a moment.

Looking in Caelan's direction, Agatha didn't notice Charles moving towards her. "Your birthday, why didn't you tell me? I would have got you something."

Agatha smiled sadly. "I didn't really celebrate it, not after I had run away from home. It was always Aunt Natalie's thing to make such a big deal of it." She rubbed her arm, looking at Charles.

"Well, we will keep it simple but I hope it will be memorable for you." Charles moved closer and brushed some of Agatha's hair behind her ear. "Happy birthday, Agatha." Charles was so close now Agatha could see all the silvery flecks in his eyes. He cupped her chin and smiled at her.

They were interrupted by Pollyanna clearing her throat, Caelan cuts into the tension, 'Right I better rouse the men then," Caelan moves out of the room quickly.

"Why, Agatha, are you married already" Pollyanna glares at Charles.

"Ahh no, Pollyanna." Squeezing her sleeve. "This is my hired, male counterpart, and ahh, close friend."

Charles moves back slightly. "I am sorry if I have over stepped Agatha, Pollyanna you are a good friend, I do so look forward to getting to know you more."

Pollyanna looks Charles over, before she can respond however, the thundering footsteps of Caelan coming back into earshot distracted Pollyanna. Charles smiled and quickly kissed Agatha on the cheek. He moved back toward the chandelier. Agatha was left speechless, holding her cheek where he had kissed her.

"Well, it's set — birthday party at the Old Squirrel." Caelan did a double-take of Agatha and Charles, who was smiling and trying to concentrate on the chandelier.

"Okay, what did you two lovebirds do? What did I miss?" Pollyanna looks between the two. "Did I miss something? Agatha, what's been going on?"

Agatha snapped out of her trance, going bright red. She turns to Caelan, who was attempting to ignore her bright red face. "Where's the Old Squirrel?"

Charles butted in. "Oh, can't we go somewhere a bit classier, Caelan? Why there?"

Caelan turned to Charles. "Where else can our lot get in and relax, Charles? Plus, they have one of my mates playing in the band to night" Grinning, Caelan elbowed Charles in the ribs which made Charles yelp.

"Caelan, I'm not as rough as you. Please be gentle, for goodness' sakes. I'm going to be a bag of mush if you keep playing with me." Agatha giggled at Charles's comment but stops as Pollyanna looks at her.

"Okay, Miss Agatha, darlin', let's pack up early. We all need a good wash."

Agatha hesitated. "I don't have anything to wear, I only have this and my travel clothes. I lost my trunk moving back here."

"Oh, Agatha that's dreadful, is there a place in town we could stop at." Pollyanna tried to console Agatha. "Perhaps I can be of assistance Miss Agatha," clearing his throat Charles glances at Pollyanna for approval. The fight in her manners is visible. "I think that is fine Mr. Charles, items will be needed as many have been lost."

"Well, put your travel clothes on Agatha, mis Pollyanna I will take you to the dressmaker's before the Squirrel. We best hurry, though. I will come back in an hour with a coach and we can all travel in together.

Think of it as my birthday present." He smiled at Agatha, who blushed ignoring the look from her new protective friend.

"All right, all right, you lot, I'm going to get sorted." Caelan packed up his tools, waving to the three as he walked out of the hall. "See you there at seven p.m. Don't be late!" Caelan called out as he left the dining hall.

Charles smiled at Agatha quickly so as not to be seen by Pollyanna, they put away their tools and broom and walked out together.

Time went quickly for Agatha as she hurried to bathe and scrub the years' old dust off her body and hair, constantly watching the clock for when Charles arrived with the coach. Pollyanna is behind the screen as she bathed, catching Agatha up on all the gossip of London and the house they both worked in.

Soon she slows down. "Agatha, who is Charles to you, I'm very wary of his brazen attitude to you, and you hardly know him! It's been a little over a month, you haven't been alone with him anywhere have you. Oh, Miss Agatha" Agatha cuts into the conversation

"Pollyanna, it's okay, you are here with me now, you can teach me what to do, I don't know what I'm doing. I feel so happy you came here, I know it's not much, but you can pick your room tomorrow, we can make sure you have whatever you want, I know I said housekeeper. But you're my friend, can we be equal."

Pollyanna thinks for a while and is silent for the first time in almost an hour.

"I'm okay with being your housekeeper Agatha, in fact I'm more than happy, yes of course we can be friends, we always will be but I have my duties and you have yours, we will be in a different style of relationship now. But I will help as much as I can. If it weren't for your birthday, I would have said no to this Squirrel place. It doesn't sound right for a woman of your place in society now. You should know this. Charles though, if you feel strongly for him, you need to solidify your place with him, tongues will wag and that is the last thing you need while trying to find your footing"

Agatha got out the bath, and with Pollyanna's help she dresses.

Brushing her long auburn hair, plaiting the edges and tying them at the back, Pollyanna stands back so Agatha could look in the mirror. Her tea-stained travel clothes made her feel shabby and awkward. It had been a long time since she had bought new clothes, and she had never done it with a male present, especially one she was so fond of. Sighing, Agatha brushed her hand down her front one more time in front of the mirror, then turns to Pollyanna, "Are we ready Miss" Pollyanna winks at Agatha and smiles the cheeky smile Agatha loved when they worked together. *So my friend is in there after all, I was so scared she would become a stranger to me.* Agatha moves out of her room with

41

Pollyanna in tow to meet Charles, and the carriage at the front entrance.

Walking down the stairs, she had barely time to think before Charles opened the front doors. Standing there, he was wearing a broad grin and a beautifully tailored outfit of green and black with gold stitching.

Agatha felt he looked breath-taking and couldn't take her eyes off him.

He helped her into the coach followed by Pollyanna and they were soon on their way to the Dressmakers. Agatha was excited to get some decent clothing. The bumps in the road made it hard for conversation. "Your hair looks beautiful, Agatha."

She smiled then looked down and for the tenth time, brushed her hands over her travel outfit. "I think we need to acquire your own carriage Miss Agatha, it won't do hiring them" The road was so bumpy Pollyanna sounded funny when she spoke, making all of them smile at each other, Charles went to move toward Agatha but found he bounced forward on his seat nearly onto the floor. "Ahh, a lot bumpier than I remember." Both the girls giggled at this. "So she does smile" Charles had been watching Pollyanna, who sat up straight and quickly looked out the window.

Agatha moved towards him and the next bounce in the road put her nearly in his lap. "I was hoping to get closer to you, Agatha, I guess I got my wish," Charles whispered, which made Agatha move backwards and blush. He slid towards her and held her hand. She leaned forward and felt a huge urge to kiss him. Shocked by her urges, she blushed even more and sat back in her seat. Pollyanna distracted from the window by Agatha moving on the seat continues to look out the window attempting to ignore the private moment Charles and Agatha were having.

Biting her bottom lip to hold back a grin, Agatha wasn't alone, though. He was smiling too and brushing his hair back off his face. Too nervous to speak any more, Agatha looked out the window, seeing the township come into view. It looked so peaceful, calming almost, at night time.

Turning a corner further into town, they stopped in front of the Dressmakers. Agatha was so excited when she saw how beautiful the entrance of the shop was. Even Pollyanna couldn't deny it.

Agatha was nervous as she held Charles' hand to step out of the coach closely followed by Pollyanna. the dressmaker was waiting at the entrance for them.

"Good evening, madam, I heard this was a special occasion so I have put out a selection of our clothing." He bowed and opened the door for them to walk in.

It was so bright in the shop Agatha had to take a second to acclimatise to the bright lamps.

The dressmaker walked around her looking her up and down. "I think let's get these clothes off. What would be the best thing to do for you my dear?" Agatha was in agreement with his comment. "I think just dispose as you see fit."

The gorgeous gowns and outfits were soon brought through into the shop both girls gasped at the breath-taking embroidery on the bodices of dresses, simple to intricate designs all laid out for her selection.

Charles stepped back and took a seat near the entrance. One of the staff had given him a whiskey which he sipped whilst watching Agatha's admiration.

"So what do you say, Miss Wilderfort? Will these suffice for your new wardrobe?"

He smiled as she turned with a brilliant smile that caught him off guard. He opened his mouth slightly, not sure how to take this lavish look of bliss on Agatha's face.

"Come on, miss, let's get you trying these on." One of the staff ushered Agatha into the back followed by Pollyanna.

The tailor met them in the other room commenting. "I think the blue to start with, then the cream stripe, and then the green. Let's see how those go on her. She has a perfect figure for those. Not many women have a figure fit for a corset, and you, my dear, have." He winked at her and wriggled his lips, making his moustache move. Agatha giggled a bit as the staff helped her out of her travel clothes.

It wasn't not long before she stepped through, very shy in the blue dress. "Do you like this one, Charles?" she said in a very shy manner.

Charles looked up, smiling, and nearly dropped his drink. He cleared his throat and stood. "Why, Agatha, I think this is the one you should wear tonight. You look, well, you look breath-taking."

Agatha blushed. "I haven't tried them all on yet."

Charles couldn't stop staring at her. He was absolutely in awe at how beautiful she looked but was excited he would see more of her clothing. "Take your time. I could sit here all night and do this with you."

Agatha giggled again and moved into the back room to the awaiting staff and Pollyanna. Her dressmaker was having a cigarette, leaning on the measuring table, with one of his other workers. Agatha was pretty sure she had caught the men in unusually close-quarters, so she looked down and cleared her throat, pretending not to have seen anything. the dressmaker's male liaison came closer again and pulled the measuring tape off the dressmaker's waist.

"My apologies, madam. I didn't think you would be back yet."

"Oh, I'm, sorry. Would you like some more time?" Agatha mentioned and smiled at them both. She knew of male's having relations and knew of its dangers, although she didn't want to cause alarm

They looked at one another questioningly but smiled. They could tell their relationship did not need to be hidden from Agatha. The other workers gave the dressmaker a quick touch on the cheek and disappeared back through the curtain behind him.

"Ahem, right, shall we get back to it? Was that not to your liking, Miss Wilderfort?" The tailor looked at Agatha, worried he had picked wrong.

"Oh no, I love it. I would like to have it for tonight, but I do need some more clothes. I only have two and we have removed my travel clothing from my wardrobe."

The dressmaker looked shocked. "What happened to the rest of your clothes?"

"Oh, my trunk was lost on my trip home. Can I ask for some items and you can see if you have them? As much as I want to dress up in these beautiful clothes, I still would like to meet my friends before it gets too late." Agatha smiled. The tailor stopped and looked at her. He stepped back and took in the dress, her hair, her eyes, all of her.

"You are very beautiful, you know. Tell me. Whatever you want, your wish is my command." He flicked his hair and wiggled his moustache again.

Agatha laughed. "I need, well, I need trousers and a shirt to start with."

The dressmaker stopped short. "Well, I wasn't expecting that request."

"Ha, ha, I'm renovating and a skirt only gets in the way. I will need some other dresses and skirts, though. Perhaps four of each. Is that enough, do you think?"

The tailor stopped short. "Four of each! You will need blouses and jackets, too, I'm guessing. My, what a big order. I will have to make some of these items. I might not have it all in stock. But we will do our best for you tonight so you have a start. I can have the rest delivered to you when they are ready. Would that do for you, madam?" The tailor whizzed over to her and started measuring.

He called for other two staff members. "Benjamin, Violet! Please bring me my book. We have some measurements to do." It took a small while before they were complete. Agatha insisted on trying on the other two dresses before she left, walking through to Charles to show him. Each time he couldn't stop staring at her.

"I'm really, really enjoying this, Agatha," he said to her as he stood up while she was wearing the last dress. He held her hand and twirled her around. "I can't decide which I like more. I'm truly stuck."

Agatha giggled again. "Don't worry, I'm taking all of them, but I think the blue will be best for tonight." She smiled at him as she walked back through to the back room. Pollyanna looked from the entrance way disapprovingly at Charles. "You may have had free rein of her before Charles but, im here now so you will need to refrain from your wistful ways with Agatha, I will not have her named sullied under my eye," turned abruptly out of the room Pollyanna left Charles standing in hesitation. "She really knows how to put a damper on things, does our Pollyanna, not here a night yet and really making her mark." Benjamin one of the staff members just smiles at Charles, showing the look of not really knowing what to say. He disappears through the curtain to the backroom, leaving Charles and his whiskey behind.

Charles took a seat, pulled out his handkerchief and held it over his face. He closed his eyes and couldn't stop thinking of her smile and how she looked.

Pulling the handkerchief off his face, he took the last swig of whiskey and with the back of his hand, tapped his cheeks, almost like reassurance he was still here.

It wasn't long before Agatha came back out with the blue dress on again. The tailor, his staff and Pollyanna followed her out with a package of some other items she had selected.

"As I said, madam, the rest of the clothes will be ready soon enough and we will deliver them to you." He wrote a receipt at the counter and she pays him in full for all items. He looked at the money and back at her.

"Thank you for your visit. I'm so glad we could do this. My name is Mark, Benjamin is my top apprentice dressmaker Please let us know if we can help in any way, Miss Wilderfort. It's been a pleasure."

Agatha smiled. "Please call me Agatha. I haven't had this much fun in, well, let's say a long time." Reaching across, Mark patted Agatha's hand.

Thanking them all, Charles, Agatha and Pollyanna left, and got back into the waiting coach.

"Are you ready for some more fun? I think you are going to take everyone's breath away when we get to The Old Squirrel, Agatha." Charles smiled. He was sitting next to her in the coach this time with Pollyanna opposite, Charles was still holding Agatha's hand from when he helped her in although it was hidden from view under the layers of beautiful blue dress.

Agatha bit her lip, holding back an even bigger smile.

He looked at her. "You really are beautiful, Agatha." Charles moved closer, Pollyanna attempted to clear her throat as a distraction but the two were too involved with each other, knowing she needed to sort out boundaries Pollyanna against all judgement chose to ignore the situation and to approach both Charles and Agatha apart from each other, she needed to teach Agatha to be proper, Pollyanna knew this. But in this instance all she could do was blend into the furniture, so she turned to the window and pretended she was invisible.

Agatha not aware of Pollyanna any more moved towards Charles she could feel his breath on her face. The rush of emotions was almost deafening. He kissed her and everything she was nervous about melted away. She reached up and touched his face.

It was only a brief moment as the coach jolted to a stop and pulled them apart, Pollyanna pushed the door open and rushed out of the coach, not waiting for the steps to be lower by the driver, willing to be away from the emotion of the temporary inhabitants.

Agatha reached up and touched her mouth. Charles smiled and brushed the hair behind her ear.

Her heart was racing. It didn't stop. She followed him into the Old Squirrel and his previous comment was correct. As he held her hand, she looked in and it was a strange sight. Her vision blurred. It was like waves of air were blowing over her, but she ignored it Pollyanna pushed past Charles and found the other men who worked with Caelan, she needed away time from Agatha, barely a day and her position was already wayward, being passed a pint she gulped down half, shocking the crew.

The music stopped and everyone glanced at the newcomers. The silence was quickly broken

"Ahh, the lovebirds have finally found us!" It was Caelan. He waved them over to the bar and slid two handles of beer towards them.

The music began to play again and the noise of chatter got louder.

"I thought you got lost in the mountains of dresses, miss, but I see you have found the best of

them all for tonight."

He winked at Charles, who smiled into his beer as he took a deep drink.

Chapter 5
The Awakening

Not sure if it was the beer Agatha was drinking that was going to her head or the atmosphere, but the waves she felt upon entering the Old Squirrel were still blowing around her, the feeling tingling in her body.

Caelan was melancholy for a moment. "I met my wife in this 'ere pub," Caelan said to his beer. He was on his fourth one from when they had arrived and a merry glow was all around him. "God rest her soul." Agatha's face fell at the comment. Caelan put his hand up. "She may have lived a short life with me but the life we lived together was the best I 'ave ever had, enough to fill my remaining years with happiness. Don't feel sad for me, Miss Agatha. I'm the luckiest man ever."

With that, Charles winked at her. She returned it with a smile. She went to turn to face the band but found her movements slowed with the previous uneasy feeling, but this time tenfold. She dropped her pint, smashing the glass on the floor. In a blurring movement, the barmaid swept around her feet and fitted a new pint into her empty hand.

Stunned by the quick clean-up and replacement, Agatha looked over to Caelan with a further double-take at his appearance, then looked at the unusual band members.

"Is this the first time you have seen these breeds, Miss Agatha?" Caelan commented his speech starting to slur as he downed his fifth pint.

Agatha replied with a look of shock, 'Breeds!' She took in the look of the band members, also those sitting so comfortably around her. She slid closer to Charles, but not looking at him. Agatha spotted the unusual anatomy of the live band — one had long ears that spiked to the top, another had what looked like ten fingers on one hand but the movement was so quick over the strings she couldn't tell. The singer was of a grey complexion and they all had black eyes, much like that of the footman that Lord Caspian had in his employment.

"I — I don't understand what's wrong. I mean what's happened, everyone looks so, so different? Even you, Caelan."

Caelan turned back from watching the band, listening intently to her stunned comment and now seeing her complexion.

"I'm guessing, lovey, with your response, that your aunt never told you of the dimension door." Caelan looked back at the band, unable to look at Agatha's queer expression.

Stuttering her response, she replied in a hoarse voice, "The dimension door? What on earth is that and why do they look so, so different?" Agatha shook with shock and pointed to the band as Charles immediately jumped into action. He took her pint out of her other hand before another slipped from her fingers. Agatha stood up.

Charles took her by the elbow and whispered soothingly, "Dance with me, Agatha. All will be explained, I promise." Stumbling a bit, Agatha regained her composure as Charles whisked her to an empty section of the pub, Pollyanna is alerted of their movements and watches curiously. They began to sway to the music as he started telling her all he knew. "Agatha, Caelan and I have worked with your aunt for many years. What you know is not the way the world really is. Your aunt protected the dimension door as did Caelan and myself."

Trying to pull away from Charles, Agatha looked at him. "But you're my age. How could you have worked with my aunt and why are you mentioning a dimension door?"

Agatha tried to pull away, but Charles held her close. "I'm sorry, Agatha, but I'm a lot older than you may think. Caelan was a foot soldier for your aunt, as was most of his crew. Your aunt protected the door, she was a keeper, and now that she has passed, that job has now been passed to you." Charles kept Agatha swaying. He turned her slightly so she could face the wall, an attempt to calm her.

"A keeper, what on earth is that?" Agatha shrilled, momentarily stopping the music whilst onlookers turned towards the two. Pollyanna stands noticing the panic look on Agatha, Charles sees her notion to come closer but bats her away making her hesitate but stay standing.

"I need air, I don't understand what you are talking about or what is going on in this pub, this is all too much!"

Panicking, Agatha pushed Charles away and rushed out of the pub. Caelan, seeing the commotion, scrambled up from the bar, swigging the last of his beer in one hand, and shoving his crew and random people out of the way he is closely followed by Pollyanna who ducks and weaves all those he had shoved. He followed in Agatha's wake with Charles and Pollyanna close behind.

"I knew you couldn't be trust Charles, what the hell did you say to her. She looked so panicked, Charles what did you say!"

Pollyanna tried to grab for Charles in an attempt to make him look at her, but with his strength he just brushed her off and kept pace with Caelan.

Agatha, gulping in the cold air and leaning on the white washed bricks of the pub, turned to see the three standing in front of her. Again, the bewildered look came over her. She looked at Caelan and Charles scared at what she saw, lastly looking at Pollyanna human, no weirdness, no change in personal being unlike the other two.

She was hugging her waist. The look she gave them was like she was looking through them, her eyes widening with each breath Agatha attempted to take in. She managed a step but her eyes closed and she slumped to the floor. Pollyanna dives for Agatha, pulling out her handkerchief and flapping it in front of Agatha's face. "It's okay, miss, we can get you home and sort this out. Whatever he did to you I will find out." Both Caelan and Charles look at each other blankly.

"We better get her back to familiar grounds, Charlie." Caelan pulled Agatha up and over his shoulder. He whistled for the coach that was nearby and gently put her inside. Caelan, Charles and Pollyanna joined her in the coach.

"Wilderfort castle and quick," he announced to the driver as he settled in his seat. The carriage groaned as it took his weight. He shut the coach doors and although lopsided, it rushed off into the early dusk of the night.

"What did you do that for, Charlie? That was too soon.

"I said slow interrogation, you stupid man, not the whole story in one go!"

Caelan, red in the face, and Charles, white as a sheet, look at Pollyanna as she tries to tend to Agatha. "What is going on you two?" Exasperation can be seen in Pollyanna's face, the men hesitated, decided to ignore her and argued most of the way back to the castle, who said what first, and when.

As they came into the driveway, Agatha opened her eyes, groaning and trying to sit up. Both Caelan and Charles rushed to help Agatha but are pushed back by Pollyanna with a fierce glare.

"I'm so sorry, Agatha. Caelan is right. That was way too soon," Charles blurted out.

Agatha held her hands up motioning them back. "Give me space, both of you. I don't know what's going on, but my head is throbbing awfully, I'm in this silly attire and how did I get back to the castle?"

Rubbing her eyes, Agatha blinked and looked first at Pollyanna with a confused glance wanting reassurance then at both of the men. Their calm and happy previous personas had gone. They were replaced by two scared and worried weird-looking men.

Caelan now had a weird orange complexion and long ears which she previously hadn't notice or never realised, and Charles had a slight grey glittery hue to his skin.

Grappling at the edges of her dress, Agatha looked at both of the men, or what she thought were men.

Closing her eyes and rubbing them once more, Agatha said, "All right, I have no idea what's going on. You both have changed, you look to diff... so not... argh I can't even explain it, you are just different okay! And I'm in the dark. Who is going to start explaining things please, as I would very much like to know who you really are and what on earth is going on!" Pollyanna attempted to assure Agatha. "I do not understand, perhaps you have a migraine coming on and it's making to see things funny, should we call for a Doctor Agatha?" Agatha had started opening her eyes again when the carriage stopped at the entrance to the castle. Agatha, unsure on her feet, was helped out and down from the carriage by the driver and Pollyanna. He also was unusual to look at, his hair only growing in the centre of his head, his ears almost non-existent, and his hands made of three very long fingers that started from his elbows.

Shocked, Agatha let go and stumbled to the ground. "Are you all right, miss?" the driver said. Agatha put her hand up to decline the help as she stood, not looking him in the face as she was scared of what else she would see. Agatha said thank you for the help and with Pollyanna helping her up they walked into the entrance-way followed closely behind by Charles and there Agatha slumped onto the red velvet lounger at the base of the staircase.

Caelan, who had paid for the carriage, followed the others into the castle. Not wasting the opportunity of the silence, he began to explain the full story and what he thought was why everything Agatha thought was how life should be was now completely different.

"Agatha my lovely, it's okay," he said in a soothing, but gravelly voice. To this, Agatha scowled at him and put her head in her hands. Caelan continued. "Your aunt must have put a charm on your sight to protect you and outsiders from what this place really is."

Agatha wasted no time in interrupting Caelan in an exasperated manner. "Which is what, Caelan? Or is that really your name, and what about you, Charles, who are you! Or should I really say how old you are!" Agatha snapped at both of them. Pollyanna feeling very much outside of what was going on, could only sit there, mouth open, staring from one speaker to the next, feeling this bizarre conversation was getting weirder by the minute.

"Agatha, now that's enough, you listen to me and you listen carefully. Your aunt died protecting who you are. I'm a chimeon. That's why I work with bricks in your world. I create fire. It's a great disguise. And Charles is a daemon immortal. Your castle holds underneath it the dimension door for the daemon realm. You are a Keeper, you keep the door. You have magic in you that you obviously haven't fully awoken yet, but when you were at the pub, the charm your aunt had put on you was wearing off. You were seeing us for who we really are, but we are good people. Well, a chimeon and immortal anyway." Caelan's accent had dropped the Irish tone and now had an unusual tang to it, almost like he had two tongues, and they were wrestling in his mouth to get the words out.

Agatha, pink with upset, looked over both of them. She turned to Charles. "You're not as grey as the others in the pub."

Charles smiled. "I'm a half-caste but still have the immortal part as my father had. My mother was your great-great-great grandfather's wife's sister if that makes sense Aggie."

Confusion came over Agatha again. "So we are related!" she squeaked.

"No, not by blood, Aggie, only by marriage in a sense. I'm sorry this is such a shock, Aggie."

Agatha turned again to Charles. "Aunt Natalie used to call me Aggie. Does that mean you knew me as a child? Only Aunt Natalie called me that and she is now dead! This is so confusing. I don't have memories of you or Caelan. Have you always been here?" Furrowing her brow, Agatha put her face into her hands.

Pollyanna felt she was in the centre of a great dramatic play, bewildered by all of this she shuffled across the lounger as Charles hesitantly sat in between Agatha and Pollyanna he mouthed to Caelan, "What should I do?" Caelan shrugging in response, made the motion of Charles rubbing her back, which Charles silently followed suit.

The weather slowly turned for the worst as the evening thunderstorms commenced. The eerie purple hue was caught by the sun's final rays and shone through the windows. "Well, I have never come across purple storm clouds before, what will I encounter next, a three headed dog!" Pollyanna scoffs looking up to Caelan, who thinks she has done so for a response and a change in subject.

"Nah, those guys are too big to squeeze through the gap."

Pollyanna is taken aback by his remark. "Do you think I am wanting sarcasm Caelan for that was not the response I gathered I would get from you!" Caelan looks at Charles. "Don't suppose you want to open her mind do you."

Charles sighs and rubs his hands together.

"What are you doing Charles, I don't need my mind open it is perfectly fine the way it is, closed and kept safe in my head," Pollyanna stands and begins backing away.

"It won't hurt Pollyanna I promise." Charles stands and with a quick movement is next to Pollyanna she shrieks and he muttered drawing a symbol on his hand, Pollyanna went to back away again but Charles was too quick and smacked her on the head with his palm.

"Usually, I use paper and place it on your head, but I don't have any handy and this gives the same result."

Gasping Pollyanna's vision blurs, she blinks and knuckles her eyes, blinking heavily. "Ow! Why on earth did you hit me on the head Charles that is not something you do to a lady."

"Well, you do if you need to give her the sight and it's to bring you into the life you need to know about, living here anyway."

Charles stands back and waits. "And what does smacking her on the head do, Charles," Agatha who had been quite forgotten in that moment moves her arm over the lounger for a better view of the situation.

Pollyanna slows her rubbing and blinks quickly squinting at Caelan and Charles. "Woah, wha… what is this magic, why are you changed! How, how have you done this." She begins to panic looking from one daemon to the other.

Charles impatient replies, "We are not changed, the true sight has been given to you, unlike Agatha here who has it from birth, but was put under a cloaking spell by her aunt, we had to give it to you, hence the smack on the head."

Aghast, Pollyanna looks at Agatha. "Well, you are not changed, please save me from this madness, they have done something to me, help me, Agatha!" Pollyanna hyperventilated and started to rub her chest, she moved forward towards Agatha for help but is overcome and fainted, like a toppling tree she had come crashing down on the floor.

"That's going to hurt tomorrow," Caelan remarks.

Leaving Pollyanna on the floor Charles moves and sits back on the lounger, finished with his exercise of true sight. Caelan, knowing he would break it, sits on the floor. The three took a moment to watch as the purple rays dissolved into darkness leaving no trace left of the day, only the eerie hue from the storm lighting the open doorway.

"We will never leave you alone, Miss Aggie," Caelan stated. "Come on, let's make some supper. If we are all going bunk here for the night, we may as well have a hearty meal to wash down the beers from the night."

Charles looked over to Caelan. "You mean that you had. Aggie and I only had a mouthful at least."

Caelan laughed and went to pat Charles on the back. This time he artfully dodged the swat and simultaneously hit a curtain on the inside of the hallway. It fell down with a crash, revealing a door that Agatha had never noticed before. Pollyanna screams starling the others, "I forgot you were laying there miss." Caelan responds, Agatha ignoring Pollyanna stepped forward and brushed her hand over the door.

"I have never seen this door since coming back, but I feel like I remember it."

Caelan replied, "Aye, Miss Aggie, that's the door to the dungeons' lovey, one that would best be avoided for the time being, I think."

Agatha moved forward, brushing her hand over it before moving on to the kitchen with the others in tow. Pollyanna was still panicked muttering and shrieking, Caelan grabbed her and threw her over his shoulder, rolled his eyes at Charles as they both continued. Flashes of distant laughter and what Agatha thought were memories of playing hide and seek with people whose faces came up blank vaguely came to mind.

Chapter 6
A NEW, New Beginning

The brilliance of another day came blinding through the curtains of Agatha's room, Pollyanna had slept on the bed next to her, as she had no rooms setup yet, it had taken a while for Agatha to get her to sleep. Agatha Rubbed her face, it felt rough, the memory of last night at the Squirrel and all that was revealed came to fruition.

"Oh, Aunt Natalie, what have you left me?" Agatha groaned into her pillow. She had pillows now and a proper bed, acquired by Caelan who felt she shouldn't be sleeping in squalor considering the amount of work she was doing.

"A decent sleep can't be had by sleeping on jackets, Miss," he had told her. Pollyanna stirred slightly, Agatha could hear footsteps coming towards her door as a light knock came shortly after. Caelan's head popped around the door, followed by the aroma of fresh coffee.

Caelan held up his giant orange hands and sat in the middle of them was a tray with two cups of coffee steaming away for Agatha and Pollyanna, who was brushing her bird's nest of hair out of her face. Beckoning him in, Agatha sat up in bed and took the coffee from his outstretched hand.

"Good morning, Miss Aggie. I hope you slept okay." Caelan looked a bit sheepish and turned his head away from the bed. Pollyanna whimpered at Caelan, who ignored her noise and handed her, her coffee, which she hesitantly took.

"Oh Caelan, it's all right. I'm still coming to terms with it but I always had a feeling of unease when I was here, and now I know why." Agatha took a sip of coffee and looked out the window. "One thing, Caelan. No more secrets, okay? Do I need to know anything else?" Agatha looked at Caelan, who slumped onto the side of the bed nearly spilling Pollyanna's coffee.

He looked at his fingers. "Miss Aggie, I wish your aunt was here to tell you. There is so much to learn and to tell. I can only tell you what I know."

Smiling, Agatha patted Caelan on his enormous rock-like hand. "Well, that's a start."

It took a bit of coaxing for Pollyanna to start working with the others, she was not her usual chatty self and was very jumpy with anyone that stepped within her proximity.

Chasing down the cobwebs and continuing the clearing of the rooms made utter chaos in the massive building that was Aggie's new home.

All the workers were covered in dust, dirt and God would only know what else. Every day was strenuous, leaving all desperately tired, with the previous goings-on with Lord Caspian's visit, the unveiling of the lifeforms for Aggie on her birthday, and of course

Pollyanna who was still shrieking, at least a bit less now, the role Aggie needed to fulfil as the new keeper of the gates. The work to exhaustion was a brilliant reprieve as the daemon realm and the gate were quite a shock to anyone especially after the first abhorrent unveiling for Miss Aggie and not to mention the constant coaxing of Pollyanna in coming to terms with the new shapes of those who worked with her in the castle.

Although Lord Caspian and his daemon footman had been spotted in a fair few locations since the previous incident, the small team of Caelan, his men, Aggie, Pollyanna (who didn't dare to leave the Castle in case she encountered more daemons) and of course, Charles, became accustomed to having a watchful eye and covering their tracks with any town visits and making sure the other realm only noticed their natural conversations and not the otherworldly ones to help Aggie with her transition from knowing nothing to gaining all she needed as the newfound role of gatekeeper.

Due to the introduction of the realm and those around her, Aggie and Charles had cooled off with their emotions for each other. Nothing had changed their affections, the wistful glances from each other, but space was granted and needed, for Aggie to learn her newfound life, her responsibilities as the new householder, caring for Pollyanna, the new gatekeeper and her role in the refurbishment of the estate. All most monumental even for one person but of this charge and calibre — it was a wonder anyone could balance sanity along with finances. Something Aggie first scorned with her aunt, although now understood and adopted the notions and habits she had undoubtedly detested when first introduced.

Coming to terms with the role, Aggie now donned her shirt and trousers most days providing manoeuvrability with work and with her ever-growing arts in self-defence provided by her team of varying daemons/workers, a subject Pollyanna was keen to observe as well.

Upon settling for lunch one day, Caelan offered an idea. "Aggie, lovely, I think it's time we teach you the main types of daemons so you know what they can do and what best way to defend yourself, if, of course, you're caught off guard and alone."

Sipping her tea crossed-legged on an old couch set outside the front oak doors, Aggie mulled this over. Pollyanna, who had just started to slow down in her whimpering and jumping, sucked in her breath. "Is there going to be fighting now?" Panic showing on her face. Aggie closed her eyes and turned her face to the warmth of the sun.

"I understand what you're saying, Caelan. I know I should be learning, although there is just so much. Surely there is an easier way." Aggie turned her face away from the direct warmth and faced Caelan.

"From my understanding, Miss, one of your ancestors had a book, almost a ledger of all that came into this realm, their abilities and how many came through and were found."

Aggie jumped up excitedly, to which Charles responded, "Aggie, this ledger has been missing for years if not decades. I haven't seen it and nor has anyone that I know of."

Aggie dropped her arms and straightened herself, with an air of defiance. "Well then, Charles, Caelan." She turned and stared both down with an almost manic grin. "I think a treasure hunt of sorts is in order. We must find that book for us to proceed with my learning and gaining all I need to beat Caspian at his game."

Her wording then panicked Caelan. Pollyanna began shrieking again, ignoring Pollyanna, Caelan responded trying to speak over the noise. "Miss, I know or should I say understand where you are coming from." He brushed his hand along one arm of the couch. "But these are dangerous waters. You're not ready for any type of altercation, be it verbal or physical."

With this, Aggie stood, straightening herself again, and stared down Caelan. "I'm not feeble Caelan," she said, to which he looked at his giant feet that he pushed through the dry dirt coating the floor. "Oh, be quiet Pollyanna for goodness sakes, you are here, there are daemons all around us but have these ones hurt us!" Aggie stared at Pollyanna who hesitated at her statement. "Good now please for all our sakes, enough! If you see a new one coming towards the house by all means shriek away, but please just stop! You are giving me a headache." Pollyanna looked hurt then flopped down on the couch next to Aggie, Aggie moved towards her and rubbed her arms to comfort her as she looked up to Caelan.

"Caelan, I know I'm still learning but perhaps you should consider the fact that maybe this is what we need to move forward with all this gatekeeper defence. I have been thinking, with all my training I have started and will be doing, I need to capture Lord Caspian and send him back through the gate."

"Woah there, Miss Aggie, I think you're getting ahead of yourself there." Caelan stood as he talked with a look of shock on his face. "Many have tried your suggestion and many have failed."

Agatha, determined on her decision, replied, "But, did they have the Ledger, did they know what every daemon was capable of?"

Caelan was thoughtful in his reply. "Aggie, from memory, no, but what you're asking is dangerous. If he goes back, all that he has summoned will follow."

Aggie looked at Caelan. "Are you part of those who were summoned, Caelan?"

"No, I escaped the realms upon one of the first splits of the gate, as did Charles and many others. What you're asking is possible genocide Agatha! Do you understand how dangerous this is?"

Agatha recoiled with shock at his drastic response. "Why genocide? Caelan, we will just be putting him back rather forcefully."

At this, Caelan laughed at Agatha and her interpretations of the danger that she was wanting to pursue. Caelan then stood and turned to her. "Aggie, my love, genocide cannot be avoided unless there is something on the Ledger that could help us. But as I said before, it has been lost to us."

From here Charles stood, brushed his rather dusty jacket and said in a voice similar to a nervous mouse, "I think we should find the Ledger." Charles looked from one to another and cleared his throat with the facial responses he received from both Agatha and Caelan, one of excitement and one of anger.

Caelan stood. "This road you're about to take, Agatha, is dangerous. I want to step away but I swore an oath to your Aunt Natalie. I will protect the Gatekeeper at all costs. I can't stop you but know I help only in protest. The wars of the Gatekeeper helped in the loss of my wife. I will not stand by and watch more die if I can help it. Please take this as my warning to you. Tread carefully."

Caelan's response posed a damper on Agatha's determination. However, her mind was set. Being the last to stand, she took one of Caelan's huge hands in hers. "Caelan, I am listening and I can see that dangers will come with this decision, but we can't just stand by. What if he finds a way to let more through or causes more wars? One war against many is a better look for the future, wouldn't you think? Help me find the Ledger and from there we can plan our next step. I make this promise to you, I will never step blindly forward. We will plan together and move together. Agreed?"

Caelan covered her hands with his other. He looked at Charles. "My lady, I will walk where you walk, I will stand where you stand and I will protect those who need protection. I guess we should find this Ledger." Caelan stresses a smile. "Where do you want to start, Aggie?"

Charles stepped towards the two. Agatha dropped her hands from Caelan and smiled at Charles. He positioned himself next to her and put his little finger out, holding hers with his all the while looking at Caelan. "I think the way forward with this is to go back and retrace the steps of the previous Gatekeepers. We continue with the restoration of the castle and not raise any suspicion with the locals. I think we should move into the premises so we can hunt and research with ease at night whilst the storms circle the castle. Our story, which is already circling the town, is that Aggie is unable to sleep through the storms. They already know we have been taking shifts in caring for her. the next step is moving temporarily into the premises to further help her. What say you, Caelan, Agatha?"

Agatha moved her hand completely into Charles's hand. She squeezed it and replied, "We go ahead with the plan. I agree to the mask of restoration by day, and storms with Ledger hunting at night. It will also prove our tired and dishevelled look if we need to visit the town."

With this, Caelan nodded in determination. "Well, it's still daylight so let's keep our daytime story going, aye gang?"

Pollyanna who had been silently biting her hand through the conversation stood up. "I don't know if I can be a part of this, Agatha, I don't have these skills like you are learning, nor do I have powers like the others, I'm scared!"

It was the first time she spoke without whimpering since her sight had been given to her, "Pollyanna, I understand this had been hard for you," Agatha continues. "But you are here and you are as much a part of this as all of us. You will not be forgotten, I'm sure we can help you in some way to defend yourself, but it is your decision to stay, if you don't perhaps you can get your old job back in London." Downcast, Agatha trails off her conversation.

Pollyanna is stunned not sure how to answer, slowly she speaks, nerves shown through her voice. "I don't want to go back, I feel like an equal here, the first time since I started as a maid, I think I'm invested now, I'm fearful though and this is all an unknown to me."

Agatha stands and hugs Pollyanna. "It is just as much an unknown for me too, but we can do this together okay. Just promise me one thing though okay."

Pollyanna hesitated. "What am I making a promise to, Agatha?"

"Only no more screaming okay, we know these men can be trusted," Agatha smiles at Pollyanna with reassurance the pleading in her eyes was obvious.

"Okay," Pollyanna responds. "But I can't promise that if we get attacked.

"Ha, ha, okay, Pollyanna." Agatha squeezes her hand and turns to Caelan giving him a nod of approval. Turning to the doorway he bellowed to the rest of the team to come into the entranceway. Five extra men, or men-shaped at least, came into view.

"It's time to introduce the rest of your guard, Miss Agatha. First, is Naga."

A pale effervescent man-shaped figure moved forward, leaving watery footprints in his stead. He bowed towards Agatha then slowly moved back to the group of Daemons. "He is a primelon, a water Daemon. He escaped the dimension door when I did and we have been friends and colleagues ever since. Second is Fervor."

A leaf-coloured shape moved forward. He also bowed to Agatha, but stepped further forward, took Agatha's hand and said, "Your aunt and I were close, Agatha. I will never forget her smile and the love she shared with everyone around her." His voice was low and had the echo of leaves rustling in the wind. His comment created a ball in Agatha's throat. She smiled at him as he let go of her hand and moved towards the other group of men.

"He is a Verdure Daemon. They are quite rare nowadays. They don't much like to fight but will suck the life out of those who cross them." This last remark made Agatha snap her head towards Fervor again, who smiled simply at her and winked. She felt he was showing a bit of cheekiness. No wonder Aunt Natalie had liked him. She had been very cheeky with those close to her.

Caelan cleared his throat. "Next, we have Oxide or Oxxy or if he annoys the hell out of you, oxymoron!" With this, the group laughed. Oxxy stepped forward. His shape was like a mini twister shaped as a man. He bent into a bow shape in front of Agatha then turned, jumped and clicked his heels together but instead of the noises it should make if a person did this, it made the sounds of crashing air against rock, almost like waves hitting a cliff, leaving Agatha eerily aware of Oxxy.

"Oxxy is a promulgate Daemon or Air Daemon. He is one of the newest to the group, an initiate you could say. Next is Ants, as in Antsy. He is a Fulgurate Daemon or Lightning Daemon and his name is his reason for not keeping still. He looks like he has ants in his pants." At this everyone laughed, even Pollyanna who seemed to be settling with each introduction to the crew. A strange mixture of human and daemon with Ants stepping forward or flickering forward. He stated, "Excuse me, miss, but I warn you, I may shock you with my wit but never with my hand."

Upon Ants saying this, Charles groaned. "Ants thinks he is a comedian, I'm afraid, Agatha. He is right in saying he will shock you, but he could shock a human to death if he wanted to. Demons, on the other hand, take only a little more. His kind are what you would call the gypsy of the demon realm."

"I may shock you with my wit, Miss Agatha, but my kind are the travelling kind. You may find a fair few in your forests as your storms are daily and we love a good charge, Miss Agatha." Ants stepped back and bowed with a grin that could beat a Cheshire cat.

"Finally," stated Caelan, directing the attention back onto himself, "we have our resident Death Daemon Alfred." Alfred looked more like a depressed teenager who hadn't slept in months or seen the sun since he was a baby. "Agatha, Alfred is our youngest recruit who escaped on the night your aunt died. Lord Caspian had managed to partially open the portal whilst fatally wounding your aunt."

Upon this statement, the ball in Agatha's throat returned. She couldn't hold back her tears this time, Charles moved in front of her, wiping away her tears. Caelan pulled out a dust-covered hanky and passed it to Charles. Charles shook out most of the dust and gave it to Agatha but Pollyanna, pulled it out of Agatha's hand. "Goodness me, you can't use that, it's filthy." Pollyanna undid her jacket and passed a white handkerchief to Agatha who took it wiped her eyes and nose with a watery smile at Pollyanna and then at Alfred.

"Nice to meet you, Alfred."

Alfred, aghast by her tears, spoke like any moody teenager. "Geez, it's not *my* fault, you know. Just because I'm a death daemon doesn't mean it was my fault. God, someone stop her crying. She might flood the hallway." Caelan swiped at Alfred. Alfred ducked. "Gosh, Caelan, I'm just trying to distract from the current philosophical dilemma of our socio-daemonic standing. We are the dominant races here."

Caelan picked up Alfred and gave him a shake. Agatha, wiping her eyes once more, pushed her way past Charles and Pollyanna, towards Caelan. "Caelan, put him down. He is young and obviously stupid in the sense of human behaviour."

Agatha glared at Alfred Caelan dropped Alfred hard on his backside. "Argh, Caelan, that was a bit rough."

"If it weren't for Agatha, my boy, you would have had a swift kick up the arse and been sent packing. You hear me, boy? Do not speak out of turn, she is your boss, keeper, and she also has the right to send you back to your realm."

With this notion, Alfred in a sulky manner replied, "Yes, sir, and sorry, ma'am."

"And another thing, don't bring your smartarse remarks unless it's for the benefit of our group. Be thankful Agatha has offered us a place to stay. No more leaky garage, for you!"

"But I like my garage!" Alfred protested, to which Caelan raised his hand for another whack. Alfred crouched down. "Okay, I'm sorry, I can't wait to see my new room, thanks, Agatha, do we still get paid?"

With this, Fervor stepped forward and yanked Alfred back. He grew a handful of leaves from his arm, ripped them off and stuffed them into Alfred's mouth. "We are sorry for Alfred, Miss Agatha. He is still very new and doesn't understand the ways of the human world. He will soon be taught, though, and we will make sure he doesn't offend you further."

Agatha and Pollyanna giggled now that everyone had been introduced, she sat back on the lounge suite with Pollyanna. Charles and Caelan stood by her side, all four of them looking at the five demons in front of them.

"The five of you have made your way into our lives. Our lives from here on out will be different, will be a new turning point and will also require teamwork, trust and loyalty. Can you prove this type of kinship? Can you be trusted with our work ahead? It will not be plain sailing and will definitely not be easy. All I ask of you is, will you work with us to create a better future, a better life for humans and daemons alike?"

Agatha stood watching their responses, the five stepped forward with full agreement. Even Alfred was over his sulky tantrum and spoke up with the others. "Yes, ma'am."

The five started to move to gather their things for their stay in the Castle. Caelan went to remind the others of the timeframe before dusk and the storms. He also put Fervor in charge of sorting the food for the night's meal and drink.

Whilst Caelan was busy with the others, Agatha turned to Charles.

"Aggie, as we are living so close to each other now, I want you to call me Charlie. You mean a lot to me and I wish to be less formal."

Charles stroked her cheek and cupped it in his hand. Pollyanna coughed, looked down. "I think I will help Caelan."

Agatha breathless and too involved in Charles' actions could not break away to respond, moved her face closer to his. She could feel his breath on her cheek as he moved in and kissed her on the other side. Biting her lip, she moved back a little but the moment was broken with Caelan standing right in front of both of them with the biggest grin on his face. Both Charlie and Aggie blushed.

Caelan said, "Oh come on, you two, pretend I'm not here!" Caelan still standing there with a goofy grin staring at the two made Charlie break away and clear his throat. Aggie followed by brushing her trousers with her hand. Both were bright pink from the embarrassment of Caelan and his blatant disregard for privacy, although his encouragement was sweet. He lifted his hands in frustration and rolled his eyes. "I give up, you two will be dead before you make a move. I swear it!" Caelan stomped off towards the vicinity of the kitchen.

Aggie, still embarrassed, could not look at Charles but didn't want to leave the area. She felt this connection with Charles much like magnets. Their moments together pulled her towards him, wanting more of the stolen moments they'd had. still pink in the face and looked at Charlie. Aunt Natalie's order of men never being needed was so faint in her head that her heart was pounding in her whole body. She felt like her skin was humming as Charles looked again to her. Aggie was frozen on the spot as he moved closer to her.

"In a hundred years, Aggie, I have never felt so nervous around someone, so thrilled to see you every day and so encapsulated by your eyes and how your character shines through them. I could write a thousand love notes to you and still not be able to explain this feeling for you." Charles stepped closer and again brushed her cheek, this time moving the hair off it and pushing it behind her ear. He leaned closer still and Aggie swore her heart had stopped. She held her breath and he kissed her neck. She let out a quick nervous breath as Charlie brought his face in front of hers and looked into her eyes. Again, Aggie bit her lip, and again their moment was broken by Pollyanna screaming, she raced in and hurried further into the depths of the castle, all they could here in her stead was her frantic words, "There's another, another daemon, oh lord help us my heart, my heart!" The footsteps of none other than Lord Caspian soon followed by the daemon himself.

The immediate mood changed from love and lust for each other, to hate and anger towards Lord Caspian.

"Well, well, well, isn't this a turn of events? Employer and employee turn love birds, is it?" Lord Caspian laughed as he pushed the oak doors open wider, and there next to him was his footman both changed in appearance from Agatha's last meeting, Caspian now had dark grey skin his hair line showed cracks filled in an angry red colouring, his hands no longer instead claw like.

His footman still tall with a malevolent look, skin grey and green, his tail swished behind him. The closer proximity strengthened the dread Aggie felt when she saw him at a distance. The feeling was like a stranglehold almost choking her breath. The footman's evil echoey laugh radiated through the entranceway. Charlie was stuck also with short rasping breaths.

"I presume this means you will be taking the head of state then, Mr Charles Ignacio What a pity, such a poor excuse of a charge, Miss Agatha."

Charlie broke his frozen state and lunged toward Lord Caspian. The footman stepped in between them and reached a hand up. He opened his mouth and it made the sounds of thousands of people screaming. Agatha covered her ears and squeezed her eyes shut. She screamed and crouched down. The noise terrifying and Aggie stayed like that until Charlie managed to pull at her arm and release it from her own grip, it had felt like hours of screaming, her mind felt as it would burst.

He kept repeating to her, "It's okay, Aggie, it's over, they have gone. Aggie, you are safe, Caelan came to the rescue. Aggie, it's okay now." Aggie, crying slowly felt the noise lessen to an echo her ears were ringing as she cried out, more so in relief, she fell into Charlie's open arms and buried her head into his shoulder.

Caelan called from outside, "They have gone, Charles, but I would say they will be back soon enough. We need protection. We need that book."

At this last comment, Aggie lifted her tear-streaked face from Charlie's shoulder. Charlie once again looked into her eyes this time, to make sure she was okay. Aggie pushed her hand through his hair which made him briefly close his eyes. When he opened them, she smiled with a bit more confidence. They both stood and moved apart as more voices came rushing closer. Charlie stepped in front of Aggie in a protective stance. It was the team returning. They had been running for a while when they had realised who had driven past on the road. The purple-hued clouds followed the men as all five and Caelan entered the entranceway.

"I thought you had only just left?" was the puzzled reply from Aggie at their arrival.

Charlie relaxed his pose of defence and turned to Aggie. "It was a spell, Aggie. You had been screaming and holding yourself for a while."

Yeah, an ye can definitely say you have a pair of lungs on ya. You been screaming for near over an hour! You must have a sore throat now Aggie'

Agatha was shocked at his comment. "It felt like days the noise, the horror of it," Caelan stated, "Well, this was your first encounter with an unfriendly spell, hey! At least it was only a warning shot. But we need to find out which daemon that footman is and the only way to do that is to find that book!" All agreed with Caelan as they all began to move down to the kitchen.

"So Fervor, what did you manage to scrounge for our supper? we are some big men here who need a big hole a fillin', and I think it's safe ter say our Missy needs a decent feed and a long drink with all that screaming."

Aggie smiled a brittle smile, exhausted from her first attack. "I think I need to learn some magic, Caelan. Physical defence is one thing but magic, I need to learn. Can it be done?"

Hesitant, looked from Charlie to Aggie. "The only lass I know that can relate to that strength o' magic lives on the outskirts of town. Be a fair day trip to get to her and back again." Caelan looked reserved in his response and they all gathered around the kitchen table, Alfred jumped as a hand had grabbed his ankle. "Argh, Pollyanna what are you doing!" Pollyanna hiding below the table looked about the group, her eyes wide and fearful. "Is it gone, did those things go?! So much screaming, so many screaming. I thought you had all been killed." Fervor placed the bags he was holding on the table in front of everyone, he lent down and slowly pulled Pollyanna out from underneath the table Pollyanna whimpered as she let him pull her out. Wearily she grabbed the chair Alfred passed her and sat down holding her chest. the others silently moved to put their bags by the kitchen door. Aggie, looking in the bag from Fervor, found a few odds and ends, enough to make a stew for dinner, with a fair few bottles, from the local tavern, the Squirrel. Brew, enough to maintain the group whilst the stew cooked through.

"I think," replied Aggie, bending down to comfort Pollyanna whilst speaking to the others in the group, "this person or daemon you speak of, is in dire need of new temporary lodgings, who if needs be, can be paid for their time here, enough I dare say to teach me magic and supply future learning once they have shown the basics."

"I want to learn," blurted out Pollyanna. "I'm so scared, I don't want to die, maybe they can teach me, can they teach a human?" Aggie looked around at the group of Daemons as she opened and passed the bottles of brew to each of the group.

Caelan looked into his bottle. "Okay, Aggie, Pollyanna, on one condition. Aggie you must have a loophole-free contract, enough to contain the Daemon in the house or premises for the entirety of the contractual obligations. It can only be broken with your say so, and they must sign it before entering the property, do you understand, Aggie? It's important." Aggie frowned but agreed. Pollyanna looked hopeful at Caelan. "I can't be like this forever I want to defend myself if I am to be here. I want to stay with you all."

Agatha thought to herself as the others found chairs to sit in around the large, girthed table used by past cooks and maids. She set to peeling and preparing the food for the stew. *If there is a contract to be made, what kind of danger is this person or daemon going to be towards us?*

She looked up at the high ceilings in the kitchen whilst Caelan got up and started to light the fire for dinner. Agatha could see Charlie trying to catch her eye, although she knew he wanted to deter her from her decision. She broke her momentary stubbornness to look at him and smile. She looked back down at her area of the table — potatoes, carrots, sweet potato, onion and a fresh leg of meat.

She peeled the last veggies and said, "Naga, can you fetch some water please?" Agatha then hesitated and looked around the room. Realisation hit. "You all can eat stew, can't you?"

Everyone turned to her with a grin. Caelan swelled his chest to obviously make a cheeky remark and was cut short by Charles jumping up, grinning while he did so.

"Yes, we eat stew. Will it have ears and snake venom though? I do like a good kick!"

The others looked at Charles. "Boo!" They all remarked, laughing.

Caelan turned to Charles. "What a bad joke and here we thought you would have something smart to say. I guess being a scholar isn't all it's cracked up to be." Charles sat down, rolling his eyes and going bit pink. He looked at Agatha who grinned openly at him. Agatha then jumped with shock. "Naga, how, what, you can just summon water!"

Naga grinned at Agatha. "Well, I am a daemon after all, Aggie. I got to have some tricks up my sleeves."

Alfred made his presence known. "Oh God, you people are so old fashioned with your jokes and parlour tricks, I might as well just kill myself now, guh!" Alfred put his head into his hands. Pollyanna gasped as the remark, not sure where to turn her head

Caelan gave Alfred a friendly swipe. "Cheer up, lad, your gothic mood will dampen everyone if you keep this up." Caelan then gave him a warning glance.

"Fine, call me when dinner is ready. I'm going to have some sanity in my room."

Caelan stood up. "You remember where you are, Alfred." Caelan sternly pointed his finger at Alfred. "Be thankful for Agatha opening her place to you. I will not stand it if you insult her kindness."

Alfred turned with his head bowed and said, "I'm sorry, Agatha, thank you for your kindness, would you mind awfully if I remove myself in search of my room until dinner is ready?"

At this Agatha looked shocked. Alfred was nice to her, and not sulky. "Well, that's definitely an improvement, Alfred, but yes, you may wait in there if that suits you better. There are rooms on the ground floor that you lot can take. Charles and Caelan will be up by me and Pollyanna on the first floor." Alfred bowed and turned sulkily out of the room and into the darkness.

Everyone was silent which brought in a timely crash of the storm raging outside. The fire flickered as a gust of wind hurtled past and gave a decent blow down the chimney in the kitchen.

Charles stood unceremoniously. Holding his beer up, he spouted out, "To Aggie, for her kindness, willingness to accept, and the future we now hold with her."

Caelan laughed. "Sit down, ya love-lusted lad, we will cheer to that but, my boy, calm yourself. The two of you are almost as bad as each other." The rest of the group laughed as Agatha hid her redness by turning to stir the stew that she had prepared and was now sitting by the fire, the water Naga had supplied was by Pollyanna who busily ladled it into the stew a happy distraction she concentrated on.

Caelan, breaking the temporary silence spoke up, "Aggie my dear, the book you are after, it will not be an easy feat. Once we have found and contracted this daemon from the south, we need to retrace your family's steps. Is the library still intact?"

Aggie replied, "I have not been into the library yet, Caelan, and we haven't reached that part of the castle. I hope it is still intact as I remember Aunt Natalie reading me stories as a child. They are all in the library."

Caelan sat straight up. "Aggie, that must be where the ledger will be held or a clue about it. Do you remember any stories being told of the types of daemons and what they can do?"

"I wish I could say yes, but that was never read to me or from what I remember, but it would be a very good place to start."

Caelan slammed down his fist onto the table with a big grin. Pollyanna yelped, "Oh my nerves!" she exclaimed clasping her chest dramatically.

Caelan spoke up looking away from Pollyanna. "Great team, great team." Caelan spoke as though the brew was warming his belly and his restraint was waning. Agatha gave a giggle to which Charles looked again at her, this time with longing, a look she returned in the same manner.

Agatha broke away from his stare. she turned towards the stew, adding dried herbs from the shelf above the mantel.

She placed her hand on the side of the fireplace as her mind wandered to her brief moment with Charles, the kiss on her cheek and the closeness of him. Agatha ran her hands over the fireplace, not thinking of what the shapes or designs were as her fingers followed the swirls and curls of the design. Her hands found a rough patch which she picked at. She looked at the area and found a curious entrance point for a key.

"Charles, Caelan, look at this, did you know this was here?" she said as she moved away from the fireplace to angle herself in front of the rough key-shaped hole. Pollyanna sat with the others cautiously looking around her to make sure no more daemons were going to jump into view or want to eat her. You could see she was drained and hated the feeling of dread.

Caelan moving closer to the fireplace to have a better look. "In all my years, Miss Aggie, I have never seen or even noticed that before," Caelan replied, bewildered.

Agatha furrowed her brow and looked closer; she mumbled to herself then turned and smiled. "That's it!" Agatha stated. "Aunt Natalie always maintained adamantly that all things hidden in plain sight are the hardest to find. She used to dress in the monochromatic clothing and when we played hide and seek, sometimes she would be leaning against a wall and I would run straight past her, looking for her but not truly seeing. 'Hiding in plain sight'."

Agatha's lifted spirits then soured as memories of Aunt Natalie surfaced. Her face now showed remorse. Charles moved and pulled her chair closer for her. Agatha sat back in front of the fire, her mind elsewhere as she aimlessly stared at the fire, the group discussing the keyhole behind her as her mind wandered off into her memories. She was pulled back to reality when Charles spoke up.

"Caelan," he said. "Caelan, where do you think this leads? It must go somewhere, and of all places to be, it's here, the kitchen."

Fervor spoke up. "I think we need to figure out first how to open whatever it is, don't you, Charles, Caelan? It could lead to something, or it could lead to nothing, Agatha is right Aunt Natalie did have enjoyment in trickery for hiding in plain sight, this may lead somewhere."

Agatha slowly stood. She moved to the pot of stew as it was now bubbling away. She grabbed a cloth and pulled the meat bone out and onto the table. Cutting away at the cooked meat, she looked up, oblivious to the conversation. "Ants, can you get Alfred? This is almost ready."

Caelan speaking with Agatha, "Lass, do you remember your aunt having a big ole key?"

Agatha again furrowed her brows. "Caelan, I don't remember any key. I didn't even know that hole existed until now. If it weren't for my hands exploring the wood, I would never have known it was there."

Alfred and Ants walked back into the room as Agatha placed the meat back in the stew. She collected bowls and spoons from the built-in cupboard. It had a bowed door with beautiful designs painted on it, faded through age but still reasonably clear in design.

Placing the bowls and cutlery on the table, Agatha served up the stew to the group circled around the table. Fervor put three loaves on the table, which Agatha then sliced two of them and put the third in the cupboard.

After a while of concentrated eating, the warmth of the fireplace and the bodies soon made it too hot for all to sit around the table.

Bellies full, a tired veil draped over the group in the room.

Oxxy stood up and put his bowl on the bench. The others followed as Oxxy stretched. "I think we all need to find rooms and have a decent sleep. I know I need one," Oxxy commented to the group whilst yawning.

"Aye, think you are right, Oxxy," said Caelan, standing up and rubbing his big, girthed belly. "Come on, lads and ladies, I think we should retire for the night and plan our week in the morning. It's been eventful and I think a good sleep whilst we can, should help all involved." Caelan started placing the chairs in the corner of the kitchen whilst the others finished stacking their bowls. One by one, most of the group left the room. Caelan and Charles hung back for Aggie as she cleared the table and wiped it down. She removed her apron and smiled at the both of them. "Ready?"

Walking out of the kitchen and down the hall to the entranceway, Charles walked next to Agatha as Caelan led on. Charles brushed his hand against Agatha's then put his hand out for her to take it. Agatha did so willingly, with a flutter like butterflies in her chest.

Gong up the stairs to their floor, Charles let go as they came to their lodgings. He was further down the hall whilst Caelan was opposite Agatha. Caelan stumbled heavily into his room; a mumble of a good night was heard before he shut his door. He left Agatha and Charles alone on the floor.

Agatha reached her door. "Agatha." Charles mentioned her name and she turned towards him, her back against her door. He stepped closer to her, lifting his hand and brushing her hair away from her cheek. "Aggie, I have wanted to be alone with you since I first met you." She bit her bottom lip, which made Charles smile. He stepped closer so their bodies were almost touching. Agatha breathed in a nervous breath as Charles looked her in the eyes. "I just can't stop looking into your eyes, Aggie. You have captured my heart and soul."

Agatha cut his further words short by closing the gap between their lips. Charles gasped as he felt her warmth whilst returning the kiss. With both their bodies touching, Agatha's mind was cleared and all she could think of was the moment. Charles ran his hand up her arm, giving her goosebumps as they kissed more deeply. Agatha's eyes were closed but flashes of light and fizzes of warm flowed through her body. She reached out and up and ran her hands through Charles' hair. She could feel the tingling sensation on his neck, the warmth of his blood circulating through his skin; she could feel the urge of wanting more from her and the passion he had for her. They both stopped briefly for air as both had ragged breathing. They stayed close and Charles kisses Agatha's neck. She felt herself pinned to her door but didn't care — she didn't care about what or where or how.

Her mind was numb from the wanting Charles. He stopped kissing her neck and moved back slightly. They smiled at each other, knowing the want was mutual. "I want to follow you in your room, my dear Agatha, but not now. Our kiss will keep me going for the night. Tomorrow I will want more of you, Aggie, for you are my drug. I am addicted to you."

Agatha bit her lip then smiled., She put her hand up and cupped Charles' face into her hand. He kissed the side of her palm then held her hand and moved it down. The want for more was present but Agatha broke the moment. "Sleep, Charles. We have so much to do tomorrow. We now know how we feel but more can wait. I still don't know much about you, but what I do know I want more of."

Charles went to step forward but Agatha had turned the handle of her door. She smiled a big, beautiful smile and whispered, "Good night, my Charles," to which he responded with a smile as he faltered to a stop. It was as broad as hers. Agatha moved her body into her room still smiling as she sent Charles on his way.

She closed the door and leaned against it. Her mind was exploding still with light and fireworks from their kiss. She sighed a deep sigh. Agatha was almost tempted to go to Charles' room now and continued their kiss, but her aunt came into her mind's eye. "Agatha, remember men are not important. Love is just a passing phase, concentrate on life, concentrate on your tasks at hand." Aunt Natalie faded away, leaving Agatha crestfallen. Charles was so much more than a passing fancy. She could feel it in her bones, how she ached for him.

The door opened slowly, it was not Charles whom Agatha hoped for but Pollyanna, crestfallen Agatha hid her emotion, but Pollyanna looking down said, "I'm sorry I wasn't spying on you, I was coming from the bathroom."

"It's okay, Pollyanna, you can stay in here tonight, we will find you proper lodgings tomorrow. Sharing the bed with Pollyanna Agatha had a restless night of fighting her urges for Charles and the ever-present swells of stormy weather outside.

Chapter 7
Unravelling Destiny

The morning slowly came through as a bright and sunny day. Agatha, although having a restless night, was full of energy and excitement, knowing she would have many more days of Charles so close to her. Pollyanna however, looked bedraggled and tired, as she slowly dressed for the day of work Agatha quickly washed and dressed, full of vigour and happiness. She left her room and Pollyanna who was still readying for the day, Agatha with her shirt open, a singlet underneath and her work trousers, shut her door. She felt warmth behind her — Charles.

"Good morning, Agatha, I hope you slept well." He kissed her neck, giving her goosebumps up and down her arms. She shivered with excitement as she turned to look at him.

"Shh, Pollyanna is still getting ready." Agatha grinned at Charles. He stepped back to look her over, his eyebrows raised as he saw she hadn't buttoned her shirt. Charles stepped forward and started to button her shirt for her. Agatha giggled and bit her lip. As he gets to her neck, he ran his hand over her collarbone and leaned in to kiss it.

The door opposite flew open with a big crash and Caelan yawned and stretched. "Aye now, that's a storm to wake the dead all right!" He hadn't noticed the closeness of the pair. They quickly moved apart and Agatha stood next to Charles, blushing as red as ever. Caelan raised his eyebrows and smirked. "Well, well, well! What mischief have I caught then, hey?"

Charles grinned from ear to ear, coughed and adjusted his cufflinks. He put his arm out to Agatha. "May I accompany you to the kitchen, Miss Agatha?" Caelan walked over and slapped him on the back, sending him jolting forward. Charles again straightened himself.

"Come on, you two love birds. Let's get some grub, no nonsense today, ya hear? We have a lot of work to do and you both need to be concentrating, okay?"

Agatha blushed again, took Charles' outstretched arm and they walked down the hall to the stairs. "Morning, boss," was heard from the bottom of the stairs. Pollyanna quickly skirted past Agatha and Charles and headed down the stairs, to where the rest of the group was waiting. The group headed for breakfast in the kitchen.

"Where is this library, Agatha? We should make a plan of attack for tonight whilst we are here." Caelan spoke whilst wiping the remaining stew off his chin. Some had opted for tea and toast, although Caelan took what he could, which was everything as he seemed a bottomless pit.

"Slow down, Caelan, or you will eat your hand if you're not careful!" said Ants. A chuckle was heard from the others in the group. Pollyanna placed more toast on his plate, Caelan swiped at Ants who ducked and nearly put his face into the table. The group laughed at the commotion Ants scowled at Caelan.

"From memory, Caelan," Agatha began to say. "It's in the south side of the castle, a part we haven't touched yet. I haven't even ventured down that far to be honest. It looks as though the roof may have caved in on that side."

Caelan thought on this, while the others continued their breakfast in silence, apart from Charles, who whispered in Agatha's ear, "I cannot wait to say goodnight to you again tonight, Aggie. I'm not sure I could last the day."

Agatha blushed as Charles sat back on his chair. His hand reached out and clasped hers in her lap under the table.

"Caelan what about the She-Daemon from the other side of town? Who is going to fetch her, and when?" Naga pointed out the keyhole as well and continued, "And what about the keyhole, Agatha found last night? We have some many unknown things to sort out."

"Oh, hush, Naga, I have already thought of everything, you should know by now I don't really sleep, my hearing is impeccable I can even hear whispering in the hallways."

Charles and Agatha stopped dead, both showing signs of red along their necks, faces and ears. Caelan looked at them and grinned to the rest of the group. The group turned and looked at the pair and started to laugh.

"Aye, naughty business were we up to, hey?" Ants looked at them both with a big grin.

"Aww, leave them alone!" said Naga, and Pollyanna together, coming to the stunned couple's rescue. Naga continues, "I'm sure you have been caught with your pants down, Ants. As I recall, it was your missus who did the catching! Is that why there was no fight in you moving into the castle, ya balardy scallon? You been up to no good again?"

Ants rolled his eyes. "Yeah, I'm my own man. I'm not tied to anything earthly or unearthly in this realm, and I'm glad of it. They's a balardy nuisance, I tell ya!"

At this the group laughed. "It's not their fault you can't keep it in your pants, Ants. Is that how you got your name, hey? Ants in your pants, can't keep them on for long enough, ha, ha, ha!" the room erupted with laughter. Even Ants couldn't help but laugh. He knew he was a mischief.

"All right, all right, you lot, let's plan the day out. Naga and Ants, you will accompany Charles and Agatha. I think your prowess and initiative will help in swaying the she daemon in signing the contract I wrote last night. Charles, I have already drafted out a copy. Agatha, you two have a look over and let me know what's missing." Caelan pulled out a roll of paper from the depth of his shirt and laid it on the table, Agatha and Charles, already next to each other, bent over the paper to read what had been drawn up.

"Alfred, you're on dishes, Fervor, you're on moving the rubbish we have cleared so far to the outside of the house. We will need to take it and dump it today to make room for more rubbish we will undoubtedly find."

Alfred moaned. "Oh great, make me the slave of the house. I have prowess and initiative too you know, too," he said sulkily to Caelan.

Caelan replied, "Well, use your initiative and prowess to hurry up and finish those dishes, then you can help Naga with the rubbish clearance. We can't have all of you running off to find she-daemons. We have to keep up with the restorations. What if Lord Caspian and his footman appears again? We will need you here, Alfred." Alfred felt a little better about the situation hearing that response, that he would be needed. Although he still grumbled whilst cleaning and tidying away the dishes.

"What would you have me do Caelan." Pollyanna's voice waivered a bit. "Erm, sorry Pollyanna you were so quiet I forgot you were there! You can work with Alfred today, I'm sure you can keep him in good spirits." Pollyanna smiled meekly, Alfred was the least Daemon looking of the bunch and had a proper face you could actually speak to.

Reading over and tweaking the contract during breakfast, Agatha and the rest of the group then began to get ready for the day's events.

Agatha gathering up her travel coat from her room saw Charles across the hall. He was kitted out in an almost army appropriate outfit. He also had an axe at his side holstered on his belt, along with large shells and a shotgun slung over his shoulder. He noticed the shock on Agatha's face as he walked closer to her. He smiled and reached towards her.

"In this line of work, Aggie, you have to be prepared for anything. Have you ever shot a gun?"

Agatha shook her head. "I never had to, before. I was a housemaid before I got the castle. I was nothing really."

Charles looked her over. "Aggie, you were never a nothing, and you definitely are not a nothing while I'm here." she smiled. Charles held his arm out for her to take and they walked down the hallway together.

Naga and Ants were already ready and waiting in the entranceway. Agatha looked at them and noticed they didn't have any weapons like Charles. "Where are your weapons?" she asked them.

They both glanced at each other and smiled. Ants held up his hand and streams of light flickered within his palm, Naga started swirling water. It glinted in the sunshine that streamed through the opened front oak doors. He then swirled it out of sight. "You know why

Caelan chose us, don't you Miss Agatha? Lightning and water together, we are a deadly pair," said Ants.

Naga shot a small shot of water into the air. Ants, with a flick of his wrist, threw a small ball of lightning at the water. Agatha could see the electricity flare up as it enveloped the water. The electric ball hit one of the old drapes by the front door and small bolts could be seen shooting around the falling water as it ran down the drape. She was surprised at the ease of the task, knowing full well it was a deadly combination.

"Well, you definitely will not need a gun, you two." Her impressed behaviour brought forward Charles' jealousy.

"Charles," Naga called as he saw the streak of jealousy. "Charles, lest we not forget, immortality bests all our powers. We may have them but we cannot survive what our other teammates can throw at us."

"Alas Naga, my immortality may seem to best yours but I tell you now, Death does visit me frequently waiting for my time to eventually run out." Agatha, shocked, looked panicked.

Alfred sauntered into the entranceway. "Geez, Charles, I don't think you're that popular. I don't waste my time with an immortal." Alfred then sulkily carried on walking outside to help Fervor with moving the rubbish. Naga and Ants smirked at Alfred's complaint.

Alfred sighed when he saw the sun was shining. "I wish it was raining," he said. "At least the day would match my mood and probably be a bit nicer to work in."

Pollyanna timidly walks out, slowly following Alfred, she smiled then hugged Agatha. "Please be careful, please come back in one piece, I still need you!" Squeezing Pollyanna back, Agatha watched her continue to follow Alfred.

Charles responds to Alfred. "Oh, enjoy it, Alfred. Remember the purple clouds will be coming every night." Alfred heard Charles but still remained sulky and moody. "Seems like a typical moody teenager to me." Agatha smiled, reciprocating his feelings.

Caelan was heard before he was seen with his heavy stomping feet on the upstairs flooring as he and Oxxy came into view on the first-floor landing. "Right! Are we ready then, lads Miss Aggie erm, Miss Pollyanna, of course?" Caelan smiled at Agatha with a gentle look, a hard feat considering that he was made of what looked like orange sandstone.

He moved down the stairs clomping his heavy feet as he went. He looked at the group and said, "I have drawn up a rough sketch of the route you must take to this she daemon's place." He went to give it to Agatha but then pulled it out of reach before she could secure it. "Aggie, you must promise me and all of you the same, do not request anything other than what you are there for. I will tell the others as well. She will see it against you. She can see your future if you touch her and it will drain you of energy which she will energise from so be warned, this is not a holiday!"

Agatha, weary of Caelan's words, took the map from his now open hand. She looked at the map and saw a few circles over the top of their route. "Caelan, what are the circles for?"

"Aye, glad you brought that up, Aggie. They are from memory, places of caution, highwaymen, robbers and Lord Caspian's lot who search the areas from time to time. You will be on foot so go quickly." Agatha passed the hand-drawn map to the others.

"What is this, Caelan? Your grammy draw this for you? It's almost illegible," said Ants with an impish like grin .

Caelan stepped down to swipe Ants, who was too fast and bolted out the door. Caelan chuckled. "The balardy cheek, I tells ya! Go on off with the lot o' yer before I change my mind about this balardy she daemon."

With that, the group moved out of the oak doorway and into brilliant sunlight. What had been an overgrown front passage was now stripped back of the vegetation and a dilapidated stone veranda went all the way across the front of the entrance. They walked down the five or so stairs onto the gravel driveway. In plain sight to the left was an enormous pile of rubbish and vegetation that had been removed from the castle. Only small weeds were left visible on the gravel driveway but the improvement was vast. The brick of the pillars near the entrance were scattered with a leafy moss giving character to the once messy, overgrown entrance.

Agatha moved her face up to the sunlight and enjoyed the warmth. Charles, still arm in arm with her, proceeded to brush some hair that had fallen down onto her face. Caelan ushered the group to get moving with his hands. Turning to farewell Pollyanna, Agatha started walking down the driveway with the others.

Caelan yelled, "You better put some pep in your step or you won't be home for a week. Come on, hurry up, you blundering blockheads. Not you, Miss Aggie,"

Ants and Naga rolled their eyes and quickened their step. Charles and Agatha moved at the same speed. "You know we will slow down at the end of the driveway, right?" Ants said with a cheeky grin.

Naga moved ahead, not turning but speaking, "Caelan is right, we have an important task ahead of us. We are avoiding the township to remove any suspicion or to alert Lord Caspian. This drawing from Caelan is rough but gives us a guide of where we need to be." He turned and looked at Ants, who solemnly nodded.

"Okay, no funny business. It's straight business, got it."

Charles spoke up. "Well, as we will be doing a lot of walking, Agatha, you want to tell me more about the house. Perhaps we can stumble upon some information I haven't come across through your memories of the house, or where your aunt might have kept the key."

"Two birds with one stone, hey Charles? Not a bad idea if you get stuck. Perhaps we can do our combo shock treatment on her to help her remember."

Ants grinned evilly at Agatha, but both Charles and Naga replied, "No, Ants, not a good idea."

The group fell silent as they reached the end of the driveway. Naga looked at the map and decided the route was to the left; he showed the others, who agreed with his findings.

"Do you think we should remain on the roadside, Naga?" Charles looked at Naga for an answer.

Concentrating on the map Naga replied, "We are only on the road for a short while, then it's cutting through the forest, and avoiding the township that way. It looks as though the daemon's land is in or near a swamp land but I cannot be too certain. Through the forest is where the markings are shown of possible raids and highwaymen so at least we will have cover." Naga moved around a big boulder at the side of the road and continued walking.

The landscape was changing whilst they walked, from bushy lands to becoming flecked with smaller bushes. There was no cover and the heat from the sun as they walked became uncomfortable for all, especially Naga.

"I need water soon," he said.

"Naga, we have only just left! Why do you need it so quickly?"

"I am a water daemon. I cannot be covered for the entirety of the trip but I can be helped with fluids. Why do you think my pack is so heavy?"

An hour had passed and back at the castle, Alfred had continued to grumble as he helped with little effort in clearing and tidying the place with Fervor, Pollyanna was trying her best to help, clearly not as strong as the other two. Oxxy and Caelan were clearing yet another room of all the items that had been in the same position for years by the amount of dust left on them. Slowly moving the decent gear to the ballroom and rubbish to Alfred, who was still moaning. "Ach, Alfred, stop bloody moaning, will ye?" Caelan threw a broken and brittle lounge chair onto the rubbish heap, narrowly missing Alfred as he dove for cover with his hands over his head.

"I wish Agatha was here," said Alfred to everyone's surprise. "At least then she can see how brutal you are with me." Pollyanna moves to Alfred. "Are you okay, would you like something to drink Alfred?" Startled by her care Alfred paused, only briefly though as Caelan took the second lounger off Oxxy and hurled it at Alfred. Alfred pulled his hood up and stepped forward and disappeared as the lounger flew into the heap and through the area where he was just standing. Pollyanna shrieked at the disappearance causing Caelan to laugh.

Alfred came into view leaning against the pillar by the entrance. "I could scream brutality, Caelan" But Alfred didn't think that part through. A giant sandal hurled through the air and narrowly missed Alfred. He let out a big puff of dust and slipped to the ground. "Got to be quick on your toes boy! and stop ya moaning we have a whole castle to fix" Caelan stomped back into the house, picking up his sandal as he passed him, leaving Alfred still grumbling although more to himself. Pollyanna unsure how to take his disappearing act; keeps a watchful eye on him as she continued to move the lighter items, clearly not having the super strength as Fervor and Alfred.

Ants, Naga, Charles and Agatha had reached the edge of the forest where their turn-off had been crudely drawn on the map by Caelan. Naga turned to the others. "Keep a lookout. It is this area that the highwaymen are drawn." Heading off the main road and onto what seemed to look like two goat tracks going into a line of head-height brush edging the forest, once they got through the first obstacle, they were met with a hefty mud patch. It is slow going for the group.

Agatha, lighter than the others, moved ahead of the three and came out first from the mud patch but stopped when she heard an unusual noise. It was like a gas light but the noise was going higher and higher in pitch. Charles had a look of shock and dove for Agatha. A net hurtled past the group as Naga and Ants also dropped to the edge of the dry ground Agatha was on. Voices could be heard as Charles, now on top of Agatha, brought his hand up to motion her to shush.

"Did ye get them rascallies, me boyo?" said an older voice.

A younger voice was then heard, "Neh daar, I can't 'ear any squawking from the she lady."

The older voice chuckled. "You're a good shot, boyo. Mebe you knocked her plum out!"

With that, the young voice agreed. "Yeah, yeah, I knocked her plum off her feet daarr. Les go get 'em ait!"

Charles, still holding his hand on his lips, was looking around the area. Naga and Ants had disappeared into the brush silently. A few seconds later, yelling, a few thumps and bodies dropping to the ground could be heard. Naga and Ants could be heard laughing at the ridiculous sight but Charles and Agatha remained on the forest floor.

Charles was looking her over and ran his hand up the side of her thigh. Agatha, looking into his eyes, couldn't help but flush pink with excitement and bit her bottom lip. Charles smiled and leaned forward to kiss her.

"Aha! That's five silver pennies there, Ants, I knew they would be kissing or some malarky." Ants and Naga pushed past a low-lying bush and came back into view. They stopped by the two still lying on the ground.

Agatha went bright red as Charles stood up. He put his hand out to help her up. Agatha, still blushing, sat up, folded her arms around her legs and looked at her feet. Charles just laughed it off, smiling sheepishly, trying to make it seem it didn't catch him off guard.

Agatha, collecting her thoughts, then turned to Ants and Naga. "You bet on us!"

Ants was the one to look sheepish now. "It was childish. I'm sorry if I upset you, Agatha, I mean no harm." He went to Naga's outstretched fist and pushed his hand holding the coins back towards Naga's chest.

Charles put his hand out to Agatha again who then took him up on the offer. Standing, she brushed her trousers and thought, *Get it together Agatha, you don't have time for a love interest right now.*

Speaking to the group, Agatha put her hand out. "May I have a look at the map please?" Naga passed the map to her. She looked at the crudely drawn picture, then pointed at the map, showing the others. "If we are here now, how much longer until we get to the next problem area?" The three looked at each other, surprised. "I can read a map, you know. I may be a female but I am not a feeble one." Agatha pushed through the bush Naga and Ants had come through.

It wasn't a pleasant sight. The two highwaymen were dead and a bit spread out, to put it kindly. "I advise from now on, no more killing or they will be discovered, especially if you decide to do this with their bodies." Agatha held her head up high and kept walking to stop her from looking any further and to hold down the vomit rising in her throat.

"Yes, Miss Agatha, won't happen again," both answered simultaneously.

Charles was the last to walk through. "God, boys, you can kill without mess, you know."

"It's been a while and we got excited, I guess," replied Ants.

"Speak for yourself, Ants," said Naga, now feeling a bit guilty at what they were leaving behind. Haphazardly covering the bodies will leaves and brush the two rushed to catch up with Agatha and Charles.

The way was silent between the four for almost an hour when they approached an unusual handmade sign nestling in the trees.

"Charles, do you know what this is?"

Charles came closer and had a look alongside the other two. Charles put his hand out to touch it, which was quickly slapped down by Naga.

"Don't be a fool, touching that could curse you," Naga said to Charles.

"I know what it is. It's a protection type spell."

Naga then cut in. "Yes, but can you not see the blood on it? That is another spell cursing those that touch the artifact."

Charles, surprised, lowered his hand, rubbing it. He stepped closer to look and this time not touch. Its willow branches were shaped into three triangles intertwined together. It took him a second to realise the triangles were moving, twisting and circulating around.

Agatha stepped forward to look and almost yelped when she saw this. "Why have I not seen this before!" She panicked.

Charles held her arms. "Agatha, your birthday, the tavern, remember, anything resembling magic or daemons was all hidden from you. I understand your panic, it is unworldly and foreign to you, but it's been around you all your life. You just haven't been able to see it."

Agatha pulled her arms out of Charles' grasp. She rubbed them, not because of him hurting her, but due to the shock and needing security within herself. She looked at Charles sideways. Were it not for her attraction to him, her reaction might have been rather different. "I'm confused," she said. "I can't believe this was hidden from me. Why would Aunt Natalie do that?"

Naga stepped forward, cutting off Charles' reply. "Agatha, Natalie did it for her reason of protection, be it wrought with misgivings and propelling you to this discomfort in the future. Her intentions were pure. Natalie only wanted the best for you."

Frustrated, Agatha moved towards the symbol on the tree. She looked it over with fascination. The want to pick it up was overpowering. She reached out to it. Her hand was grabbed by Charles.

"Agatha, what are you doing? I was just told not to touch, why are you now trying?"

Struggling, Agatha reached over Charles. "I must touch it! I must have it" Agatha scrambled with Charles and Naga stepped forward to help. She shoved Naga out of the way and tried again for the Symbol.

"I must touch it!" she screamed at them. With this turn of events, all the men dove on her. The three grappled her to the ground as she screamed at the top of her lungs.

"I MUST HAVE IT!" As Agatha breathed in for another bellow, she was cut short by Ants who punched her and knocked her out. The men stood up, startled.

"What the hell was that, Ants? You could have caused permanent damage!"

Ants in panic replied, "I… I'm sorry, I just was trying to get her to stop, she was…"

Giggling behind them began to become an outright high-pitched laugh. Charles crouched over Agatha to protect her from whatever next was happening. Ants and Naga, saw a small what looked to be a child, with green hair that went right onto its face and stopped by its cheekbones. Its giggle could have passed off as a child but the laugh, that definitely sounded like a more mature malevolent person.

"Aww, is the wee girlie fallen?" it said as it walked behind a tree. It disappeared then reappeared right next to Charles, looking down at Agatha. "She is beautiful, Charlie-warlie. I suppose you will go to the ends of the earth to keep her safe, hey!" It looked at Naga and Ants. "So would you Naga and possibly you, Ants, but your feelings are still mixed. Not sold on her yet, is that it?" It grinned at Ants.

Ants stepped forward to swing a punch at the thing and it twisted and disappeared. The group were left puzzled and on guard. Agatha was still knocked out on the ground. Charles looked down and swept his hand across to move her hair out of her face. His face was completely covered in worry.

The thing reappeared inches away from Agatha. "Looking so good even close up. She is a special one, my daemons."

The thing went in and kissed her, which Charles reacted to by swinging at it and yelling, "Get away from her, you mad thing! How dare you?"

It laughed and swirled away into nothing again. Charles picked up Agatha and tried to gently shake her awake. She drew a breath and opened her eyes, looking at Charles straight away.

"Your eyes!" Charles said.

Agatha's eyes, which she was renowned for, were black. She looked at the others, surprised by Charles and his comment. "What's wrong with my eyes?" As she looked from one to another, the group noticed they grew lighter and lighter until they went white. She then went stiff and started fitting, with the look of surprise now fixed on her face and she writhed about, falling from Charles' arms and dropping on the ground. In panic, the three tried their best to help her as she calmed down and slowed to a stop. Agatha was now in a relaxed position not dissimilar to before the stranger stole a kiss.

Laughter peeled through the edge of the forest. It bounced off the trees and came from all areas. It confused the three who tried to pinpoint where it originated. After what seemed many minutes had gone past, the laughing stopped. The group huddled over

Agatha. They knew they had to get out of the forest and fast.

The trickster swirled into view, leaning against another tree. "Wondering what I did to you?" It looked at its talon-like nails and crossing its legs as it remained leaning against the tree, it laughed again, but this time no echoes bounced off the trees in the forest.

Naga stood. "What did we do to you? Why have you done this? Who are you?"

The stranger then rolled its eyes and stepped forward with feet like a horse. "And then the questions, it's always the questions. Never, oh my God, am I going to die, is she dead, are we all dead? It's why!" Exasperated, the thing stood up straight and in a now formal tone explained himself. "Well food, for starters yes, you are probably going to die. You are my food and I'm playing with you. My name is Gnargoyle. I am a forest daemon. I have kissed your plaything, Charles, which has paralysed her. I know your names because I can hear your thoughts. I can also see what you are going to do next which means while I see you, I can see what you next want to do." Gnargoyle rolled its eyes. "So yes, Charles, I can hear you wrestling with how to kill me or how fast you can get to me."

Gnargoyle then looked at Ants. He could see Ants was wrestling with himself and laughed. "What was that Ants? I am your enemy, ha! Of course I am your enemy, you silly lightening daemon. I am greater than you, I can use you as my bug zapper while I suck the flesh off this silly human and your tasty daemon friends."

He grinned and looked at Naga, searching for what he might be thinking but was puzzled. "You seem blank to me, Naga. What are you doing?"

Slowly and clear headed, Naga moved forward. Gnargoyle was upset they had ruined his game of panic. "What are you thinking, Naga? I know I will make you slip." Gnargoyle moved forward and, distracted by Naga, he danced around looking at him, whilst Naga slowly moved forward again.

Charles and Ants looked at each other, following Naga's stand point, but noticed Gnargoyle wasn't reading them or picking up their quick plan of attack. Charles pulled out his ankle blade and Ants slowly sparked his hands. Charles threw the knife at Gnargoyle while he was distracted with Naga. The blade caught his arm and Ants threw his lightening charge that caught the knife.

He stopped suddenly, looking down at the electricity current cursing through his arm. Ants gathered up a much larger charge of electricity and threw it towards the knife., Gnargoyle rattled in a breath, it spat out black blood. "Well, that was quick, you're no fun." Upset, he tried to stamp his feet but the ground opened up. He screamed with shock as he was swallowed down through the hole which sealed up after him.

Stirring, Agatha wiped her eyes. She looked about and the group was calmly squatting down and looking at the map, not too far from where Agatha was laying down.

Charles spoke up to the other two. "Do you think we should keep going? This area seems to be pretty bad. We have not even walked a mile in here and two attacks of differing daemons and bandits have come towards us. Ants, Naga, we need to get back to the castle before nightfall. We need a faster route. I know a cloaking spell I can buy from the bookkeeper in town. If we get that, we can hire horses and use the roads. It's a darn sight safer than this." Both daemons looked down.

Naga rubbed his chin in deep thought. "Okay, we have already wasted a few hours here. It's time to play catch up. But we can't leave empty handed, we can use the horses hired to get to the she-daemon." Before Charles could protest. Agatha moved into a sitting position which spurred the group to turn towards her. Charles started to get up but then hesitated. He looked at her eyes, remembering what had happened the last time she woke up

He relaxed seeing the bluey green with startling silver rims and flecks. "It's all right, I'm here. Are you okay? Do you know what happened?"

Charles stood up and moved forward. Agatha moved and welcomed his arms around her. Agatha started to cry. "What happened to me? I was here but not here. I could hear and see everything but I couldn't control anything. I tried to scream but I don't know what

114

happened. All I remember is you talking about some shape in the tree and then I felt a sting on my neck."

Charles looked at her with his brows furrowed so Agatha pulled her hair back and on her neck was a red angry welt. Charles was shocked and Naga jumped in between. He summoned water and held his hand over Agatha's throat. She writhed and screamed in agony as more and more water flushed out of Naga's hand. Agatha in pain and too stunned by what was happening, couldn't even attempt getting away from them.

It didn't take long before the blue icy water flushing her neck began to turn grey then darkened to a cloudy black. Agatha slowed and again passed out while Charles continued to hold her and Naga continued to flush her wound.

It took a while for the water to turn clear. Relief was shown on Naga's face as he stopped the water. Ants stepped in and bound the wound with a poultice made from moss and lichen. He held it to Agatha's neck and started to mutter an incantation. The poultice turned into an almost green bandage that had a shimmery hue.

Charles then gently laid Agatha down; he brushed her wet hair back and pulled out a cloth from his pocket to gently dry her face. Her eyes opened, suddenly stark white at first, then a glow. The glow slowly faded the more Agatha blinked. Again, she looked to Charles, this time uncertain. She then looked at Naga, it was the first time her impulses had gotten the better of her and she lashed out. She went straight for a punch.

Naga flew back and fell on the ground. He started to laugh. "Boyo, boy, that's the first time in a while someone has caught me off guard. Agatha, you have some strength behind you too, darling. I'm sorry I did what I did with no explanation but that was a dangerous mark of the goat, but you're better now. No more flushing or pain, just healing. Ants made a poultice and has wrapped it around your umm… cut." Naga looked at Ants, who shrugged.

Agatha looked at them. "I'm so sorry for being so out of turn! It was horrible right from the sting until now. Now I feel no pain, just exhaustion."

Charles looked down at her and put his hand out, which she took gratefully. He helped her back up to a sitting position. "How do you feel now, Agatha? It has been quite tumultuous for you. I have been worried."

Agatha looked him in the eyes and weakly smiled at him. "I think a rest will help, Charles, but it will have to be once we get home. I know time has wasted while we have been here." Agatha rubbed her head and gingerly touched the green bandage.

Ants cut in. "Yes, time has wasted, a lot of it. Charles has devised a plan we are to go to the book keeper for a cloaking charm. From there, we can hire horses and ride to the she-daemon on the roads without suspicion." Agatha looked at the group hopefully.

"How far is the town from here?" she asked the group.

"If we cut back through the way we came and cut across the forest on the other side of the road, we can be there by lunch, and that will mean two hours riding to the she-daemon and we should just make it back to the castle before the storms come in for the night."

At this Agatha stirred to stand. Charles helped her up, holding her arm. Apart from a dizzy spell, Agatha put on a brave face.

"Okay, you three, I say we get a move on then, enough time has been wasted." Charles, still holding Agatha, looked at her. "You are riding with me, Agatha. I'm not having you fall off the horse and break something."

Agatha attempted to protest but before a word of protest could be said, Naga cut in. "Aye, listen to Charles. What you have been through will take a few days to come right. You need all the help you can get. And I'm not having your death on my conscience, Agatha, I mean it." Naga gave a warning glance at her; Agatha looked at her feet and nodded silently.

The group managed to retrace their steps quite quickly to the edge of the forest. Here they cut straight across as planned to the other side of the road.

The forest on this side looked much more welcoming, with lush green ferns, moss-laden ground and beautiful shades of every green on trees, leaves and other varying plants. The sun was also shining through the tops of the trees, giving warmth the other side did not give.

Agatha took a look back at where they came from and shuddered.

Charles, still holding her arm gave her a reassuring smile. Agatha smiled back and moved into the forest. They enjoyed the walk on this side. After a few minutes, they were all talking about past life experiences. Agatha spoke of her work before coming home and how she was a maid.

"I worked so hard to become the scullery maid, fetching the snacks and lunches for the owners of the house. It was a blessing I got to leave when I did; the boys at the house were coming of age and had started to display obnoxious behaviour with the staff. One maid was fired as she had become romantically involved with one of the boys, never mind that she was the same age."

Agatha continued, on moving onto the kitchen cook. "Awful woman, she was, always testing the food for the house, to make sure it was perfect, but in turn gave us the bland meals that needed a packet of salt to bring it even close to acceptable to eat."

Hearing the horrors of employment as a scullery maid, Naga shuddered. "Agatha, why did you work in such conditions?"

Ants stepped in on this comment. "Agatha was obviously working to improve her station. Sometimes you have to sift through the silt to get the gold, Naga, you should know that!"

Naga rolled his eyes at this remark. "I was once a gold miner in my earlier life on earth, before all these fancy houses were here and before I was killed for my naïve approach to human life. Many who come back more than twice will have a meaner countenance then the first; it makes you bitter and hate human life." With that, Naga pushed aside a bush and there to the relief of the group was a fence and further back was a small house.

"Excellent, we have made it to town. Now to the bookstore Charles, you lead, I have no idea where the bookstore is," explained Ants. He continued to hold the bush aside as Charles and Agatha walked through while Naga followed.

It did not take long for them to reach the store and enter with a pleasant greeting from the owner. Charles asked for the cloaking charm without any delay.

The owner went towards the door and turned the sign to closed. He locked the door and in his bent down shape shuffled past the group and beckoned them through to the back. The shop was deeper than what Agatha had previously remembered as they turned this way and that after the owner who guided them through the maze of book towers, cupboards and shelving that were full to bursting towards the back of the shop.

From here he lifted a red velvet curtain dull and faded through age. red dust fell off the curtain and billowed slowly to the ground. It looked like a protest from the curtain being moved. Here an old gas light was lit and turned up, blanketing the room in a warm light. The group entered with ease as there were no books here. The floor was clear and the room was very tidy, a stark contrast to the bookstore behind the now closed curtain.

"There we are," said the book keeper smiling. He turned towards them. "Now, your group has caused a few episodes with some of the townsfolk," he said whilst looking at Agatha with his eyebrows raised. The group look surprised at each other as the book keeper continued on. "I have been watching from afar as many children and young folk have run past with messages for none other than Caspian." With saying Lord Caspian's name, the bookkeeper looked as though saying the name left a nasty taste in his mouth. He spat on the ground before continuing. "I have had the bastard daemon in my bookstore almost every day wanting potions, spells, charms, and information on the forest folks." With this last lot of information, the group looked at each other

Charles angrily voiced, "Yes, we have met some today, in the forest. Not the greatest welcome, but they won't bother anyone any more."

The bookkeeper raised his eyebrows again and looked around the group. They all could see him mulling over Charles' response.

"It's been my busiest month in years," he said with a grin. "The great thing about selling charms and potions is how each can be so intricate I can charge a fee that is rightly deserved for each spell and client. I bet this month, Caspian" — again he stopped to spit on the ground after saying the name — "is rather short on funds, I'd say." He stopped and grinned again at them all.

Ants chuckled while the others smiled. "No harm in extortionate pricing when you are the only place that makes them, Helgam." Charles patted the book keeper on the shoulder and smiled. Helgam winked at the crew.

"So what can I do you for, boys and of course milady?" Helgam smiled and bowed at Agatha which startled her and she went pink with embarrassment.

"Helgam, thank you for seeing us and telling us what you know." Charles, getting straight to the point as time was precious

Helgam replied, "Well Charles, I gathered you coming here was obvious you needed my assistance. Is it only the cloaking charm you require or an energy flare as well?" Helgam looked over Agatha, still pale from her previous entanglement.

"Free of charge of course, for you." He gently patted Agatha on the arm.

"I spent many hours with your aunt over wine and books, my dear. She was loved by many. Which reminds me. I have something for you." Helgam furrowed his brows and started lifting things off the tables that edged the room, with many neatly labelled bottles corked sitting in rows, all varying colours. He looked about the room, passing two bottles to the group.

In the end he stood by the curtain with a furrowed look on his face. He pointed his hand to the air. "Ahh ha!" Helgam shuffled over to one table and lifted the cloth, residing underneath the table were many, many boxes of varying sizes and shapes. He rummaged around and found a small wooden box. Its thin rectangular shape looked like it would hold glasses.

Helgam brushed the box saying, "Yes, that will do." He passed the box to Agatha. "Your aunt would have wanted you to have it, my dear."

Helgam grabbed one of the bottles from Ants; he uncorked the stopper and attempted to pass it to Agatha, but Agatha was busy looking at the box in her hands. She turned it over and heard a clinking noise from inside. She looked at the others quickly before returning her gaze to the box. Agatha figured out it slid open and upon doing so revealed a large but unusual key. The group gasped. "Oh, Helgam we thought this was hidden in the house!" Agatha rushed and hugged him.

Helgam, surprised by her kindness offered the drink to her again. "Drink this, my dear. It will help you restore yourself. It is sweet. I made it taste like apple pie. My favourite pie. It's always good when feeling dreadful to have something taste delicious, I find it helps with the healing process. You should have a warm tea before you go as well, it will help put you back on your feet." Agatha passed the key to Naga who turned it over in his hands. He handed to the others to check it over Charles then pocketed it for safe keeping.

Helgam had already disappeared. He was heard calling out from another room held behind another curtain.

He put his head back through and much like the first red velvet curtain, a spray of red fell on him. "Sandwiches, anyone? Tea?" he mentioned in a muffled tone whilst wiping off the velvet. The group thankful for the offer of food and followed him through into the new room, careful not to get sprinkled by velvet.

This room was larger again and very tidy. A fire was alight and sitting on a table next to some very comfy chairs were a pile of sandwiches, a large tea pot and enough cups for everyone. Helgam beckoned Agatha to the largest, most comfortable chair. The others found and sat in chairs, all varying in size, shape and colour. Helgam passed around the plates of sandwiches. Whilst he was doing so, a teaspoon lifted off the table, the lid of the teapot opened and the spoon went in and stirred the pot.

"Would anyone like milk? Sugar?" The milk jug and sugar lifted as the group voiced their preferences, the milk jug and sugar bowl measured out into each cup as the teapot lid placed itself back down, the spoon put itself back on the table and the teapot rose and poured into all the cups.

Agatha was fascinated by this magic. She touched the sugar bowl which bowed at her then put itself back into place. The milk also bowed to her and returned to its original position. "Oh my goodness," Agatha exclaimed, her cup rose and moved towards her hands. She carefully took the cup and had a sip. The warmth went right down to her toes, relaxing and calming all the stress and strains from the day's events. She sat back in her chair as the cup gently lifted itself out of her hands and floated back to the table.

Helgam passed Agatha a plate of sandwiches which she thankfully took.

With the morning the four had, eating became a concentrated effort in silence, Helgam watched curiously as all manners were clearly forgotten.

"I suppose it's been a rather busy morning then."

Helgam inquired with lifted, dusty eyebrows

Charles cleared his throat. "Helgam, I am mightily impressed. These are delightful." Stuffing his face full of another sandwich. "I have quite forgotten my manners. We have had one hell of a ramshackle morning and this albeit brief break from the madness has left us all famished."

"Yes, it looks like you haven't eaten in days, Charles, but never the matter. The cloaking potion I gave to Naga, it is most important you say these words as each of you have a drink from it. You must all say them and you must all say them right. Mantine-mă, acoperă-mă, păstrează-mă în siguranță. This will keep you safe, all safe, but please be careful."

Charles grabbed his serviette from his plate and found a pen on one of the tables. He wrote down the incantation and pocketed the serviette.

Helgam after some time of reflection, rose slowly and put his now empty teacup on the table. The others were just about finished when they heard the door open from the front of the shop. Helgam put his hand up, motioning the group to stay there and be silent.

He left the room and soon after voices could be heard. Ants slowly got out of his chair. He lowered his cup to the table and crept out the room, following Helgam. The others were left straining to hear the conversation. Ants voice was heard, the new customer spoke loud and clear, the notion was obvious in gaining Agatha's attention. "I am here for Miss Agatha. I saw her come into the shop and I come bearing a message."

"Your message is not wanted, you waste of space. Go crawl back under the rock you came from"

Agatha, Charles and Naga silently stood and walked to the curtain, nudging it back so all three could see. None could get a clear look at the messenger. they all slowly exited the back room, back through the potion room and into the shop, cautiously walking through the piles of books, nearing the counter. Agatha hesitated once she saw who the messenger was.

None other than the demonic footman of Lord Caspian. The footman sensed Agatha and looked over to the counter. "Miss Agatha, I can sense you there, I have a note from my Lord." The footman quietly held up the note and calmly waited for Agatha to take it. The tension in the room could have been cut by the knife.

Agatha cautiously stepped forward and hesitantly took the note, he bowed and silently walked out of the shop.

Agatha stared at the now vacant space.

"Are you going to read it, Agatha." Charles had moved towards her. She looked at her hand realising the envelope she had taken. Agatha turned it over, it was a simple white envelope with her name written on the front in a very beautiful calligraphy. She turned it over again and slipped the v of the envelope out. Pulling out the card within, she found it was a formal invitation.

It read:

Miss Agatha,

You are formally invited to dinner tonight with Lord Caspian at his manor. Please arrive in a timely manner at seven p.m.

There was a signature underneath, presumably Caspian's.

Agatha stared at the card with her mouth open. Charles looked at her then looked down at the note. He was shocked also.

"Oh dear, not the best time for an invite. Will you cancel, Agatha?" Helgam looked at her blankly. "He wouldn't do anything, as this is the first time I have seen a formal invitation from him, to, well… anyone for that matter."

Agatha looked at the card again. "I think I will go." She said letting the contents of the invite digest.

Charles stepped closer still almost shoulder to shoulder with Agatha. "Agatha, you can't. What if he does something to you or takes you captive?"

"He won't, I will make Caelan come with me."

Naga snorts a laugh. "Do you really think Caelan will go with you without trying to kill Caspian on the spot? Caspian killed his wife."

Agatha startled at this unveiling of truth, held her heart with a sorrowful look on her face. "As much as Caelan may hate him, he will be able to keep me calm, and can also help in relieving or deterring any mischief."

The others nodded in agreement although doubt flickered across their faces. Ants moved towards the front of the shop. "Thank you for the sammies, Helgam, and the tea. We had better get moving if you have to be at a dinner party tonight, Agatha. Time's a wastin'." Ants stood sideways and bowed at Helgam who smiled comfortingly towards the group. Waving their goodbyes, the group head out onto their next step of the journey.

Securing horses was an easy feat, geared up the group trotted out of the township on their way to the She-daemon with Caelan's crudely drawn map as their navigation.

With the sun beating down on the group, Charles and Agatha, being on the same horse, chatted away about the castle and what room would be next to be emptied. "I cannot wait to have my vision finished," Agatha exclaimed with excitement.

Ants and Naga rode silently as the sun reflected off Naga's silvery skin. Naga was a varying colour with light and dark brown and green hues. It looked as though underneath a very thin film of skin, his whole body was a tree of blue, with the sun flickering on him. He looked as if any moment he might finish his transformation.

Ants rode ahead slightly as they came to a fork in the road. On one side was a very forgotten track overgrown and in desperate need of a cut. The left was gravel with very little weed growth, mainly from frequent use. Checking the map, Ants turned his horse so the others could see him and point down the overgrown path.

"She is down there."

The others sidled up to Ants and looked down the path too. Agatha lifted her leg over the horse and Charles helped to steady her. Slightly hesitating she jumped down onto the road. "How far do you think it goes?"

"From the map, it isn't that far, around the corner over yonder and into a small glen with her house or camp. I think that's what it shows." Ants leaned down and passed the map to her.

"Do you think we should take the horses with us?"

"We don't know what she will be like, Agatha. I think take them in a little way and do the rest by foot so

128

they are at least off the road and not in sight of possible thieves. But we will walk the rest of the way from here." Ants dismounted. Pulling the straps over his horse's head, he steered it a little way down the path. Naga, and Charles also dismounted, meeting up with Agatha and following Ants lead. As soon as the road was gone from view, Ants found a decent tree to tie the reins of his horse to. He went into the saddle bag and gave his horse an apple.

Charles and Naga tied their horses to the same tree and also fed their horses

Naga stepped back and took in the scenery. It all seemed peaceful enough except there were no birds chirping or noises from nature here.

"I think we should move with caution." Naga stepped forward, now taking the lead further onto the overgrown road. The others followed silently with a watchful eye for their surroundings.

The path made a turn to the right and it was not long before the glen was visible. "Be on the ready," Ants remarked as they walk closer to the edge of the glen. The She-daemon's lodgings were a very old, thatched cottage. She had an open fire pit in front of the house and a walnut tree to the left of the house. There were beautiful bluebells all over the ground and with the sun flickering through the walnut tree, it made the place look quite welcoming. The four moved down the slope nearing the fire pit which was alight. There was a blackened pig on a spit over the top of the fire pit and a big pot with a lid popping and bubbling away in the embers of the pit.

A branch snapped, making the four turn sharply to their right. There in front of them was a lean tightly dressed mature woman. She has a thin mouth and pale skin. Moving towards the fire, all the while not letting her eyes leave the group, she reached the pit. From here she spun quickly and changed her look to a kindly, again mature woman with gold bird-like eyes.

"I thought you would nearly be here," she said. "It took you long enough but then, I guess that nasty piece of scrotum Lord Caspian is to blame for that. I have made lunch with tea coming as well. Ants, would you be so kind as to bring some seating from the house to the fire and perhaps a table of sorts so we can eat?" She looked over at Ants expectantly.

Ants hesitated. He looked questioningly at the she-demon but stepped forward and put his hands on the ground. Up shot nine rods of electricity from the ground. They shot into her home and dragged out a rickety looking table and enough chairs for everyone. The furniture slowly assembled by the fire for the waiting group. Ants did a slight pant before sitting on the stool in front of him and clearing his throat, making it seem it was effortless.

The She-Daemon stepped over to the now bubbling pot and did a flurry of movements. Cups, plates saucers and cutlery came flying out of the cottage and placing themselves neatly in front of all the stools. She lifted the bubbling pot with a cloth by the handle. A teapot finished its travel to the table and she poured the boiling water into it. The rest of the group sat at the table silently waiting for her to join them, unsure of whether to appreciate what was in front of them or be wary of it.

The She-Daemon placed the pot on the floor and took her seat opposite the group. She put her elbows on the table and crossed her very long fingers, waiting patiently for someone to start talking. After a couple of minutes had gone past, she rolled her eyes. "Fine, no introductions or an attempt to explain why you have come. Give me the contract Agatha and I will sign it." She spoke sharply to which Agatha responded by removing the contract and placing it in front of the She-Daemon.

"By the way I have a name. I am a She-Daemon but doesn't mean you can keep repeating it in your heads when looking at me." Again, she rolled her eyes. "My name is Variwen. I am four hundred years old and this has been my home for almost thirty years. I like it here. I can grow what I want and be who I want when I want." Variwen flicked her hair with her hand and she immediately changed again. This time Variwen was a blonde woman although her hair looked at the roots to start off as part of her skin before trailing down her back as hair. She was wearing a green dress but had the same golden eyes as before.

"It's the only thing that doesn't change with me," Variwen exclaimed, pointing at her eyes to the others as they take in her new appearance.

Agatha finally was able to gather her thoughts. "Nice to meet you, Variwen."

"Is it, my dear?" Variwen looked towards Agatha and glared at her. "You have all had quite the start to your journey all to bring this thing, this gatekeeper to my glen. And for what? Why do you waste your time with mortals? We are eternal beings — they are just a blip on our radar." She flicked her hand at Agatha who was not impressed but attempting to keep her head clear and remaining calm.

Variwen smiled as she looked at Agatha. "Not taking my bait, hey? Your aunt would have stewed on that." Variwen almost spat aunt out. "She was a menace around here, upset all our hard work. We may be daemons, you know, but it doesn't mean we are all bad."

Variwen sneered at the contract and signed. "Very well, maybe a trip out of my little life will help me get a fresh look on the town. It has been so long since I walked through there."

Agatha, trying not to show too much excitement, looked briefly to the others who still remained silent.

"Looking for approval, are we, Miss Agatha? You won't get it from me, you dirty thing. Eighteen and only seeing our world for the first time. Your aunt was so stupid. She should have given you away." Agatha tried to stand but Charles who was by her side held her arm

132

and pulled her down again. "Ha! You are no match for me my girl, can't believe you think you could have a go at me. How insulting!" Variwen walks around the table and comes up to Agatha and sniffs her, she stops abruptly. Variwen grabs hold of Agatha's arms and in a shocked clipped tone. "Who were your father and mother Agatha, where were you born?" Agatha tries to pull her arms away but the grip is too tight, Variwen keeps a cautious gaze.

"Well, I'm not sure. They died when I was very young."

"Yes, yes, yes, we all know you to be the poor little orphan girl taken in by your foolish aunt but what were your parents? You're a mongrel human, my dear." At this Variwen sniffed with a look of disgust.

Agatha was shocked. All of the group were looking at her intently now. "All I was told was that they loved me but both died in different parts of the world. I don't think I ever met my father, and my mother was my aunt's sister."

"Would you like to know your mongrel blend, my dear? I find it fascinating, really." Variwen reached towards Agatha and with a nod from Agatha, Variwen placed her right hand on Agatha's temple and flicked her left at her neck, cutting Agatha, which made her jump and yelp. "Be still, Agatha," Variwen growled as she licked the blood from her nail. "Arghhh!" Variwen screamed and spat out the blood on the floor. She moved quickly away scared to look at Agatha.

Agatha was shocked. "What is it? What am I?" the group, puzzled by the goings on, turned to the now-cowering Variwen.

"Variwen, tell us what Agatha is," Charles spoke with a worrying glance at Variwen as he put a protective hand on Agatha's wrist.

"She must be released," Variwen said. "She is caged in her own body. Many spells and many potions are within her. I also taste the poison from the goat. Her blood mixes like the smoke of a fire in the air. Agatha, you are powerful, you have magic within you that far supersedes my own, I am but dust to your strength but you have been subdued, put to sleep." Variwen cautiously sniffed the cut. "It smells like human spells mixed with" — she took another sniff — "Helgam! That mad sorcerer. He will be the end of us!"

Agatha shook her head. "He gave me some energy, that is all, and we had got a cloaking charm for later." All were puzzled by Variwen and her antics. "Mark my words girl, there is more to you than you all know." Variwen pointed at all of them, "Helgam has also done more to you, I taste more than just energy my dear girl." Too much had been given to her of who and what she was and many more questions piled in her head. Shaking it helped clear and focus herself. "Variwen, we need your help, we don't have time for what I can become. You need to come with us."

Variwen stood up with a big sigh. "You people are always rushing, never any politeness or manners." She got the dishes to go back into the house, the teapot and milk jug emptied on the fire whilst a rather large handbag and what looked like a toy horse came out of the remnants of fire. The untouched pig folded up like a piece of paper and went into the now opened handbag and slotted into one of the pockets. Everything was packed away in a matter of seconds.

"Can't waste the pig now. That could be pork sandwiches for later," Variwen exclaimed as they all stood watching the table and chairs disappear into the bag, there was no other option but to leave the glen.

"Such a pity, first time I have been unsure of an outcome and now I know why." Sighing, their new companion strode wide and in the direction of the horses. Of course she knew where the horses were.

Agatha thought to herself, *This woman knows everything, I swear it.* Agatha rubbed her temples tracing her finger over the new cut Variwen had done to see her history *she knew more about me in a matter of seconds.*

Variwen looked behind her at Agatha with a wary questioning look as they turned the corner. Charles, Naga and Ants showed signs of being in the same train of thought.

"You know it is very bothersome when you think about me behind my back," Variwen stated whilst she strode towards the horses. "I think once the contract is complete, we may want to explore the depths of Agatha. I would rather be on her side than against." Variwen looked again at Agatha as the group came to a stop by the horses.

Charles beckoned Agatha to his horse but Variwen cut in. "I think this will be the prime time I utilize your services, Charles. I'm sure Agatha, now back to her restrained self, is more than capable to go with Ants, who would have openly offered if I had already heard him think it."

Ants, rolling his eyes, knew she could hear what he was thinking but thought it anyway.

"Yes, Ants, most people do find my telepathy bothersome. Why do you think I chose this place to stay? As much as it annoys you, it annoys me too." Ants stood next to his horse patiently.

Charles mounted the horse and moved back on the saddle to let Variwen on. "I'm fine at the back, Charles." Charles moved forward and Variwen jumped up and sat astride the back of the horse.

The remaining three mounted and they were soon on their way. With the afternoon sun showing the return route, it was clear they would get back on the cusp of the storms.

"Agatha, as you know, I know what you know," Variwen stated. "You are expected at Lord Caspian's manor tonight. I think it will be in your best interest to allow me to accompany you. Tip the scales for the mad idiot and his possessed footman. We will need outfits, so boys, you can drop us in town and head your way back to the castle."

"I think I need a drink," said Ants, rubbing his forehead.

"I second that," Naga replied and Charles nodded in mutual agreement with the two.

Agatha gulped in reply. Ants squeezed her arm in comfort. The next while was in awkward silence as they got back to the township.

Agatha dismounted next to the tailor's and so did Variwen. Charles followed and openly kissed Agatha, not only in comfort for her, but in showing support in a nonverbal sense. He mounted the horse again and winked at Agatha. The men headed off to the stables to return the rented horses, leaving Variwen and Agatha still standing.

"Are we going to get this over and done with or are we going to stand here staring at the men all night?" Variwen grumpily stated before grabbing Agatha roughly and taking her into the same shop Charles had taken her too. What almost seemed like another lifetime ago when last entering this shop, it was only a few weeks but the circumstances in life showed such a complete turnaround for Agatha.

The tailor was in the shop and had such a huge grin when he recognised Agatha. Agatha almost jumped as he looked completely different. *Of course*, she thought to herself about the spell lifting. Agatha, regaining her composure, smiled back at the tailor. He looked like a spiky hedgehog. As Agatha moved further into the shop, she stepped aside and Variwen became present. the tailor stopped short, rolled his eyes and said, "Of course you're bloody here, madam, or should I say mad woman." He sniffed at Variwen and started to laugh.

Variwen was laughing too which confused Agatha. She looked at the two whilst they hugged and had a small catch up before Variwen informed the tailor of the night's endeavours.

He rolled his eyes again and looked at Agatha. "You know he is just trying to find your weakness. He wants your castle and he wants you!" he exclaimed to Agatha.

"I know, but I have to see what he wants. If we cause too much upset now when we are not ready, Caelan says he may wipe us out before we can even begin."

The tailor raised his eyebrows. "So the whispers are true." He looked from Variwen to Agatha. "This is a very dangerous road you're heading down, ladies." The tailor shared a worried glance with Agatha although no more was said about the matter. He moved behind the counter and behind the blue curtain. He returned in the shop with an assistant. They were both holding two dresses each. Agatha was surprised at how rich and vibrant the colours were.

"Lord Caspian reacts better to vibrance, he thinks they are elegant," the Tailor replied with a frown and brief glance. The assistant gasped although didn't speak. She placed the dresses on the counter, turned and busied herself with something in the shop.

It wasn't long before Variwen and Agatha were in their new outfits. Agatha was in a gorgeous red dress with white detailing, Variwen was in a yellow dress with green detailing. Both looked elegant although very awkward.

"I will tell you something, Agatha. I have to say I openly hate these types of dresses." Variwen attempted to adjust herself in a rather un-elegant fashion. Agatha laughed and pulled her massive bustle up at the side to adjust the pantaloon underwear she had to wear with it.

"At least we are in agreement. This is awful. I think I am more than willing to do that terrible prank young people do." Agatha furrowed her head as she spoke wanting to show bemusement at the task ahead but felt the dread creeping in.

"Ding dong ditch hey! Well, well, well, I didn't think it would be in you." Variwen looked sideways at Agatha lifting her eyebrows in surprise.

Chapter 8
Caspian's Manor and Mannerisms

Walking towards Caspian's manor, Agatha and Variwen sighted Lord Caspian's black and blue, coloured carriage turning the corner coming towards them. The footman steered the carriage closer.

Agatha's face dropped at the sight, realising it was here for them.

"Are you ready?" she exclaimed to Variwen.

"I think we need to go in with an open mind. We know he will disappoint. He is a very disappointing creature." Variwen's cheeky comment made Agatha grimace as the carriage pulled to a stop.

"Oh footman, I have missed you so," Variwen swooned at the footman. "I am Agatha's companion tonight." She didn't wait for approval, opening the carriage door and stepping in. Agatha nodded worryingly to the footman who looked ahead, no words, just silence. Once the door was shut, the carriage jolted to a start.

"And we're off," Variwen stated, looking through the curtain at the township as they drove away. "You know, at the moment I can't see our return. But because you are a big screen of grey to me, I really hope that is the case here." Variwen showed concern in her voice.

"I am in the unknown myself, Variwen. Maybe we should just do the wait and see." Agatha smiled although her sentiment fell on deaf ears. Variwen pulled back the curtain and was watching the night sky start to move in.

"Are you ready?" The footman had stopped and spoken in a clear manner. The ladies could feel him slide off the carriage with little movement. He came around the carriage and opened the doors. Looking out, Agatha could see they were outside a rather large manor with the sun setting to the left of the place. Variwen, stepping out, had the footman bow to her. She huffed at him and Agatha giggled quickly masking herself she returned to her blank composure as she came out of the carriage.

He bowed to Agatha, then turned wordlessly to lead them up to the entrance of the manor.

It was obvious the hesitation in Agatha. Variwen put her hand out and she gladly took it. "Here we go" she said under her breath. Agatha went to keep moving but Variwen looked like she was being shocked with electricity. Agatha tried to remove her hand but Variwen had clamped onto her. As Variwen's head was jolted back, a stream of light shot from her mouth for a few seconds. The footman bolted back down the steps and ripped Agatha's hand out of Variwen's. She dropped to the floor and lay very still.

Shocked, Agatha hesitated to move towards her, the footman grabbed Agatha by the arm and dragged her inside.

"W-what about Variwen? We can't just leave her there."

"Leave her, she is her own demise." The footman shoved a stunned Agatha through the doors and shut them behind them. He stopped and looked her over. Straightening her outfit roughly, he then grabbed her by the shoulders and shook her. "Miss Agatha, the Lord awaits you. I think you need to be on your best behaviour and do not mention Variwen to his liege."

Anger flared on her face and Agatha slapped the footman across the face.

Snickering was heard behind them, and Lord Caspian came out of a room not far from where they were standing. "Already getting used to my staff, I see, my dear Miss Agatha."

Agatha spat Caspian's name out. "Caspian, I am not nor will I ever be your 'dear'. My friend is outside lying on your steps. She has had a shock and your nasty servant left her there." She glared at the footman who remained motionless and showed no sign of emotion.

Lord Caspian looks from one to another, "Well, you have already put a damper on things, Hesiss. Go and get the woman."

Not looking anywhere but straight ahead, the footman replied, "My Lord, I did it in your best interest.

That daemon should not be present at your table. She is a disgrace to our kind."

Lord Caspian speaking sharply said, "I think in my best interest," he continued, whilst moving his arm towards Agatha, motioning for her to take it. "You should go get her and bring her to the table. How can we have any fun or enjoyment tonight if it starts with upset, Hesiss?" Giving up on Agatha taking his arm, Caspian watched Hesiss.

Emotionless, Hesiss bowed and went back the way they had come. Agatha rubbed her arm where Hesiss had grabbed her.

"Miss Agatha, please follow me, you must be cold. We have lit the fire to warm you from your journey." Lord Caspian smiled at her, trying again. Being civil did not sit with Agatha, although the 'best behaviour' notion stewed in her mind.

Attempting politeness, Agatha remarked, "Thank you so much, Lord Caspian. Please though, I would just like to wait for my friend to accompany us, then I would very much like to take you up on that offer." Agatha felt sick to her stomach talking politely to Caspian. All she wanted to do was find the fire poker and shove it through his heart. But pleasantries were needed to find out what his endgame was.

Hesiss came back to the entrance with a now awake although feigning weakness Variwen. She looked at Agatha and winked, relieving Agatha of any ill will, she might have caused. Variwen's arm was around Hesiss's shoulder which looked very awkward as he didn't enjoy the temporary partnership still he walked with his back straight refusing to bend for her. He stopped next to Agatha who continuing the act worried over Variwen.

"Variwen, this is Lord Caspian. Have you two met?" Agatha stated sweetly as she turned toward Caspian.

Returning her favour, Caspian replied, "We have known each other for many years Miss Agatha. No introduction is needed for her kind. I mean, Variwen is known very well in my area of the world." Caspian tried his best to smile but it turned out more like a grimace.

"Variwen, Lord Caspian has offered us to warm by the fire. You must be frozen. Shall we go through and get you warmed up?

Glaring at Variwen, Caspian replied to Agatha's request to Variwen. "Please do come through."

"I'm so sorry to be such a poor host, Agatha. I must speak with Hesiss a moment. Do carry on through, I shan't be long." Caspian turned to Hesiss as the women walked through to the fire.

The door to the room was shut behind them and immediately Agatha placed her hand on Variwen. "Are you all right Variwen? What happened?"

Variwen looked about her in a vexing way, steering Agatha towards the fire. "Speak into the flames, Agatha," Variwen said as she pulled something out of the top of her skirt. She moved towards the fire and threw in a handful of dust. "We must be quick before

144

they return. Crouch down with me, Agatha, we don't have time."

They both leaned into the fire as the smoke turned black. It looked like a portrait but was moving. They could see Caelan and Charles talking. Caelan turned and was stunned to see heads staring at him from the middle of the room. Charles turned, saw this and rushed closer.

We don't have much time," Variwen said. "I had a vision. Agatha is in grave danger. A war is coming, Caelan, we must stop it."

At this both Agatha and Charles stared at each other, baffled at the words. Caelan, however, furrowed his eyebrows. "Do we have a timeframe, Variwen? What else did you see?"

Variwen put her hand to her mouth. Agatha and Variwen could hear footsteps approaching. "Will talk soon but be wary of any that come to the house." And with that, Variwen threw another handful of dust at the fire. She stood quickly, turning away, and the image was gone.

It was the first time Agatha had seen that and she was spellbound by the flicker of the flames. It took Lord Caspian touching her shoulder, before she realised he was back in the room.

"Hmm-mm." Agatha pulled herself away from the fire and looked up at Lord Caspian, quite forgetting where she was for a moment. He stood over her and smiled which brought back all that he had done so far in causing the wrong sort of attention from Agatha. Her

145

smile turned from happiness to hatred, she quickly masked this by turning her head to get up, composing herself and hoping Caspian hadn't seen her expression. "Goodness, I quite forgot where I was then. I just get so spellbound by your fire." Lord Caspian smiled and looked back at the fireplace.

"I could have sworn there was a male voice in here," he stated, looking from one to the other. But both Variwen and Agatha had composed themselves quite well as Agatha stepped away from the fireplace, not answering his question.

Hesiss walked in. "Dinner is served my lord, ladies." He bowed and walked back out of the room.

"Ah ha! I do hope you like the game, we found a lovely piece from the forest on the other side of town." The women smiled as Caspian led them through to the dining area.

Here both women looked up. The high ceiling was covered in slowly moving cherubs in battle with each other.

Lord Caspian also looked up and smiled. "Ah, when the upper realm opened and war pursued, such a wonderful war, bloodshed and mayhem, confusion for our dear little cherubs who we smattered all through the human realm." He turned and smiled like he had shared a delicious treat with them both. The look of horror on Agatha's face was clear. Variwen elbowed her and Agatha refocused and regained composure.

"I love the lighting in here, Lord Caspian," Agatha managed to strangle out of herself, knowing that if any type of misleading or anger towards him was felt, he might turn on her and Variwen, such a juxtaposition they all faced.

Agatha walked towards the large table with the three places set. Lord Caspian was obviously in the centre of things, and Variwen was set a few spaces further down from the other two, obvious in the attempts to push her away from Agatha and Lord Caspian.

'Oh dear!' said Variwen. "Your servant Hesiss has muddled up the places. Look, he has put me further down the table. I should be next to you both. After all, Agatha isn't married and we don't want people talking," Variwen retorted in an innocent manner, knowing full well what Caspian was doing, helping herself to collecting the tableware and moving it next to what she assumed to be Agatha's place.

Lord Caspian was aghast, mouth open and speechless as Variwen then pulled the chair out next to the head of the table and plopped herself down, patting Caspian's seat with a marvellous grin across her face.

Agatha slowly moved forward to the chair next to Variwen. Caspian dove forward, almost knocking Agatha. "Well, here let me at least help you with your seat," he said as Agatha sat down on the chair. He obviously attempted to whisper in her ear, which she quickly retaliated to with a pull of her napkin and flicking it on the side Caspian was on, rebuffing his advance and pretending she didn't see or hear anything in his regard. He turned in an attempt to cool his anger. Agatha cheekily smiled at Variwen, who squeezed her hand under the table.

Lord Caspian was clearly not impressed. He moved and sat himself down, he gulped down a large part of his red wine readily poured for him, and at that moment the doors were opened and Hesiss came through with three plates well balanced in his arms. He stopped and hesitated when he saw the new position of Variwen. faltering momentarily before introducing the meal. "Slowly stewed game with new potatoes, butter, garlic, and seasoning. You also have game terrine and steamed spinach finished with slivers of almonds and a whiskey jus."

He placed the plates in front of the guests and lastly to Caspian.

The women looked at each other. They smelled the food but something faint stopped them from starting. Agatha picked up her fork and picked up some of the stewed meat. She sniffed it and turned to Caspian. "What type of game did you say this was?" she remarked while turning it over on her fork.

"Oh, I didn't," Caspian said with a smile as he looked at both women at the table. He then stuffed in a large portion of stewed meat into his mouth.

The women were still hesitant to start.

Lord Caspian finished his mouthful, turned to Hesiss. "Beautiful and tender. I admire your technique,

Hesiss, your patience with skinning and removing everything not needed is amazing!" he exclaimed as he stuffed another mouthful in his mouth.

Agatha picked up her knife and went for the new potatoes. She felt safe eating those and had one. *He is right,* she thought to herself. *This food is delicious.*

Caspian, after his second mouthful, put his fork down, dabbed his mouth and smiled. "I love eating fresh meat. Nothing better, especially when it's been under stress and fear of death. It gives such a unique taste to it."

Variwen put some meat in her mouth and she chewed a bit then glared at Caspian.

"You didn't!" was all she had to say before he started laughing. He was in hysterics, slapping his hand on his leg and looking at a very confused Agatha. "How dare you think it okay to do this to us! To us, Caspian, you dirty downright evil malevolent being." Variwen spat the words and mouthful of stew at Caspian. Hesiss, Agatha noticed, was having a very slight giggle which he coughed and ended as quickly as it started.

"What is going on? Is someone going to tell me what is the stew from and why you are acting so weird? Please, I do not like being left in the dark."

Variwen smacked the fork out of Agatha's hand. "We are going," she said as she stood up, throwing her handkerchief at Caspian. Hesiss dove forward and pushed Variwen over. She conjured up a ball of light in her hands while Caspian was still laughing.

He wiped his eyes with his hand and started to calm himself down. "Ha, ha, all right, you two. That's enough," Caspian lightly aid, although both Variwen and Hesiss were ignoring him, both ready to pounce. "ENOUGH!" Caspian shouted exasperatedly.

The ball of light went smaller and Hesiss bowed and moved towards the wall.

"Okay, my fun is over now," Caspian announced. "What you are eating there, Agatha, is the remains of the men you and your team dismantled, shall we say, in the forest." He waited for the sentence to sink in, the look of horror as the scene came back so vividly to Agatha. "In saying that from memory, I think you are eating a bit of stomach" Caspian reached over to Agatha's plate with his fork and moves the stew about. "Oh, yes, and the terrine, Hesiss, its leg, isn't it?" He grinned nastily at Agatha who had dropped her fork and pushed the plate forcefully away from her it skimmed across the table and landed on the floor.

Caspian pouted at her reaction. "Oh blast, do you really have to make a mess of things, Miss Agatha? I thought we were getting on so well." Caspian laughed again. It was short and clipped as his expression changed.

"I brought you here, woman, because your family owes me a debt. My last life was stolen from me. And your family owes me a life. A life for a life I think is fair. My peace-making instead of outright revenge," he announced to no one in particular.

Variwen could see Hesiss nodding as he moved towards Agatha. The ball of light was still in her hands and she threw it towards Hesiss. "Run, Agatha!"

Variwen conjured up another as Hesiss was dropped to the floor by her first.

Caspian remained seated as he watched the commotion. He yelled over the noise, "I think your life should do nicely, Agatha, or better yet, take my proposal and be my wife! Don't worry, I will be nice to the others at your castle. I will give them a day to leave and I won't hurt them too much, ha, ha, ha!"

Agatha felt her body vibrate with anger. She kicked back the chair behind her which hit Hesiss and smashed apart. Hesiss was momentarily stunned before he regained himself and dove out of the way of another orb of pain from Variwen.

Caspian, laughing even more, remarked, "Oh Agatha, did I upset you? Oh, poor thing. Would you like a tissue? Or better yet, why not have some dinner?" Another round of laughing came from Caspian, as Hesiss rebuffed another glowing ball from Variwen. Hesiss ducked her next attack which flew past him and shattered the wall at the back of the room. Caspian was happily eating some of his food, grinning at Agatha while the chaos of fighting between Variwen and Hesiss continued.

Variwen got up, stumbling a little before holding her stance firm.

It was complete madness in the dining room. Variwen was destroying everything with her balls of exploding light and Hesiss was throwing everything he could find at her. His anger getting the better of him, Hesiss summoned a bubble of sorts with which he encased the fireplace. It started to lift the fireplace.

But before he could get any further, Caspian was now red-eyed with rage and a new addition to his attire was showing a tail! It flicked from side to side as Caspian stood up, his claws extended from his fingers.

"A tail!" Agatha, shocked, yelled out loud, pointing in astonishment. This distracted both Hesiss and Caspian enough for Variwen to conjure up a portal. It showed the entranceway of the Wilderfort Castle. She ran over and grabs the stunned Agatha. Kicking away the chair in the direction of Hesiss, she covered her hand with her dress sleeve, stopping the skin to skin contact with Agatha. Variwen threw Agatha through the portal with brute strength. Agatha looked like a ragdoll as she was tossed through.

Caspian rushed to standing flinging his chair backwards also threw the table forward, yelling after Agatha, "I guess that's a no to marriage then, is it?" He laughed again manically.

Variwen not hesitating, jumped through the portal that quickly closed behind her.

Caspian and Hesiss were left standing looking at the wall as both Agatha and Variwen had gone. The mess left behind was massive with holes in the walls, food all over the floors and table along with Agatha's chair in pieces, the fireplace still sitting within the bubble Hesiss had conjured up.

"Well, Hesiss, I guess we should tidy up and gather the forces. We have a little rabbit to hunt down along with her babies."

Agatha and Variwen were panting in the entranceway. Rumbling footsteps were heard from the kitchen.

"What just happened Variwen? Were those really human remains in the food, Variwen? What's happening?"

Variwen, still panting after the skirmish, patted her hand. Agatha was grey with shock and had a crazy unfocused look. Her eyes were searching everywhere, but not really seeing.

Caelan was the first to break the reverie, he slid to a halt and grabbed Agatha to check her over. She was unhurt but the look of shock and the fact that she was still vibrating made him look back for the others.

Charles was already there he moved Caelan with force to hug Agatha. "What did they do to you, Agatha? Please talk to me, please!" Charles hesitated as he could feel her vibrate. Pollyanna pushed Charles aside. "Agatha are you okay? Hello! Agatha, oh dear please talk to me!" Pollyanna desperate tried clicking her fingers in front of Agatha's face hoping the action would snap her out of whatever stun she was in.

"They were human, it was all human," was all that Agatha said. She looked unfocused straight in front of her. Pollyanna tried waving her hands in front of Agatha again trying to pull her back to the present. But again, still distant, only got louder. "They were human! It was all human, Charlie, all of it." Agatha started screaming at the top of her lungs, Pollyanna raced and dived behind Alfred. Charlie unsure what to do stepped back.

"Oh gods, she is gonna blow this place apart! Caelan, grab her and get her outside now!" Variwen yelled the order, he didn't hesitate but showed confusion at Variwen's words. He pulled Agatha outside into the rain and storms of the night. This didn't deter her screaming. Caelan yelled out and dropped Agatha arm standing on the driveway. He rubbed his hand and looked back at Agatha. The rest of the group were under the veranda of the Castle staring at Agatha who now had the same white glow as Variwen did; differing in Agatha being completed cloaked in it.

The ground began to vibrate and lighting hit Agatha. Charles yelled and tried to run to her but the others held him back. Agatha was untouched by the lightning strike and a force field was now showing around her. Her screams were almost ethereal. Her mouth was open but the noise was coming from everywhere. All of a sudden like a bomb, the white flash exploded from Agatha. It blasted the group clean up into the air and pushed them back into the entranceway. The heavy oak doors folded up on themselves like a crumpled piece of paper, the ground was scorched with the outwards blast, trees and shrubs nearby were either broken or sent flying, the windows within the first floor were all smashed and parts of the brickwork broke and disappeared inside the house.

Charles, covered in blood, got up, his broken ankle now clicking back into place as he waited for it to be fixed enough to walk on. He stumbled at first, then walked hobbled for a few steps. Through determination he continued to walk gaining normalcy with every step. "Thank the realms for immortality," Charles stated as he scanned the area for Agatha.

The screaming had stopped, although stepping off the veranda, Charles realised the rains had stopped. The clouds were not purple any more but were now black. "Hmm, interesting," Charles stated to himself. In the background Pollyanna could be heard sobbing. "She's a daemon, they turned her into a daemon," Sobbing turned to early stages of hysteria. It was short lived though, Variwen soaking wet slaps Pollyanna. "Grow up, you petulant child. Get inside."

Charles Hesitated slightly, as he continued to walk towards the now unconscious Agatha on the ground metres away from where Caelan had left her. He checked her pulse. Relief showed as confirmation of a heartbeat was felt. He put his hand up by her nose and mouth and felt the warmth of her breath. Picking Agatha up, Charles walked her back into the house. He walked straight past the others without muttering a word and straight up to her room he felt the presence of the others starting to assemble and follow him, Variwen pushing the rear with Pollyanna roughly grasped in her hands.

Getting to Agatha's room, Variwen ditches Pollyanna at the top of the stairs, she caught up and opened the door for Charles while the others waited in the hallway. He walked in and Variwen stepped forward and pulled the blankets back for Agatha. Variwen helped to take off the skirts, Agatha's boots, gloves and the reminder of her dress, leaving her in her undergarments.

Charles could not help but take a moment to look at her. "It's not the way I wanted to first be in your bed chamber, Agatha, nor be under these circumstances see you undressed but Agatha, all I hope for is for you to be okay." He brushed his hand up her cheek as Variwen pulled the blankets over her. Variwen vexed and hesitant. she beckoned Caelan in.

"What was that, Variwen?" Caelan asked as he looked over at Agatha.

"It's a warning, lovey, a warning that was meant for Lord Caspian, I'd say, but we got the short end of the stick." Variwen talked of the evening and what had transpired at Caspian's while the others looked intermittently in on Agatha while she lay so still in bed, sleeping off whatever she had just conjured.

"I would say, boys, child, whatever was holding Agatha back, whatever had been pushed deep down inside of her, restricted by potions and magic, has finally found a way to come out." Variwen finished her recount of the evening's events.

"So you're saying this has been inside Agatha all along?" Charles commented, never looking away from Agatha.

"Charles, my little sweetie, your girlie here is no ordinary daemon, my love she is more than that by far, she is one of possibly two, the only one that I have ever seen. Agatha is a Choler Daemon or part thereof. Not an angel, cherub or run of the mill daemon, but a half-human who has been chosen to help us. Now I'm not sure who is able to do that, or how, but what do we know about her father?"

Caelan was the only one who understood Variwen. "Damn, poor thing, no wonder they locked her in her own body." Caelan came up to her. "Aggie, my poor love, are you there, honey?" Caelan spoke gently and calmly to Agatha. He put his hand on her head. "She feels warm. Variwen. Is there anything we can do?"

Charles was in almost shock. "I-I don't understand, she can't be a Choler. I have read about them in ancient texts. Are you really meaning she is that?"

As Charles came to his senses, he started to link it all together. "If Caspian finds out..." Charles trailed off as the whole group turned to him. "Caspian is to never find out! He will use her for what he wants."

"Choler never had lives. They were caged and kept angry, they were used as weapons, there was never a text of a kind person having a Choler as a wife or

157

husband, and most never lived past their twenties. It was almost unheard of for a Choler to live into their thirties." Variwen spoke trance like to the group.

They all turned back to Agatha. She was sound asleep. "Maybe she will be different, she is only a half breed, maybe that will be a difference for her," Charles said as he looked around the group.

Oxxy, Naga, Fervor, Ants, even Alfred looked sadder than usual. "Charles, me boy, I think we best leave her to sleep it off. Let's makes a brew in the kitchen. Aye, we can talk more there and let her rest/" Caelan put his rough arm around Charles. He pushed the arm off but then superseded his emotions and silently agreed to follow them all out. Pollyanna who was cowering in the hallway grasped at Charles. "What is happening will she kill us all!" He threw her arms off him. "How dare you Pollyanna that is your friend unconscious in that room. Think of her and what she will be going through. You stayed here for this life, be the friend she needs not the coward you are being!" He stomps off towards the kitchen, leaving a fraught Pollyanna, Variwen motioned she would stay with Agatha, she also calmly holds Pollyanna. "Come with me, child, I will calm you and you can help me help her through this." Variwen stunned Pollyanna with her change of tone, she brushes Pollyanna checks muttering under her breath a small incantation. Relaxation and calm comes across Pollyanna, and they both enter the bedroom.

Chapter 9
The Lament of Agatha and the Choler Within

As the big pot bubbled, Caelan was busying himself with the tea cups. "One thing I know fer sure is how to make a decent cuppa, me lad." Caelan winked at Charles, although Charles had a faraway look.

Alfred didn't even moan about having tea, which of late he usually would. "Oxxy, can you pass me the biscuits?" Alfred asked, in an almost normal tone. Everyone at the table stopped and looked at Alfred, shocked. "I am normal, you know I have hurt feelings too. I do feel sad you know. It's just those other times it's a different type of sad. Agatha loves us all, she may not say it but we all know it." Alfred spoke his mind to the group,

"Well, well, well, the death daemon does have a heart, eh!" Oxxy smiled and nudged Alfred. He grimaced at the notion but shrugged his shoulders and grabbed another biscuit.

"Variwen." Caelan stuttered. The others stood when she came followed closely by Pollyanna. She raised her arms and beckoned them back into their seats Pollyanna found a spare chair near Alfred, her countenance was a lot calmer than upstairs. "I won't be long" she said. "I want to read to Agatha, I think it might help" Alfred passed Pollyanna one of his biscuits and she quietly settled. "How is she" Oxxy chimes in but is cut off by Variwen. "It's all right, it's all right, I have made sure to cloak her emotions for the evening so she can sleep, but I have some serious discussions with Helgam when I next see that bastard, that's for sure.

"Oh, hello Alfred, darling, how's your mum?"

Alfred rolled his eyes. "Back in hell. Probably a good thing. She was eating children again." Alfred rolled his eyes. Pollyanna chokes on her biscuit at the response.

"Ahh well, that would do it. She does have a sweet tooth for them, hey? Silly thing."

"Humpffft." Alfred answered by pulling his hood over his eyes and largely covering his face.

Variwen smiled at the group. "Been awhile since I saw the looks of most of you. Oxxy, is it? I don't think I have had the pleasure." She smiled a sweet smile as she looked him up and down.

Oxxy got up and offered her a seat. He then got another and sat next to Ants. Ants had been quiet this whole time. "You all right, Ants?" Oxxy noticed the faraway look Ants had on his face.

"I'm not sure, I need to speak to my kind before I say anything."

Variwen looked at Ants. "It's all right, lovey. She is, like I said, a Choler, or as they used to call her, a Fury

160

daemon. She can knock the socks off any one and thing. Back in the ancient times, Choler were many. The monsters and daemon that plagued this earth with fire and vengeance for their previous incarceration were wiped out by the Choler. It's a sad fate for them, but maybe it's different for our Agatha."

"She is not your Agatha." Ants stood up. "You only met her today! How can you be in the same league as us?"

Caelan gave Ants a warning glance as he stood there with a pot of boiling water in his hands, his hands glowing red from the heat as he poured the water into the teapot. "Ants, sit down before you get yer knickers in a twist." Caelan carried on speaking as he busied himself. "You are upset because Agatha caught you off guard. You're upset because you're a light daemon who got blasted back by an orb of light. Speak to your elders if you want, but I would say do so with another agenda in mind. Lord Caspian will be wanting war after what he stirred tonight." the group, even Charles, looked his way.

"Talk about putting an even bigger damper on things, Caelan," Alfred sulkily stated.

Naga laughed. "Ahh, I missed you, Alfred. Glad you have your sense of humour back, mate." Naga folded his arms and legs and leaned back in his chair.

"Well, what a turn of events this is. How will we take the next move from here, Caelan? Our goal today was to get Variwen to sign the contract and come back with us, which of course we have done, but now we have the wage of war encroaching on us, Agatha is a half Choler, and her protection from it has been broken, and Caspian wants Agatha."

Charles turned to the others. ``Does he know? Does Caspian know what Agatha is?''

His desperate eyes reached Variwen who was passed a cup of tea. "Well, unless they somehow followed us through the portal, which I doubt, he would had to have a telepath within his ranks to have seen this. Unless his arrogance has stopped him from checking, I would say we have one- or two-days' head start on him before he finds out, safe to say." Variwen sipped her tea. "Oh, Caelan, I forgot how good you make your tea. Once this is over you must come and visit." Variwen spoke warmly, although Charles was at the stage of hyperventilating rage. Pollyanna grabbed her tea, silently thanked Caelan, and darted out the room.

Charles almost yelled, "Once this is over! Do you have any idea what we are facing? Do you know that we could have died? We may still all die." Charles stood up harshly and his chair crashed back against the back wall. It clattered sideways onto the floor as he glared at everyone. "How can you all act so casually, what is wrong with you?" He glared at them all. "What is wrong with who, Charles?" Charles sharply turned to the door and Agatha and Pollyanna were standing there, Agatha in her underwear with a blanket thrown over her.

"I could hear the chatter and didn't want to be by myself. Can I join you?" Agatha asked with a croaky voice. They all jumped up offering her their seats. Agatha thanked them and sidled up to Charles. "Can I sit with you, Charles?"

She smiled a shy smile which Charles then gushed over. "Of course you can. You can always sit by me, Agatha. I will never say no to you." Charles helped her down as the others went back to their seats. Pollyanna quietly settled back into her previous seating by Alfred, Variwen winked at him, he rolled his eyes in an attempt to ignore her

"Are you hungry, lovely?" Variwen said to Agatha. "Would you like a cheese sandwich? I have some made up in my bag." Variwen pulled a small bag from her skirt, no bigger than a coin purse. She pulled on it and tugged on it, stretching it and helping it grow until it was the size of an oversized baggy briefcase. Variwen opened the top and rummaged around. "Anyone up for some pig? I still have one on the spit. I also have a few loaves of bread if any of you want to make some sammies up. Have you had dinner?"

The men looked at each other hesitantly. "Well, come on, then, you bloody useless lot. Grab some knives and plates for our guest," Caelan yelled.

Oxxy and Fervor jumped up to grab the necessary items while Variwen pulled out a small package from the front pocket. She unfolded it over and over. Once it reached full size, she shook it out and a popping noise was heard. A full-sized pig on a spit rested against the table. Oxxy reached out and swirled his hands, setting the table with the cutlery and plates he and Fervor had just collected. He then swirled his hands again and a knife came up from one of the drawers. He lifted up the pig, and in the air it started to be sliced up, Fervor grabbed a knife and started to slice the bread. Naga picked up another knife and started to butter the bread. Soon enough there were ten sandwiches sitting in front of everyone, tea had all been made and enough was remaining for Agatha to have one as well.

"A hot sweet tea, my dear, will help you feel better. You must feel so drained after that. Do you remember much?" Variwen casually looked at Agatha all the while squinting and trying to read her. She gave up and took a sip of tea.

Agatha furrowed her head. "I felt strong anger rising in me. I felt like that when I was at Caspian's manor, he was so evil I felt he needed to be stopped. I wanted to stop him. I wanted him to explode, and the more he laughed and the more he mentioned our dinner, the angrier I got. I felt like I was shaking, slow at first, then it came on faster and faster. By the time we came back here, I was vibrating with all that had happened today and tonight was circulating around in my head. I wanted to stop him, but a part of me wanted to calm down. I felt like I was releasing myself when I was screaming. Every time I took a breath to scream some more, I felt further release somehow. Although I got louder and louder, it wasn't until the final scream and everything went white that I calmed down. I went to this place, I'm not sure where it was, but I could see you all like I was looking through glass. On my side it was all white but there were people there, all in white and hiding. They were whispering. I didn't have a chance to look around. When I wanted to take a closer look at them, I all of a sudden woke up in my bed. That was it, really."

Charles rubbed her arm. "It's all right, Agatha. It's over now. Here, have your tea." Charles passed the tea to Agatha who took it nonchalantly.

No one else really spoke about the events further that night. They all ate their food and drank their tea, in relative silence. As the group walked to the entranceway, Oxxy offered to show Variwen to a room. "Pollyanna, we had better set one up for you too, Agatha will need space to rest." Pollyanna looking for reassurance for Agatha, didn't get any, Agatha was exhausted, Ants offered to help set the rooms up as well and as they said their goodbyes, Alfred waved to everyone and sulked off to his room. Naga and Fervor wished the remaining goodnight.

"Agatha, have a rest, it's been a big day, don't worry about waking up early. You take all the time you need." Fervor hugged Agatha, they wished her goodnight and walked away, leaving Caelan, Charles, and Agatha who turned and slowly made their way up the staircase.

Caelan hugged Agatha. "I'm glad you're safe, rest tomorrow and we will continue to hunt for the book the next day." Agatha jumped at the reminder but was held down by Caelan. "A day's rest, Agatha, my lovely, you have been through a lot today, more than most can handle." Caelan pointed at her neck, hugged her and walked to his room, quietly shutting the door.

Charles turned to Agatha. Both were alone now in the hallway. Agatha hugged him tightly, surprising Charles at her strength. "Please, Charlie, stay with me tonight. I can't be by myself."

Charles held his hand up and cupped her check, he looked from eye-to-eye thinking. "Promise me something, Aggie. If anything were to ever happen to me, you would let me back through."

Agatha frowned at his cryptic question so he tried again. "Agatha, please you must promise. If something ever happened to me, you would open the door for me. Open the dimension door."

Biting her lip, she replied, "Charles, if it came to it yes, but please don't put yourself in harm's way. I need you. We need you, but I need you most." She looked worried and glanced from one eye to the other, looking for some sign as to why he should say this. Nothing was there but a slow smile. "You worry for an immortal. Come, let's sleep, you need rest and I need to lie down. I haven't had this much action since you aunt was alive."

"Can you tell me about my aunt Charles?" Agatha asked.

Charles turned her towards the door. "Only if you get in bed and do as you're told." He grinned as he stepped through her doorway after her. Agatha giggled and closed the door behind them. Agatha jumped into bed, Charles grabbed some pillows and moved to sleep on the window seat in her room. She looked forlornly at him.

"I'm sure just this once we can share a bed, Charles."

He turned and looked at her and smiled. "Only, if you're sure. Your reputation and womanhood are at risk, you know. What will people say, Agatha, if they find out?"

She smiled. "I think they will let us have a pass tonight, Charles. Come lie down next to me. I need you near me, Charles, please."

Smiling and sighing at the same time, Charles walked over and sat on the side of the bed. He took his shoes and his jacket off. Agatha was under the covers, holding them up to her nose, watching him. He turned and grinned. Climbing into the bed, he held her head in his hands and kissed her nose, her forehead, then her mouth. Agatha slid across and wrapped her legs around him and kissed him deeply. They slowed to a stop and lay there looking into each other's eyes.

"My, how you have captured me, Agatha. Never have I been so encapsulated by a woman, never have I met anyone like you before, in all my years." Agatha smiled a watery tired-eyed smile.

Charles kissed her forehead. "Don't worry, Agatha. I will stay here for the night. I will hold you all night if you want me to."

"Hold me for as long as you can, Charles. I don't want you to let me go." At this Agatha was already drifting off.

Charles brushed her hair with his hand and watched her drift off to sleep. He looked at her intently before placing her head on his chest and drifting off himself.

The morning came with a light drizzle, the clouds were light and fluffy, making the sun come through the curtains. Charles looked down at Agatha and was shocked to see her beautiful auburn hair was a stark white. All the colour had drained from it, leaving an almost pearlescent shimmer as the sun crept around a cloud and shone on the bed.

Smiling as she stirred, he brushed her hair out of her face and held it back in such a way so that Agatha could wake up first. He didn't want her to be shocked straight away.

"Agatha," Charles said softly. "Good morning, Agatha." Agatha smiled and looked up. She was still half asleep on his chest with her arm around him. She reached up and touched his face.

"Good morning, my beautiful woman," Charles said as he smiled at her. She sat up and looked out the window. Charles had to let her hair go as she moved although she didn't notice the change just yet.

Agatha turned smiling, then stopped dead. She reached up to her hair. "Oh, my goodness, what happened?" Agatha jumped up from her bed and rushed to the old mirror that was set up in her room. She turned around trying to see the back and realised all her hair is white. "I don't understand! Why?" Crestfallen, she turned back to Charles, who sadly smiled at her.

"Oh, Agatha, do you remember last night? do you remember what you did?"

Agatha looked at Charles and a vague realisation crept over her face as she recounted what happened. "Agatha, don't cry, it's okay, it will all be okay." Charles stood up and came to her. He hugged her, which she accepted for a bit, then pushed him away.

"What am I, Charles?" A flicker of further recognition came in. "Does this have to do with the vision Variwen had on the steps? The white light, did she see what I was going to do?" Her eyes desperately looked Charles over who calmly looked at her.

Charles picked up her hand. "Agatha, I think we should go down to breakfast. Variwen has been researching your kind all through the night."

Agatha dropped his hand. "My kind, my kind? What do you mean my kind? I'm a human, aren't I?" Panicking, she pulled over her shirt and trousers resting on her chair by the door. She laced up the front and pulled her hair back behind her. Remembering again the colour of her hair, she sighed a heavy sigh.

Opening the door, she turned to Charles, trying to sound calm. "Come on then. I need to know, is this to do with my father? Because my mother was meant to be a gatekeeper, right? So what does that make me, a halfblooded witch and the other half daemon?" Agatha sighed. She was standing in front of the doorway and put her hand out for Charles who got up, pulled on his jacket and shoes and went to her.

They made their way down to the kitchen. Alfred saw them first, "Wow, Agatha, if I had known you were going for a new look I…" Agatha glared at him. A flash of anger flickered across her face, and her eyes shone pearly white for a moment, which shocked Alfred into putting his hands up. The colour came back into her eyes and she walked to the kitchen.

"Holy Heck!" Alfred exclaimed to Charles who had hung back to make sure Alfred was okay. "Well, this is new, Charles. What's up her nose?" Alfred sulked and sauntered down to the kitchen, following Agatha.

Oxxy and Ants came jogging up to Charles. "How's the patient?"

Charles is standing there unable to speak. "Well boys, she fell asleep Agatha, but this morning she has woken up something else. Agatha is still there but I'm not sure how much." The two were curious with Charles' response and they made their way also down to the kitchen.

"Oh, and don't say anything about her hair!" Charles yells after them hesitant on whether to follow.

Caelan and Pollyanna were walking down the stairs when he heard some arguing from the kitchen. Charles, who was still at the bottom, turned and glanced at Caelan. They both started bolting down to the kitchen as fast as they could. Caelan came crashing in when Agatha was standing there, legs apart, holding an orb of white light. Her eyes were pearly white and Naga was holding his arms over his head while sitting on a chair on the far right of the kitchen.

"All I did was ask about her new fashion statement," Naga said to Caelan as he came over to Agatha.

"Darlin', Naga is being cheeky, he means no harm by it. You need to calm down or you will blow the house up."

Agatha, shocked by the last remark, turned to Caelan. "Blow the house up? What are you talking about? Is this because of my hair? Is this why my insides feel like I'm bubbling?" Agatha lowered her hand. "Sorry, Naga, I don't know what came over me." Agatha breathed through the anger as her eyes' colour drained back in and her orb disappeared.

Variwen had been cooking over the fire this whole time, ignoring the commotion. She turned and ladled out porridge for everyone, hot and steamy, into bowls. She added a blob of fresh butter on top and some milk around the edges of each bowl. "Well, now that you lot

171

have calmed down, I think we should eat. Agatha, we have a story to tell."

Agatha's full focus was on Variwen, who picked up a bowl of porridge and passed it to Agatha. The group all found seating around the table and soon everyone was shovelling food in. Agatha got halfway through when she looked up at Variwen, who winked at her.

"A little bird told me you were given a key yesterday." Variwen leaned back and brushed her hand over the mantel where the keyhole was found by Agatha. Agatha looked at Variwen, distracted by her previous outburst at Naga, then her excitement got the best of her. She smiles and goes to stand up. Pollyanna shrieked as the table started rising, as did her hair. The others stopped eating and moved their chairs back from the table, Alfred next to Pollyanna, stood her rigid body up, and moved her and her chair away from the table.

"Hmm-mm," Variwen said as she also stood up, put her tea on the table and walked around to a shocked Agatha. Variwen patted her on her shoulder and the table dropped to the floor. Bowls and spoons clattered but thankfully nothing was broken or spilt. "Go on, boys, child, finish up. You have a lot of tidying up to do today."

Groans could be heard from the others as Variwen looked at Agatha and winked. "It's all right, Agatha. You just have something new. You will get the hang of it. You are a Choler, or Light Daemon, very rare, thought to have been extinct. Your powers are tied to

172

your emotions, my dear. It's all right, we can get you under way. But first eat your porridge, there is nothing like a decent breakfast to get a good adventure underway. You need your energy." Variwen patted Agatha's shoulder again. Picking up her teacup, she took another sip.

"Oh Alfred, why do you have to eat like that? You're an adult and you have more food on the table than in your belly."

Alfred rolled his eyes. "Well, you try stuffing food in your gob when your teeth are all spiky and uneven," Alfred moaned to Variwen. Variwen calmly lifted her lips and showed her teeth to Alfred, who sat back. "Urrrr," he remarks as Variwen carefully brought her lips back down.

"You think you're the only one with unfortunate teeth, darling boy? Well, we will have to be more polite next time, and stop spilling your food!"

"Yes, Variwen," he mumbled as the others laughed.

"Alfred, you found a new mummy." Naga elbowed him as they were sitting next to each other. Alfred rolled his eyes and moved his bowl to the centre of the table. "He is old enough to not need to be mummied" Pollyanna shocked the others with her defence, even Alfred stopped and stared. She got up and collected his bowl, He went to get up to follow her.

"Alfred, be a dear and do the dishes,'' Variwen stated.

173

"*Oh why? I do them every day!*" Alfred had a tantrum. Variwen glared at him as he looked down at the floor. "Fine then," he mumbled and started to move the dishes to the sink.

"I will help you," whispered Pollyanna, as Alfred went to walk past with a pile of bowls.

The others finished their food. "Thank you, Variwen," they all simultaneously stated to her.

Variwen chuckled and flicked her hand to shoo them out of the room, leaving Agatha, a moody Alfred, Pollyanna and Variwen. "Right, my dear, I like the new look. Would you like me to plait it for you to get it out of your face?" Variwen smiled at Agatha and flicked her hand again. Agatha jumped as her hair picked itself up and started to plait itself.

"Oh, why can't you clean the dishes like that too?" Alfred moaned Pollyanna grabbed a tea towel, and joined him at the sink, Alfred wasn't sure how to take her new attention to him, so decided on ignoring her.

Variwen glared at Alfred but answered in a sweet voice, "Because, Alfred, you need to learn about duties and who should be listened to. You also need to wash the dishes properly. Look at that chunk of porridge stuck on that bowl!" Variwen shrieked and pointed at the bowl in question.

Alfred sheepishly looked at Variwen. "Sorry, I will wash it again."

"You better, my boy." Variwen turned to the now finished plait on Agatha's head. "Much better. Now, do you have the key? I think we are ready for today to begin, don't you?" Variwen winked at Agatha, who noticed Variwen hadn't changed her image today. Agatha frowned a little. She was still the blonde woman that stood before them yesterday. "Oh, you think I should change?" Variwen could see Agatha's expression.

"Oh no, no, I was just surprised you didn't change, considering you did it three times yesterday."

"Ahh well, I was going by what you all would deem most acceptable, ha, and it works, doesn't it?"

Variwen winks at Agatha who passes her the key. Variwen gives an excited jump as she goes over to the keyhole in the mantel.

"I'm really excited. I haven't been on an adventure in years," Variwen exclaimed to Agatha. "Oh, would you like to do the honours, Agatha? Sorry I do get carried away sometimes." Variwen held the key out to Agatha who smiled and took it.

Chapter 10
The Ledger

Alfred was wiping down the benches and draining the sink. "Variwen, I finished, can I come with you?"

Variwen looked over to Alfred and Pollyanna. "Only if it's all right with Agatha."

Agatha nodded in response then turned towards the mantel. "Oh, do you have to go, Alfred?" Pollyanna objected, Alfred turned to Variwen, with a queer look. "What did you do?"

Variwen laughed. "Oh, nothing really just a few drops here and a few drops there."

"Argh, you didn't." Alfred looked at Pollyanna who smiled sweetly at him.

"Variwen, how long does it take to wear off,"

"Well, goodness I'm not sure what you are on about."

"Argh you are as bad as mother,"

"I'm sorry sweetheart it was my twisted way to make you smile. You would be a good match. Don't worry it will only last until tonight." Alfred grabbed Pollyanna by the arms. "I will be okay" he said. "Wait here or if you get bored go help Caelan." Pollyanna pouting tried to touch Alfred's face. Stifled giggles could be heard behind him as Alfred pulled Pollyanna's arms back down to her sides. "Stay!" Alfred said to her. He turned glaring at Variwen who covered her mouth.

Taking a deep breath Alfred moved towards Agatha trying to regain a form of composure. "Sorry, I just wanted you to be less sulky."

Alfred held his hand up. "Stop! Just stop, I don't want to know."

Agatha grinning about the commotion behind her put the key into the hole. It clicked into place. and Variwen clapped excitedly as Agatha grinned at both Variwen and Alfred. She turned the key in the lock and it took both hands to turn it. Clunking sounds were heard behind the wall. The mantel started to push forward, it then moved to the side, scraping the grate forward, showing a narrow entrance.

"Agatha, you know that ball of light you had before. Do you think you can summon it?" Variwen asked.

"I-I'm not sure," Agatha replied. A worried puzzling look showed across her face.

"Okay, what were you feeling when it grew in your hand?"

"I was angry at Naga for talking about my, hair colour, making fun of me."

"Hmm-mm, well, what about when you lifted the table? You were excited then, weren't you?"

"Well, yes, I was but that was a different feeling. I was excited."

"Exactly. Are you excited now?" Variwen asked. Agatha nodded in reply. "Okay, so let's try this. I want you to concentrate on your excitement, imagine you are holding it in your hands and think of it as a ball or orb."

Agatha looked at her hands. She shuffled her feet, glancing at each of them, before closing her eyes as a small amount of light came from what looked through her and not in her hands. Agatha became the lighting.

"Hmm-mm, we may need you to practise that some more." Variwen patted Agatha on the shoulder and the light was gone instantly. Agatha looked down at her hands and was disappointed she hadn't created the orb.

Alfred came forward and patted her. "It's okay, Agatha, you will get it." A very rare smile came from Alfred and for once he looked like a nice normal, young man.

Agatha did a double take and smiled back. "Oh, why does she get a smile Alfred, you can smile at me." Pollyanna looked like Ants, jiggling around in his chair. Alfred crestfallen but not wanting to hurt Pollyanna. "It's okay Pollyanna, we can talk when I come back."

Agatha whispered to Alfred, "You are being so nice to her."

He bent his head down. "It's not her fault, it's Variwen's'." They turned to where Variwen was, but Variwen had left the room and the two standing there were puzzled with her unannounced leaving.

Moments later Variwen returned with three sticks. She wrapped wet cloth around the tip and shoved them in the remains of embers of the fire. "This will do for now." She smiled, blowing them and handing each one to Agatha and Alfred.

"Right, who will do the honours?" Variwen smiled and winked at Agatha who smiled back, took a deep breath and went into the narrow gap.

The torch lit the passage as it showed a narrow hallway. It seemed to go straight for a while but the height went right up into the darkness. They all shuffled along sideways in this narrow dusty long forgotten hall. They came to some stairs that widened out a bit, making it easier to walk down.

At the bottom of the steps, a room with no door awaited them. Agatha turned back to Variwen and Alfred who were waiting behind her. Variwen beckoned her forward swishing her hand and Agatha moved into the room.

There in the centre of the room was a wooden stand. The room was covered in dusty cobwebs. There were attachments on the walls for the torches and Variwen and Alfred placed their torches in them. Agatha handed her torch to Variwen as she moved forward to have a closer look at the only furniture in the room. The book stand was empty. She ran her hands over the stand and found some symbols on the side. Looking at the symbols, one reminded her of the mark on her neck, the sign of the goat. It made her shiver as she placed her hand over the green-hued bandage Ants had placed over her wound. The next sign looked almost like her family crest, and the last was a simple arrow pointing down the arrow looked like a nob she could twist.

Agatha went to twist it and Variwen grabbed her arm. "Do you know what you're doing? It could be a trap," she warned. "I can't see the outcome with you, remember, Agatha?"

Agatha smiled and brushed the symbols with her hand. She picked out some dirt from her family crest and pointed to it. "This is my family, Variwen, this will be the right way." She grabbed the knob and turned the arrow towards the crest.

Agatha stood up and moved back to the others. They stood there listening to the clinking and clanking of the stand, holding their breath waiting for something bad to happen. They were relieved when a side popped off the stand and fell to the floor. Excited, Agatha went around the stand and looked in. Looking at the others, she reached in and pulled out a very large, very old book. It was leatherbound, with uneven pages sticking out the top and bottom. More clinking could be heard and a sharp clank.

The entrance that had no door was suddenly closing. The floor was lifting up and the group pelted for the entranceway. Clambering through, they started to run up the stairs and the walls started to narrow. Running out into the narrow hallway forgetting their torches, they ran in the dark towards the light of the kitchen. The ceiling was slowly coming down on them as they ran as fast as they could through the narrow hallway.

Agatha burst through into the kitchen first. Alfred was second and Variwen was not far behind. She started to scream as she was trying to get closer but the ceiling was almost on her head. Agatha and Alfred both tried to reach in and grab her but only Alfred's arms were long enough. He pulled Variwen out sideways as the ceiling moved further and further to the ground. Agatha was staring in a panic whilst Variwen got to her feet out of the room just in time as the mantel moved and enclosed the hallway they had just been in.

Panting, Alfred checked over Variwen, who had collapsed and was lying on the ground staring up at the ceiling. She coughed. "Ye gods, that was bloody close."

Variwen looked up at Agatha, who was looking at the book. Their eyes caught. "The ledger, I presume." Variwen smiled at Agatha. "So, want to find out who you truly are, my dear?" Variwen winked at Agatha, who excitedly looked at Alfred. His eyebrows were raised and he swept his shoulder-length hair out of his face. They had forgotten about Pollyanna sitting behind them. "Oh, there you are Alfred, oh you were gone for ages, I missed you!" The excitement of the small adventure drained from Alfred as he turned to Pollyanna, she had jumped up from her seat and was attempting to brush off the dust. Annoying him as she kept touching him. The ladies behind him giggled as they stood staring at the spectacle. "She is going to be so embarrassed tomorrow isn't she," Agatha said, transfixed on the entertainment of poor Alfred. Alfred with Pollyanna in tow walked briskly out of the room, all they could hear was, "Oh Pollyanna, please stop touching me."

"But, but Alfred just a bit more, please you're nearly tidy."

"Variwen, that was cheeky you know, poor Alfred has enough by being picked on by the others, I don't think he will forgive you for this one though."

Variwen thought on this for a bit. "You're probably right, but I did it yes, for a bit of entertainment but also have you seen how he hasn't been sulky or grumpy since I did it." Both starring at the doorway after Alfred they decided to go find the others.

Agatha held the book for the others to see. "We found it!" They all dropped what they were doing and excitedly yelled out.

Chapter 11
The Mudslinging

With the Ledger in tow, the group carried on with the previous arrangement, restoration and sorting the castle by day, and work on the otherworldly means including Agatha's and Pollyanna's training by night, their only differences were that the clouds were no more purple but black in the evenings, the lighting had stopped and the rain, which used to be fierce, was now just a drizzle, making their sleeping arrangements, a less torrid affair. Windows were replaced and rubble was piled up, ready to be moved.

On one such evening, Agatha turned the page of the book during dinner. She yelped, stood and pointed at the book. Everyone craned over to see the image of the footman, drawn exactly, right down to his outfit.

A strange look came over Agatha. "Is that his… Is that a part of him, his clothing?" Variwen, leaned across to glanced over the book.

"It doesn't say much along the lines of his appearance or attire, does it? In fact, it doesn't say much about him at all, does it?" Variwen frowned at the book. "So much for the ledger of all daemons."

She sat up and picked up her fork again. They were having fish for dinner, caught by the ever-moody Alfred, who today, for some unearthly reason, decided it was a good enough day to skive off from work like he usually did, although today he walked back with a bag loaded to the brim with fish. The group had all stopped and stared with amazement as he walked in his usual stooped fashion past them. He said what he said again at dinner. "What, you never seen a fish before?" Rolling his eyes, a usual reply to most of what was said to him. Pollyanna was in the kitchen when he came in.

Since the love potion incident Pollyanna hasn't looked at Alfred, she had avoided his gaze, which now, was constant.

Alfred sat in his seat quietly eating when Caelan patted him on the back. "Well done, lad! You actually did something for our rough tumble family, eh!"

Alfred was shocked by this. "We're a family?"

"Well, yeah, might as well be!" said Caelan.

"Oh God, no wonder you're so annoying!" Alfred slumped even more, he was smirking under his hood.

Caelan grabbed the hood and pulled it down. "You know I don't like your hood up at the table." Alfred scoffed but carried on eating while the others laughed. Caelan was sitting next to him tonight and patted him on the back, which nearly shoved Alfred face-first into his dinner. "Hmmf, Caelan, you nearly ruined it," Alfred responded, much to the amusement of the others.

"Agatha, why don't you put down the book and join us?" Charles invited Agatha who blushed and placed the book flat on the table again.

"Sorry, I just get so enthused by it all, I forget what I'm doing half the time."

It was a Tuesday night. Agatha had been learning ways to help control her new powers. She had a temper — they learnt that one quickly as a fair few more holes were present inside the Castle. Although she had managed to 'grow' a light orb and be able to provide it whenever she wanted now, she also made them really quickly and threw them whenever anyone triggered her. The others were learning a new defence, a game Oxxy had called 'duck and weave'. Agatha was always apologetic afterwards. Even Pollyanna who had been training was almost keeping up with the group, although a lot of her clothing had singed parts.

The group had got used to the new addition of Variwen to their group, who had fast made herself at home with the group, becoming an almost camp mother so to speak, or a head Maître d' which surely Alfred would have agreed upon considering his luck at causing problems right before dinner had finished. Then remanding him to the washing up and banning him from whatever he had originally planned for the night, which was usually nothing but sulking and moping around annoying everyone, except of course Pollyanna. The others had tried to tease him with it, he was left speechless giving the group a good laugh, Agatha even though so busy in her escapades still had the time to defend Alfred, and when it came to a point of being too much, Variwen stepped in with a glare enough to vaporize the sun.

It would have been a month of this monotonous behaviour, clearing and cleaning during the day and reading or helping Agatha by night. The book was almost completely deciphered when on this particular night Agatha was turning the page and there was a very familiar image.

"Variwen, who is that?"

Variwen, by now knowing she was Agatha's constant call upon for questions within the book, was shocked to see an image of a Choler. "Well, I never, Agatha, you found your kind." Smiling she stood and patted Agatha on the back. The others crowded around. Charles, of course being next to Agatha sidled in to take a closer look.

"Oh," he exclaimed by surprise. The group all looked at him. "I remember him here!" he exclaimed. The others now stared.

Agatha turned with a hope in her eyes. "Do you know him, Charles? Who is he, how do you know him, when was he here?"

Charles making sure he was right looked back at the book. He nodded for Caelan to come closer.

"Well, well, well, Agatha, don't you have an uncanny resemblance to that bloke?"

Shocked, she stood. Her body started to vibrate and the group moved quickly to the edges of the room.

"Oh, not the kitchen, Agatha," Variwen stated. "Anywhere but here. Go outside, for god's sake. If you bloody explode in here, I'm going to be very cross with you."

Abashed, Agatha guiltily took deep breaths to try and calm herself. Charles holds her hand as she attempts control of her feelings.

"Sorry, love," Caelan said to Variwen. "I forgot myself for a minute."

"Only a minute." Variwen perplexedly looked at Caelan and scowled. "I would have had your balls years ago if it weren't for your wife too, bloody idiot."

Caelan looked down at the ground. Variwen rolled her eyes. A half-hearted apology came out of her mouth and Caelan gathered himself and winked at her.

"Oh, you bastard, you did that on purpose." Grinning, Caelan moved back to his seat, attempting to look innocent as the scathing look from Variwen would have melted iron if he so much as looked her in the eye.

Agatha, now relaxed and collected, went back to the book as the others returned to their seating. Agatha touched the page, for she could only guess this image was of her father. She found the image description down at the bottom.

Choler: Aged thirty-four, rare species, named Archimedes, only known of his kind.

Agatha muttered his name and ran her fingers over the image, she looked down again and saw some more writing, it was different to the rest.

Offspring: One child, half-blood, named Archeal.

Agatha gasped and pointed again to the page but this time at the scrawl at the bottom. "Look, is that me?

'Archeal'. Oh my gosh, so many questions! Do you think he is still alive? Do you think we can find him?"

A glint of hope could be seen in her eyes. The others looked downcast, at the table.

"Oh Agatha, dear, your kind are unheard of living past forty, my love. Their emotions are too highly strung, the older they get, the more unstable. See, it says so here." Variwen pointed to the middle of the page, there are two columns and on the left column there it states about the age of her kind.

"Well, that doesn't help me any more than before!" Agatha said. She walked away from the table. "I think I lost my appetite, sorry, Alfred. I'm sure someone else will eat my dinner." Agatha walked out of the kitchen She brought up an orb in her hand and flicked it around her fingers. Stopping by the entranceway, she sat on the bench looking outside at the evening rain and black clouds.

Charles soon followed out and came up to her. He smiled at her and felt her head. "You're warm, but not too bad."

Agatha smiled meekly and slid down the seat she was sitting on and onto the floor. She looked down at her hands, still playing with the orb.

"It must be such a hard thing to come to terms with Agatha," he said.

Agatha cut in before he finished. "Oh, Charles, everything is hard to come to terms with. These last few months of my life has been turned upside down. I don't know how much more I can take. The more we sort through the castle the more my temper destroys, or my upset, or my excitement. I'm like a bomb that's almost ready to set off."

Charles bowed his head down. Agatha bit her lip. "Charles, I'm sorry, but it could be true. The amount of power I seem to have only grows stronger each day that passes. I am learning to control one type of emotion at the moment and that's anger, but what about the rest? No wonder my kind are all dead. We were bombs, living bombs." Agatha started crying.

Charles crouched down in front of her. The orb she'd had disappeared and her body was humming. Tears rolled down her face and Charles wiped them away with his thumb. "Agatha, I'm here, I will always be here, you can blow me to bits and I will still find a way back to you. I will still heal and make my way back. I can't leave you. You mean too much to me." Agatha looked up and the humming in her body slowed down, as did her tears.

"Oh, Charlie, I'm so tired of all of this." He wiped away her tears again and bent down to kiss her on her head.

"I don't want to hold back, Agatha, but I don't want to have to tidy up another hole in the floor or wall."

Agatha looked up with a watery smile. She moved into a kneeling position looking Charles in the eyes. Her eyes searched his for anything resembling hatred, anything to push him away from her, to make it easier for her to push him away too, but there was only love, affection and kindness in return.

"Charles, I know we must be apart from each other. but the more I fight it the more I am drawn to you."

Charles reached out and cupped her cheek in his hand. "To hell with it, I would rather deal with your explosions than have to stop being close to you."

Agatha showed panic but it was short lived. Charles closed in and kissed her. The want between the two was inevitable. He brought his other hand up and cupped the other cheek as he kissed her more. Agatha's body hummed the deeper they kiss. Her body lifted her up and Charles followed. Agatha hovered slightly above the ground as they continued to kiss. The carpet behind them started to lift as did the curtains. A humming noise started low then rose as they continued.

Charles grabbed her waist and pulled her closer to him. Agatha responded by running her hands up his chest. The kiss deepened even more as Agatha lifted her hands to Charles' head and ran her hands through his hair. She grabbed the back of his neck as they continued to kiss, still hovering.

Charles opened an eye to make sure she was still okay. The slight hesitation was felt by Agatha as she too opened her eyes, pulling away ever so slightly. She smiled at him. Her eyes told him everything as he kissed her again and picked her up. Charles carried her to the staircase in his arms. Agatha caressed his chest and kissed his neck. They moved up the staircase. He looked down and smiled at her. Agatha smiled in return, reaching again to kiss him. He stopped kissing her to check his footing and continued up the stairs. Agatha could feel his heart racing as he climbed the last steps.

Charles looked at Agatha again and was encouraged into walking the remaining way to her room. He booted open the door, which raised a giggle from Agatha and shut it with a side step and a push with his backside. Striding to the bed, he flung her onto the bed. Agatha happily shrieked as she landed.

Charles kicked off his boots and took off his jacket, all the while looking at Agatha with a brilliant smile. Agatha was also taking off her boots, jacket and outer shirt. She propped herself up by her elbows. Charles climbed onto the bed and on top of her. She lay back as he moved above her, smiling all the while. He bent down and kissed her, making the hum louder. Agatha wrapped her arms and legs around him and pulled him down to lie completely on top of her. He could feel her body vibrating even more than before. He kissed her lips, neck and chin. Charles opened the top of her shirt and kissed further down her neckline. Agatha moaned with excitement, wanting to feel his flesh on hers.

Charles pulled his shirt off. Agatha ran her hands all over his chest, never taking her eyes off his. Lowering himself, he could feel Agatha's body was hot now, and was vibrating. The room around them, everything was vibrating. Items were falling off the chest of drawers. The books were clattering off the bookshelf.

"Agatha," Charles said her name as he kissed her. He pulled up slightly. "Agatha, you're burning up." Agatha moaned again and grabbed him. She kissed him more and the loose items started to float in the room. Charles tried to pull up from her. "Sweetheart, slow down, you're burning up." She kept moaning. The whole room began to shake as Agatha slowed and started to writhe around underneath Charles. "Agatha calm down, open your eyes!"

Charles started to panic as she opened her eyes and the colour drained out. He jumped up and yelled for the others but no sooner did he start to yell than the door was thrown inwards. Charles yelled at Naga, "Ice her, Naga, she's burning up!"

It was hard to hear as Agatha started screaming. She began to levitate. Naga ran forward and threw everything he could at her, completely covering her from head to toe in ice. Agatha was still vibrating so it didn't take long for the ice which was steaming to shatter. Her screaming was coming from all around them that ethereal noise heightening. No one could help but feel the panic from themselves and her. Naga iced her again. The screaming quieted a little as the ice broke and flew all across the room. Charles, still bare chested, got the brunt of the next wave of ice. Naga covered her again and again as each time she broke through. Slowly, slowly though, she lowered back to the bed as each layer of ice started to cool her off. Agatha was silent with her eyes closed, the room and its items had stopped levitating and vibrating.

Variwen disappeared, pulling Alfred with her. "Alfred, we need dry blankets, warm water and... and..."

"It's okay, I can get some soup made up with the leftovers," he said as they ran down the hallway to the stairs.

"Oh, you are a good boy, Alfie." Variwen smiled at Alfred as she ran down the stairs for the Ledger. "I can help you," Pollyanna called out as she ran down the stairs after Alfred, she concentrated on the stairs as Alfred also running stared at her, "Agatha needs us, Alfred come on." For the first time since the love potion Pollyanna had strung a full sentence to Alfred. She held out her hand, he grabbed it and they ran together.

Caelan still in the room, started sweeping off the half-melted ice from her bed. Fervor was checking her pulse and her eyes. Agatha had passed out.

"Is she okay? Will she be okay?" Charles was asking, panicking all while hopping from foot to foot.

"Jesus, Charles, talk about a hot night. You're lucky. It could have been explosive," Oxxy stated, sweeping up the ice and throwing it out the now broken window.

Caelan grabbed Charles as he went for Oxxy. "Woah boy, he was only playing. Too soon, Oxxy. We are not out the woods yet. I think we should move her into another room. We can't cover that window tonight. Ants, go tell the others that she is moving rooms."

"Move her to my room," Charles said. They all stopped and looked at him. "I won't touch her, I don't want her to leave me, I love her." Charles looked wrought with worry.

"Oh, Charlie, me boy," said Caelan, still holding him. "We know you do, we all do."

He looked at Caelan and saw him clearly since they came into the room. "Is she okay? Please tell me," Charles begged turning to Naga, who had stopped covering her in ice.

"She is breathing faintly, her heart beats strong. Charles, she will get through this."

Naga looked at Charles and threw his wet shirt at him. "No offence, Charles, but put a shirt on, your hairless chest is reflecting the moonlight."

Charles smiled weakly. He hesitated but left the room to get a dry shirt. Meanwhile Oxxy, giving up on sweeping, started to use the wind from outside and blew it through the room. All the ice flew out the now broken window. Oxxy swirled the wind again and picked up the broken glass. He twisted and turned it and placed it in her rubbish bin with a slight clatter. Moving his hands, he turned the wind towards all the books on the floor. He swirled them into stacks on the chest of drawers.

Alfred, Pollyanna and Variwen returned with blankets, the Ledger, warm water. Caelan moved to pick up Agatha.

"Wait!" Variwen said as she ran towards Agatha. "You need to wake her first. If she feels your warmth, it could start all over again." Caelan looked confused but let Variwen past him.

Variwen climbed onto the now soaking wet bed. Putting her hand up, she beckoned Alfred forward with the warm water and a blanket. "Agatha dear, it's Variwen. Agatha, you must open your eyes." Variwen looked at the others then tried again. "Agatha, you need to wake up. It's Variwen." Variwen gently touched her hand which made her stir. Variwen gasped as Agatha shoots her hand out and grips her hand.

Her eyes flickered open. With a croaky voice, she whispered, "Variwen, I'm here," and closed her eyes again.

"Okay, Caelan, you can move her." Variwen moved off the wet bed and stood up. Charles had re-entered the room as Caelan picked up Agatha. Alfred and Pollyanna gathered everything up and followed Caelan and Variwen out of the room, down the hallway and into Charles's room. His room was dimly lit by the fireplace. It was tidy and welcoming with desk, drawers and bed opposite the mantel.

Charles followed close behind. "What can I do? Please give me something to do." He was wracked with guilt, feeling it was all his fault. She had nearly died for a stupid moment of passion that he knew he should never have encouraged Agatha was now lying on his bed being watched over, risking death because of him.

Alfred put the towels on the floor and handed the bowl of warm water to Charles. Charles took it. He looked down blankly before looking at Alfred

"It's okay. Do as Variwen says, Charles. Pollyanna and I can start the soup, Agatha needs to regain her strength."

Charles smiled at Alfred and handed the bowl back to him. "I will do it. Alfred, you stay. I shouldn't be here." Before Alfred had the chance to reply, Charles was already halfway to the door. He didn't look back leaving Pollyanna and Alfred in his stead.

It was a small while before the others joined Caelan, Variwen, Alfred and Pollyanna in the room. "Where's Charles?" the others asked.

"He is sorting the soup. Can you go check on him?" Alfred asked Oxxy. He nodded silently, looking at Agatha for a bit before he turned and left, heading towards the kitchen.

As he entered, he saw Charles so crestfallen, looking at the fire. The soup was boiling away as his mind was elsewhere, recapturing the night's events. Charles looked up to see Oxxy standing there. "I can never touch her, Oxxy, I can't kill her." Charles was so broken by it.

Oxxy moved a chair over and sat by the fire with him. He sat up to check the soup, grabbed the spoon from behind him, stirred it and relaxed back into the chair. "Charles, mate, it's early days yet," Oxxy tried to sympathize with him.

"No, it won't happen, I will not be able to be with her."

Oxxy patted him on the back. "It's rough now, mate, but stop being so melodramatic and put some seasoning in the bloody soup. Don't make me slap you back to your senses, Charles."

Charles looked at Oxxy and smiled a wistful smile. "Okay Oxxy, whatever you say." Charles went to the pantry then seasoned the soup. He picked up a bowl and ladled some soup into it. "Shall we?" Charles said as he held the steaming soup.

Oxxy collected a soup spoon on the way out of the kitchen and they made their way back to the room. Agatha had been propped up in Charles' bed. She was covered in blankets. She was talking but in a very raspy manner. Charles could hear her and hesitated to enter the room. He passed the bowl to Oxxy

"I can't see her like this, Oxxy." Charles handed the bowl over and walked away.

Oxxy, watching him go, re-entered the room with the soup and cutlery for Agatha. She sat up a little as he came into view. "Where's Charles?" Agatha asked as Oxxy as he sets down the soup on the bedside table.

He looked back before turning his head towards her. "Uh, he is just taking a walk. It has hit him really hard, Agatha."

"Hit him, I'm the one that nearly died. I want to see him." She looked upset.

Variwen rubbed her arm with a sympathetic smile. "Charles will probably be wanting to work through some things, love. Don't blame him, it's a confusing time for the both of you."

At this, Agatha slumped back into the bed and looked away. "I think I'm quite tired," she announced to the others.

Caelan clapped his hands. "Okay crew, let's leave Miss Agatha and Variwen alone now." Pollyanna said. "Agatha, would you like me to stay, I can read to you if you want, like we used to when we were sick!"

Agatha shrugged her shoulders indifferent to Pollyanna's suggestion, Alfred turns Pollyanna to the door. "I know you mean well, let's just leave her for tonight and visit with a nice breakfast tomorrow" Alfred tried comforting Pollyanna, the love potion incident forgotten as Agatha sat forlornly in Charles' bed. The group said their goodnights as Caelan ushered them out of the room. He turned and winked at Agatha then shut the door behind him.

Looking down at her hands, Agatha spoke in a raspy voice. "Variwen, will I ever be able to be with Charles?"

"Well, my dear, if your dad figured it out, I'm sure you can," she said with a wink. "But for now, how about you settle for some soup? Get some energy into you, eh?" Variwen helped Agatha sit up. She was so weakened from the event that Variwen picked up the spoon and fed Agatha.

"You know, when you were a very little girl, you got the measles and nearly died. Your mum, bless her, called upon my services and I came to this very house and met with a very hot, very upset and moody little girl, who had a tear-streaked face. You wouldn't let anyone near you and every time someone got close, you tried to bite them." Variwen smiled at the memory and Agatha chuckled a little.

"How old was I?" Agatha looked at Variwen, who spooned in another bit of soup into Agatha's mouth.

"Oh goodness, Miss Aggie, I think you were two, and what a wild two-year-old you were at that!

"I crept into your room and changed my face four times by sweeping my hand up and down in front of my face, each time pulling a different face as you oohed and ahhed. It was when you started clapping that I asked you if you wanted me to do some more magic. You laughed and said yes please. You made me promise if I did more magic, you would let me bathe you, feed you and put a cold towel on your head to make you feel better. I remember you saying, 'oh Variwen do I have to take a bath, I hate baths,' so we agreed on you standing in a pot of warm water and I rinsed you down in front of the fire."

Variwen was smiling as she recounted the memory, talking about magic bubbles and making Agatha's toys float on clouds. "I nursed you until you were better and didn't see you again until you were a year older, your mother asked me for a specific spell which wasn't in my area of expertise. I showed her toward Helgam and that was the last I saw of you until you came into my Glen. I thought you were your mother, or a daemon disguised as your mother, until you spoke and I saw your beautiful eyes." Variwen smiled and spooned some more soup into Agatha's mouth. They were silent for a while, thinking of previous events. Variwen gave sigh and put the last of the soup in her mouth, smiling at her.

"There, all done now. Charles made that for you, my dear."

Both women looked up as the floorboard by the door creaked. Charles was standing in the now opened doorway, holding his arms across his chest and looking at the floor. "I think I might be needed down stairs," Variwen said to Agatha. She took the soup bowl and spoon, winked at her and walked towards the door. In a low voice, Variwen said, "She has some energy back, Charles, but don't let her speak too much." He nodded as Variwen left the room.

Still standing at the entrance, hesitant on moving further into the room Charles asked, "Are you okay?" Agatha smiled and nodded and patted the space next to the bed. Charles walked in further but didn't sit down next to her.

In a croaky voice, Agatha spoke. "Charles, why won't you sit with me?" Looking upset, Agatha searched his eyes.

Charles looked blankly at her. "I'm not going to sit with you, Agatha. You need rest, not me. I can't bear the thought of knowing you almost died from my acts of selfishness."

"Our acts, Charles, it was the both of us." She was raspy and tried to push her voice, which only made her cough.

Charles rolled his head slightly. "See, you're still trying to coax me in even though I did this."

"Charles, it was me, too! Why can't you see that?" she tried to shout as he turned and walked back to the door.

"I'm sorry, Agatha, I can't see you like this knowing it was my fault." Charles went to leave the room and shortly after exiting, a pillow came flying out of the room. He heard her exasperation in a scream that was short lived and soon after coughing. Variwen was speaking with Caelan when the cushion came flying out of the room.

She turned and looked at the cushion, then up at Charles. "So much for being a romance specialist, hey, Charles?"

Caelan stopped talking and peered into the room. He turned back and Charles was staring at Variwen, unable to speak. "Well, Charlie, I think you right done it there." Caelan and Variwen walked up to Charles' room which was commandeered by Agatha.

Variwen spoke to Charles, "Why are you trying to hide your emotions, Charles? I know your heart is breaking, but did you break hers?"

Charles furrowed his eyebrows at Variwen. He looked, confused, from Caelan to Variwen, then spoke, "No, I don't think so. I think she is just mad at me. And hurt."

Variwen relaxed a bit. "Okay, okay, we can deal with an angry Agatha, but a broken-hearted one, that is not a Choler I pretend to want to know. Highly volatile from my understanding. Do you understand, Charles?" Variwen looked at Charles, frowning at him. "Don't do anything stupid, Charles. An upset heart is one thing but an upset mind is unpredictable."

She turned and walked into the room. "Oh Agatha, you have made a mess of things. Come on, miss, you need to rest. All this anger will make you worse."

Caelan walked through the entrance to the room but turned to Charles. "Do I need someone to watch you, Charles?"

He looked at him with a troublesome, confused stare. "No, no, it's okay, Caelan. I will be fine. I just need to sort some things out. Agatha needs to stay safe." Charles turned and walked down the hall. He disappeared from view, leaving Caelan pondering on his words. Caelan turned and closed the door, slowly walking toward Agatha, taking his time to get to the bed so he could process what Charles had just said.

Chapter 12
The Uninvited Guests

Charles kept to his word. He was barely seen by the others at Wilderfort Castle over the past week while Agatha was mending. Variwen kept a close eye on her and provided distractions to nullify her outbursts of emotions. Pollyanna would also come in giving updates of the castle clean up. Her anger towards Charles grew deeper and deeper as the days went past to a point where no one could say his name in her presence.

It took all of Caelan, Pollyanna and Variwen's coaxing to get Agatha out of her room when the new week began.

"Agatha, it's spring. Come and see the bluebells in the fields." Variwen had been trying to get Agatha out of her 'dungeon' as they all called it as she almost always kept the curtains drawn whilst in their making it ominous and smelling musty.

Agatha, getting properly dressed with Pollyanna's help felt like an age to her, she felt apprehensive in stepping out of Charles' room. Agatha stood at the doorway, looking up and down the hall, taking deep breaths of clean air. The doorway of her old bedroom was now boarded up, making it another area that was due for repair as rubble and the last of the rooms on the lower level were being cleared. Caelan had also been giving Agatha updates on the progress of the Castle, which helped in some ways to distract her daily asking of where Charles was and why he wasn't coming to see her.

Walking down the stairs, she was pleased to know that the banister she used to slide down as a child was still fully intact, and recently scraped back and polished. It gave the impression of the rest of the entranceway to too far dilapidated and better off to be broken down for removal than repair, although this room was by far the most damaged of late with Agatha's previous outbursts.

The group had been working hard on the final clearance with the exception of Agatha and Charles. Even Variwen was having a go at sorting and clearing when she wasn't babysitting Agatha and her tantrums.

Agatha walked outside and breathed in the fresh crisp air. It was cold and made her cough a little. She smiled whilst looking around. Variwen and Pollyanna and Caelan were relieved at seeing her do so as they followed her, almost like apprehensive sheep.

The group were outside piling up the latest broken unfixable items in the house.

"Excuse me, miss, but did your face just crack?"

Agatha rolled her eyes. Although still raspy, she replied, "Ha, ha, very funny, Naga." He smiled and walked up to hug her. She welcomed the hug, closing her eyes as he held her. Naga let go and Agatha looked around hopefully to see Charles with the men.

"He isn't here, Agatha," Alfred stated in a rather demure manner. "He is always skiving off, he starts to help in the morning and then come morning tea he has gone, disappears for most of the day."

Agatha looked from one to the other and up to Caelan. "Best to leave those with a troubled mind to find their way through, Miss Agatha. Not much point in trying to get them to listen if their mind is someplace else. I'm sure he will pick up once he finds out you're up and walking about." Caelan tried reassuring Agatha.

Variwen took Agatha's hand. "Enough about the work and Charles. Let me show you what you really came out here for."

"Oh, did you all come to see me?" Oxxy said and laughed. Variwen whacked him over the back of the head as they walked past. Agatha smiled as Oxxy winked and carried on rubbing his head.

Walking around the castle to the back, Variwen followed by Pollyanna gave a show-and-tell of all the herbs that were there and new additions she had planted with the help of Naga and Pollyanna.

They walked around, enjoying the time in the open for nearly an hour. "I think any more time outside, Miss Agatha and you will either get yourself a cold or you will plum wear out!" Agatha smiled, looking out at the fields beyond.

Variwen took her back the way they had come and around the corner. The group were no longer near the pile and a coach was now visible at the entranceway of the castle, Agatha sighed exasperatedly

"Great, another visit from Caspian." Agatha rolled her eyes as she, Pollyanna and Variwen came closer to the carriage. The footman was waiting on top. He had been watching them with an ugly turn of his head.

"Ahh, there she is," Caspian said, as he turned from the footman Hesiss to Agatha and Variwen, smiling as if nothing bad or untoward had happened between the pair.

Agatha screwed up her face and looked at Variwen. "Speak for me," Agatha managed to get out in a raspy whisper.

"Of course I will, Agatha." Variwen comforted Agatha, patting her hand Pollyanna had taken a few steps behind Variwen as Caspian walked towards them.

"Hmm-mm, a bit under the weather there, dear Agatha?"

Agatha glared at Caspian. "Never underestimate me, Lord Caspian," Agatha snarled at him. Variwen glanced at Agatha as she could feel her temperature rise.

"Oh, just so you know…" Lord Caspian leaned in a little, stopping, then pulling out his handkerchief to cover his face. Sniffing to make sure nothing was too odorous for his taste, he looked puzzled at Agatha then, as fast as his confusion showed, it went.

"You both left in such a hurry from my place the other night, I never was able to give you your party favours." Caspian smiled innocently at them both as Hesiss clambered down off the carriage and entered the seating area. He pulled out two rather large items wrapped in plain brown packaging paper. "Oh, excuse the wrapping. I'm not much of one for gifts but felt these should be wrapped."

Agatha took the large parcel from Hesiss and so did Variwen, who narrowed her eyes at both Caspian and the footman. Both kept their heads clear, making it hard for Variwen to sniff a trap.

Agatha shook her box, which brought forth tiny voices screeching. Variwen's eyes opened wide. She opened a portal straight away and threw her box through.

As she turned to grab Agatha's box, though, it had already started to rip itself apart. Agatha dropped it in shock as Lord Caspian and Hesiss quickly got onto the carriage, waving as they went.

"Oh, I do hope you enjoy your presents, Agatha. Until next time, Variwen, or should I say dinner?" Caspian laughed at his terrible idea of a joke. Hesiss whipped the horses and the carriage started to move. Whipping them again, the horses neighed an angry neigh and started to race back down the driveway.

The box Agatha held was now rattling like mad, making Agatha panic. Variwen tried to grab it but it jolted around like a bouncy ball set off in a box, with Variwen chasing it as it flew out of Agatha's hands.

"Hurry!" Variwen cried, managing to catch it, although it was too late.

Hundreds of tiny little people had fallen out of the gaps in the box and they were streaming out like the Greeks from the horse of troy. Some ran towards the trees in the distance, while others ran towards the rubbish pile. The remainder divided up again and some attempted to enter the house.

Variwen grabbed her belt, unhooked it and whipped it onto the ground. The remaining little people started running towards Agatha. "Queen, Queen!" they all cried.

"Don't listen to them!" Variwen yelled as Agatha started to step backwards with her hands up.

"What are they?"

"Fey! And they will dig under your skin and try to take over your body. They can sense your power."

"'Err, that's disgusting," Agatha rasped to Variwen.

Oxxy, Alfred and Ants were attempting to stomp on the Fey before they entered the pile of rubbish they had been throwing more onto. "They're getting through Variwen," Oxxy yelled.

Agatha was holding Pollyanna's hand for balance as they both lashed out stomping on the Fey Agatha's anguish and hatred for Caspian brought on the vibrations again. Bringing about an orb of light, Agatha threw it at a small gathering of the Fey. It made the small group scream and exploded as the ball hit. Agatha let go of Pollyanna's hand as she created more and more orb's and threw them in all directions towards the Fey as they screamed and ran to hide.

One had escaped and ran off in the direction of Lord Caspian. Oxxy pointed at the escaping Fey. "Alfred, get him before he reports back to Caspian. He can't know about Agatha!"

The rest of the group defended their area by stomping and utilizing anything, they had near. "How is it these things keep coming," Agatha yelled over the top of the screeching Fey as they were killed.

One of them had attached itself to Ants arm in an attempt to claw its way under his flesh. It was finding it difficult. "Well, they are stupid things, aren't they? I am made of lighting, you stupid Fey! Right, that's it, I have had *enough*!" yelled Ants. He grabbed and shocked the one on his arm, throwing it to the ground. Ants summoned the positive and negative charge from the ground around him, and from the air above, shocking the little Fey and burning them to a crisp.

He turned to the others. "Okay, turn sideways, I'm going to shock them all." Ants built up the lightning and Agatha heard the noise of the build-up over the screams and running of the Fey. Ants shot lines of lighting, killing off the Fey as they ran around attempting to hide or attempting to find a host. Ants seemed to be controlling them until the group from the forest came back out but in the guise of the animal hosts they had managed to find and take over.

It was a weird sight where foxes, a bear, some wolves and a badger all had either a patch of blood near a gaping wound or their fur was too dense for the wound's visibility and the fur was matted with fresh blood.

The eyes of the animals were white. They stood united growling furiously at the group. Agatha could see them clearly and yelled to the others of what was coming.

The bear was the first to take a run towards the group, initiating the rest to start running, galloping or speeding across the ground towards Agatha and the rest. The first in their path was Fervor who was drawing up a wall of trees, vines and heavy bush growth to help deter the animal hosts from the others.

Oxxy was flying wicked amounts of wind like a miniature twister, pulling the Fey without hosts inside, spinning around and knocking each other in a furious manner. It was so harsh the Fey began to break apart as their parts remained inside the twister. Blood flew outwards, spraying those near it. Pollyanna screamed at the gross spray of blood, continuing to fight off the Fey with a long broom handle she had found, panting and darting her eyes about looking for her next fight.

Agatha's eyes were blurring as she breathed deeper and deeper, attempting to control her outburst but the control was slipping. The ground around her started to shake as her friends all fought the animal hosts and Fey around them. She locked onto the bear that was going for Naga. She screamed and reached out. A stream of light and sound came from her and hit the bear, blowing straight through the centre of it. The bear crumpled to the floor as Agatha looked for another target. Naga, shocked with what had just happened, patted himself down, accounting for all his limbs.

She found the foxes attacking Fervor. As quickly as he threw one off, another had jumped back on him in it' place. Agatha, concentrating on the three foxes this time, created another stream of light and sound, enveloping all of the foxes and Fervor.

Variwen screamed out, "Nooo!" panicking for Fervor but the light just blasted past him the noise was deafening for him. He had squeezed his eyes shut as it shot past, Fervor patted himself down finding he was untouched as the foxes controlled by the Fey disintegrated.

Agatha turned and Charles, who had appeared, was now covered in Fey biting and attempting to dig into his skin. She could hear him scream as she ran towards him. Agatha jumped on him and they were enveloped in light as she held him. Her screams turned to the ethereal levels. Through the blinding light she squeezed him even more, deafening was the noise around them.

"No, Agatha, you will die," he yelled as the sound and light intensified. Charles felt them both lift up and the Fey were stunned and floating within the orb around them. Agatha reached up and put her hands around Charles's ears as the Fey popped like balloons. Agatha floating in the air in front of him smiled at Charles briefly, drops to the ground then passed out. The light and sound went as soon as her eyes closed and she fell to the ground.

The Fey that were in the orb, were now small puddles of blood on the dirt.

The rest of the group had fended off and killed the remaining animal hosts and Fey that were attacking them. Charles laying on the ground had blood coming out his ears, nose and eyes. He Pulled himself over to the unconscious Agatha lying on the gravel, his face was desperate as he looked and searched for Variwen.

Variwen, stamping on the last Fey showing signs of life, looked up and straight away ran over to Charles, skidding over the gravelled ground to Agatha. She checked for a pulse then reached for her head. "It's okay, Charles. She is still alive, and her temperature is dropping as we speak." Variwen tried to smile at Charles who moved Agatha onto Variwen's lap.

He stood, looking more upset than ever. "When is this going to stop? She has barely recovered from her last outburst and she has flared up again." He paced next to Variwen, who stroked Agatha's hair.

"Charles, you have been bitten a fair few times, love. You need to wash them out or it may get infected." He didn't hear her at first as his face was twisted with anger.

Alfred returned to the group, panting. "I found it and dealt with the escapee," he remarked as he went over to Pollyanna. She too, was out of breath, her clothes were ripped from the fighting. Alfred spoke in a concerned voice, "Are you okay, Pollyanna? Did they bite you at all?"

"No, I'm okay, just scratches here and there" showing him that she wasn't hurt too badly.

Charles trying to wipe away some of the blood went to Agatha. It was the first time he had reached over and touched her arm. She was in daze after the fight. "Charles, be calm, Agatha still has a lot of life in her."

Alfred said looking curiously at Charles. Variwen reiterated about Charles' cuts, although he immediately shut her down. "I don't care right now, Variwen. I'm immortal, I can just walk through the gates again and come back, but Agatha, her human form and her kind do not."

Alfred walked over to Charles he reached out to placing his hand on his back. "Charles, be careful the road you take, for Immortality will find a way of running out." Charles faltered. Alfred, confused by his own remark, took his hand off Charles and turned to Variwen. The rest of the group were now finished in stamping out the remaining fighting Fey and joined the four on the ground.

"Caelan, we need to take her in. Lord Caspian has only just started in wreaking havoc. It's only going to get worse and Agatha needs rest."

Caelan came over and picked up Agatha as if she were light as a feather. They all walked into the entranceway. Ants immediately held the others back and yelled, "Wait!" Some turned to look at him. "Remember some Fey came in here. We will need to be on guard in case they try to jump us."

Charles rubbed his head in anguish. "That's it. I can't take this!" he yelled at the group, turning and walking back out the entranceway.

"Where are you going?" Variwen called out to him.

"I-I need to think." He didn't turn or say goodbye but walked with intention down the driveway.

Charles was gone for the rest of the day as the others set up camp of sorts in the kitchen — the warmest place and the most available for something sharp in case a Fey popped up. It also meant they could keep an eye on each other and take shifts on watch.

Agatha was lying in a cot bed near the fire, asleep. The others were playing elemental the card game on the table whilst Variwen stirred a pot of soup. She had a loaf of bread on one part of the table which she turned and sliced.

"We should look at flushing out the Fey from the castle," Fervor said as he placed a card down. Fervor's card had a flame glowing slightly above it.

"How do you propose we do that, Fervor?" Caelan was looking at his cards. It was his turn as he held up a water card that blasted the flame on Fervor's card.

"Damn water card, how is that stronger than mine?" Fervor went to grab the card from Caelan who pointed it at him and it sprayed him with water too. The group laughed while Fervor grumpily stood up and wiped some of the water off his not-so-dry clothes.

Grinning, Caelan flipped the card and pointed to the back. "Level thirteen, mate, what was yours?" Caelan laughed again and the fire card dissolved into nothing.

"I remembered why I don't play elemental cards with you," Fervor remarked. "Playing aside, what say you, do we flush them out? We can't stay in the kitchen forever."

Caelan's smile dropped a little. "Yes, we do need to, Fervor, but what plan do you have in doing this?"

"I don't have one." Fervor shrugged. "We can't just sit here in our bloodied clothes. You reek, we all smell, they will find us a mile off. Especially as we are sitting ducks."

Rubbing his chin, Caelan resorted to his cards as Fervor placed an earth card on the table. "Level sixteen, mate!" he remarked with a grin.

"Ahhh, not your turn yet, Caelan. I have a coin to add."

Caelan rolled his eyes as Fervor, grinning away, placed a dry dirt coin on top of his card on the table. He grinned even more when his card and coin linked together and the table started to vibrate. Caelan placed a whirlpool coin on his card and played to fight Fervor. Fervor's eyes betrayed him and he looked desperate

215

when the whirling water came up out of Caelan's card and Fervor's rose in retaliation. Dirt in a square rose upwards. The whirling water hit his wall, slowly dragging the absorbent dirt away. It didn't take all of it but depleted his card's strength. The level sixteen disappeared and turned into a twelve. Fervor, frustrated, placed another earth card next to his depleted card. It was also a level sixteen. He then attacked Caelan's water card, making the cube of water a muddy patch. More absorbent dirt flowed over the top, drying out the water. It cracked up and fell apart.

Caelan threw his cards down in frustration. "Gah, that was my best card." He stood up. "I'm all itchy. I need a wash,"

"Ahh, Caelan, I think I just won, right? Are you hiding that I won?" Fervor was gleeful, slapping his hand down. "Yes! I did it! I finally did it!" he said, jiggling around in his chair.

Caelan rolled his eyes, not a good loser ignoring the rest of the game. "Right, we need to sort teams for washing. Alfred, you and me first. You smell like you crawled out of a death pit."

Alfred rolled his eyes.

"Caelan," said Oxxy. "Mate, you got it all wrong. Alfred always smells like that." Oxxy slapped Alfred on the back, who rolled his eyes.

"Come on, Caelan, before they decide to join us."

"Oxxy, you and Fervor keep watch at the front here. Naga, you watch the walls with Ants. We will circulate in these groups of two, Variwen."

Variwen put her hands up. "I can go with Agatha when she wakes and Pollyanna you can too, if someone can keep watch while we are in the bathing room."

"Alfred can watch out for you," Caelan replied.

Caelan and Alfred made their way out of the kitchen into the hallway. They decided to use the upstairs bathing rooms due to there being fewer holes for the Fey to gain access. Oxxy moved to shut the door behind them. "Don't be too long, Caelan," he said as both Caelan and Alfred nodded on their exit.

A few miles away, Charles was entering Lord Caspian's grounds. He was hesitant, but in his heart he felt he must try to sway Caspian in staving off his attempts at the castle, and Agatha.

He walked up to the entranceway of the manor. Straightening his ruffled and dirty clothing, he knocked on the big doors with the brass knocker. It attempted to bite him, making him drop his hand. "Ahh" he exclaimed in shock.

"Frr brr argh rr," the knocker tried to say but the handle was stuck in his mouth. It was a gargoyle head.

"I don't understand you," Charles replied whilst rubbing his hand. The knocker rolled his eyes, glared at Charles then pointed his eyes down to the knocker. "Oh, you want me to remove it." The gargoyle gave an excited look at him, confirming Charles' attempt at figuring out what it wanted.

Just as Charles reached up, the door opened. "I wouldn't do that if I were you," Hesiss the footman stated, grinning evilly at the gargoyle head, who moped and they could hear him grumble. Out of curiosity, Charles asked why. "Because as soon as you take it out of his mouth, he will charm you and put you in his place."

The head was heard saying, "Ohhhhhh, rwuin fy fun."

Charles looked at the head. "I was going to help you then. Not nice, Gargoyle, not nice." The head rolled its eyes as Charles was welcomed into the manor.

"So soon, Charles." Lord Caspian entered the entranceway with his arms open. "Well, Hesiss, you win that wager,"

Hesiss bowed to Lord Caspian. "Thank you, my Lord."

Hesiss walked out of the entranceway and down the hall. "We made a bet to see how long it would take for you to come. I knew you would come to defend your Agatha. I know all about the heart and how even you can be swayed to do stupid things."

Charles narrowed his eyes and stepped back. "Oh, going so soon? You could at least stay for a cup of tea before you go on your way." Charles hesitated.

"We have much to discuss, you and I, Charles," Caspian exclaimed as he showed Charles towards his drawing room.

They walked through and both took seats by the fire. Hesiss joined them with a tray of biscuits, tea cups, sugar, cream, and lemon, with a large teapot steaming through the spout. Hesiss placed the tray on the table in front of Charles and Caspian. He walked out of the room and Charles' gaze followed him.

"He is a loyal servant, is Hesiss," Caspian said to Charles, who looked over at Caspian.

"He is very loyal. What did you do to have such loyalty from him?"

Caspian smiled, picking up a cup. "Sugar?" Charles nodded his head. "I saved his life, Charles, and because of that, he is indebted to me until it is paid." Caspian smiled at Charles. "Although between you and me." Caspian continued to make his tea and passed him the cup.

Charles thanked him and sipped the tea. "Mmm, is that lavender and lemon in it?" he asked.

"Yes, yes, lovely, isn't it? Anyway, between you and me, that Agatha looks good with white hair. When did that change? It's funny, it reminds me of a certain daemon from a few decades ago, was wiped out. Oh, what's the name?" Caspian furrowed his brow whilst slowly making his tea. Charles took another, larger sip this time. He felt relaxed even though the worry of Caspian's remark normally would make him run.

219

Wow, he thought to himself. *I should be on my toes, more alert, but I feel so relaxed here.*

"Charles, Charles my God, man, are you listening to me?" Caspian offended, stood up. "You look a mess, Charles. Did they not like my Fey present?"

Charles looked up at Caspian. His head was feeling foggy as he dropped his cup. Smiling, Caspian walked around the table to Charles. "Hmm, you really like my tea then, don't you?"

He smiled wickedly as he clapped and Hesiss came back into the room. Charles, trying to make himself alert although he was fighting the sleep, tried to stand, and fell to the ground.

"Argh, you drugged me! So much for a parlay" Charles fought to get up from the floor, although on his way down he caught the tea tray and sugar cubes. He smashed bowls and plates all around him. He cut his hand trying to pull himself up.

"Do you really think I would let the likes of you into my home and offer tea? My, you are stupid, aren't you, Charles? It's been too long for you. You have been out of the game and on the wrong side." Caspian laughed and Hesiss entered the room, Hesiss grabbed Charles by the ankles and started to drag him out of the room. "You can't save your little girlfriend, Charles, my dear boy."

Charles sluggishly tried to grab the doorframe in a weak attempt to stop Hesiss. Hesiss just turned, sighed and yanked harder on Charles' ankles. It was all it took to pull him off the doorframe. Charles rolled on his back, eyelids so heavy now. He tried to blink but each time they got heavier and heavier.

Caspian was following closely behind. "You, my friend, are going to help me send a message to Agatha. I think it will put thing into perspective." Caspian smiled an evil smile as Charles could no longer keep his eyes open. The last he remembered were a door opening and being pulled down some rough wooden steps into a basement.

Hesiss tied Charles to a table. Behind him were different types of blades and cutting tools. "My lord, what would you like me to send to Miss Agatha?"

Caspian laughed, looking at the now unconscious Charles. He held Charles' chin and moved his head from left to right. He dropped his hand and walked over to the table. He picked up the hacksaw. "I think a limb in pieces should be about right. Hmm-mm, but which one should we send? What do you think, Hesiss?"

Hesiss pointed to the left arm. "Our scally-wag scholar won't need that any time soon, I'd say."

Caspian smiled and walked towards the unconscious Charles. Lifting up the hacksaw, he placed it on Charles' shoulder on the left side. Hesiss put his hand up to Caspian. "Wait, don't sully yourself with such mundane tasks, my Lord. Is this what you really want? Once we start it, will only end in blood."

Caspian had a flare of anger. He shoved Hesiss back and snarled in response. "Blood is what I want,

Hesiss. Too many of our kind have fallen because of Agatha's family. Enough of the pleasantries. I grow tired of your indignation. Where is my allegiance, Hesiss? You are mine!" Caspian turned to the table and dropped the hacksaw. He grabbed the axe, aimed and swung at Charles but Hesiss grabbed hold of the handle of the axe before it hit.

"MY LORD!" he yelled. "I will do this with precision. Let me take this task while you find the perfect boxes for his arm."

Caspian dropped the axe and hit Hesiss across the face. "Fine, I will find these boxes, but your allegiance to me is still in question, and don't ever hold me back again." With that, Caspian walked out, leaving the still unconscious and untouched Charles strapped to the table. Hesiss placed the axe back on the table and turned to Charles.

The room was dark with running water in the corner slowly dribbling out of parts of the wall creating a small stream on the floor, exiting out a drain in the centre of the floor. Hesiss turned to look at Charles. He saw the bite marks starting to show infection. "I'm sorry, my friend, I will make it as painless as possible for you. Why you had to come in his path, I do not know." Hesiss took out some scissors and started cutting Charles' sleeve up the side and to his shoulder. He pinned back the material, sighed and got a scalpel.

It was early morning when outside the Castle a cart drew up. Four packages were taken off the carriage and placed in a line on the front entrance floor. They had been wrapped in beautiful red wrapping paper with a red bow. A large white card had been placed in front of the boxes with Agatha's name clearly written on them.

The driver knocked on the hallway wall as the oak doors were sitting in dire need of repair against the pile of rubble. The driver climbed back onto the carriage and whipped the blinkered horses. They responded by slowly moving forward, turning and heading back down the driveway.

The group were sitting in the kitchen where they had been since last night. All including Agatha were awake when the knocking sound was heard. Looking from one to another, they stood and went to the entranceway. They looked out to see at a distance the horse and carriage nearing the end of the driveway and turning the horses back towards the town.

Agatha was the first to see the boxes showing her name. She stepped forward looking from left to right, making sure nothing was going to jump out at her. She bent down and picked up the card, turning and showing the others. "What does it say, Agatha?"

Caelan and Variwen stepped forward and inspected the wrapping and the boxes while Agatha opened the card and started to read. "Parts of Charles," Agatha read out with confusion and looked down at the boxes. It dawned upon her and she started to scream, diving onto the first box and tearing at the wrapping. Screaming again, scrabbling backwards, Agatha rushed to stand and she ran towards the edge of the front landing, vomiting on the grass.

The others, puzzled by this, walked forward and looked in the first opened box to find Charles' fingers neatly displayed in red-stained tissue paper. The look of shock went through the group as Oxxy dove on the second box and Ants on the third. Fervor grabbed the fourth and they all found the rest of Charles' arm again neatly placed in tissue paper. Pollyanna screaming hysterically was grabbed by Alfred, she hid her face into his jacket sobbing.

"Oh my God, oh, my God." Variwen went to Agatha, who was saying the three words over and over, between vomiting and crying.

Naga collected the boxes up. "We need to hold onto these. Charles can't regenerate and heal if he doesn't have the pieces."

Agatha looked at Naga. "He can't regenerate if we do not have the rest of him, Naga! Where is he?"

Oxxy ran out and onto the driveway. "Where are you going, Oxxy?" Caelan called after him.

"We have to find him, Caelan. What if he is in pieces? What if they have killed him?"

"He isn't dead yet," Alfred said in a quiet manner.

They all stopped and turned to him. "W-what do you mean, Alfred, can you feel him dying?"

224

Variwen walked up to Alfred who had been holding Pollyanna quiet the whole time. "Did you know something, Alfred?"

"I can't play around with fate, Variwen, you know that."

Agatha turned her rage onto Alfred. "What did you know, Alfred? What didn't you tell him or us?"

Alfred prying Pollyanna from him, backed away as the pillars of the veranda crumbled through the shaking. The stones didn't drop but floated out and stayed in the air.

"Oh, cut it out, Agatha. We are all in a panic. You are going to destroy all of us if you keep flaring up like this."

Agatha was panting and heaving in her breath. Caelan had caught her off guard with his flippant response, and she blinked. Her eyes quickly drew back the colour and the floating stones dropped to the floor. She rubbed her arm and looked at the boxes opened in front of them. Caelan stepped forward and held her shoulders. "We need to find him, Agatha. Concentrate on that, okay?"

Agatha nodded while Caelan turned on Alfred. He backhanded his face and Alfred fell to the floor. "How did you know? What did he say to you? I want to know every detail."

Alfred wiped his mouth and looked defeated as he went to stand up. "I-I'm sorry. I can't play around with fate."

"You can when it comes to us. We need you and we need your help, tell me now." Caelan stepped closer to Alfred as he talked, his eyes flaring, showing the fire within him.

Variwen stepped in front of Caelan. "Enough! No fighting and from you, Caelan, you should be ashamed of yourself, hitting Alfred like that." Variwen turned and helped Alfred up. Pollyanna ran to Alfred as Variwen spoke. "You okay, Alfred, honey?" He nodded. "Alfred, the way Caelan asked you was wrong, but what he was asking was correct. We need your help. You need to tell us what happened, darlin'." Variwen looked at Alfred, kindly wiping the blood from his nose and rubbing his shoulder in a caring manner.

"I shouldn't, it's against my kind, if anyone finds out I will be caged…" Alfred looked at the others, who were blank in expression waiting for him to explain. He looked at Agatha then back at Variwen. Alfred dropped his eyes and started to explain. "My kind are linked to the room of time. We can feel those that are drawing near to death, we can feel what they feel by touch and senses. Charles has had a link to the room of time with no expiry, so to speak. When I touched him, his time was running, which has never happened before. He doesn't have much left." Alfred looked at the others who were stunned.

"So you mean he is now mortal?" Caelan asked in confusion. "How did that happen?"

Agatha looked at the others. "It must have been those bites. Remember, the Fey bit him? A lot of them did. They swarmed him like bees on a hive."

Oxxy, frowning. looked at the floor where a dead Fey was still lying. "You don't think he was the target, do you? I mean, no one else got swarmed like he did."

The others looked at each other. "Has he been bitten by Fey before?" Naga asked, looking around.

Caelan replied, "Charles has been in many wars, he is very old, so yes, I would say he has. So, what's different this time?"

Oxxy walked around and found a dead Fey with a head still attached. He picked it up and sniffed the mouth. "You said he was bitten a lot, right?"

"Yes, that's right," replied Agatha, frowning at Oxxy. "What is it, what have you found?"

Oxxy picked up another and smelled the mouth. He threw it back down and repeated what he was doing to a few more. "Where was he standing yesterday?" he asked Agatha, although not turning around.

The group stepped past the boxes to help look for Fey. "What are we looking for, Oxxy?" Caelan asked as he started rummaging around the rubble for some dead Fey.

"Staining, or an unusually sweet deathly smell from their mouths." Agatha and Variwen looked at each other.

"Oxxy, I killed all the Fey that were on Charles, they disintegrated." Agatha looked at him. "I know but there will be some stray ones around."

Agatha began to look, as did the others in the group. It took a while to find what they were looking for. It was Alfred who pulled the body of a Fey from the dead bear. He handed it over to Oxxy, who smelled it and checked its mouth. He wiped its face that still had bear blood on it. Compared to the other little skinny green Fey creatures, this one had a distinct purple staining around its mouth and on its teeth and tongue that were visible.

Oxxy held it up and showed the others. "It's been poisoned; those bites on Charles won't heal until we get the poison out, so yes, Agatha, we really do need to find him now."

Agatha showed panic and turned from Variwen to Caelan. "We must leave now and find him!"

"Oh, hells bells, Agatha, we do, but we also need someone here in case he comes home. We also need someone to clean his…"

They all turned and looked at the boxes sitting on the ground by the entrance. Fervor shuddered. "I can't believe they removed his arm like that."

Variwen went up and picked up the part with his elbow. "They are clean cuts though. Whoever did this did it with the intention of care." Agatha gagged while Variwen put the section of limb back into the box. Pollyanna ran to the grass it was her turn to vomit. "We need to put these into the cold store, Agatha. You and

228

Pollyanna and I will stay here and prepare. We need to clean or cut out the wounds from the Fey and we will need to reattach his arm. These must be sewn together as well before the reattachment so it's not too painful for him." Agatha looked green, Pollyanna still vomiting could be heard moaning, "Oh my, oh my," Agatha trying to focus nodded to Variwen.

The men paired up, Caelan with Alfred, Naga with Oxxy and Fervor with Ants, walking down the driveway. They organise themselves — one pair would go left away from the township in case he had been dropped somewhere, and the others headed towards town in search of Charles.

"If you don't find anything, be back by sundown," Variwen yelled out to the parting pairs at the end of the driveway.

Turning around, Variwen sucked in a deep breath. "Well, we had better get these sorted." Variwen moved over to the sections of Charles's limbs. She pulled the wrapping over and stacked them into two piles. Agatha, glad she could not see inside the boxes, grabbed one pile and followed Variwen, Pollyanna shaking and holding her stomach followed behind them into the house towards the kitchen. They were still careful as the noises of the Fey remaining could be heard scurrying around in the upper levels of the castle.

Levels even Agatha hadn't had a chance to go through yet.

Agatha walked with blurry vision as streams of tears fell down her cheeks. Her chest ached for not knowing where Charles was, worried in what state he would be found in.

Variwen entered the kitchen, placing the boxes on the table. She collected the boxes from the tearful Agatha. Ignoring the over-welling emotions of Agatha, and the shaky and pale Pollyanna, Variwen organised everything. She brought forward the teapot, stoked the fireplace and placed it on the embers. Turning, she saw Agatha was still crying.

Variwen sighed, stepped closer to Agatha. Rubbing her arms, she said, "Lovey, you need to pull yourself together. When he gets back, we will need to reattach his arm and he will need you strong. You can't sit and be a wet mess. Hold it together. You can hug and make up once we have put him back together and got the Fey bites healed up."

Agatha tried taking a few deep breaths. "That's it. Take a few more, wipe your face and drink some water. We need you clearheaded. Charles is going to need you." Variwen let go of Agatha's arms as Agatha tried again taking deep breaths; she wiped her face and collected two glasses from the cupboard. Pouring some chilled water from the store room, Agatha gulped down a glass, and passed the other to Pollyanna, she then poured another drinking in quick succession and poured another. She took a deep breath, put the glass in the sink, turned to Variwen and her eyes were white, all the colour had gone.

"Oh, Agatha." Variwen's voice showed sadness as Agatha collected the boxes and put them into the cold store. She wordlessly helped Variwen with anything she needed, mute, emotionless but able to help with any task. Pollyanna was useless unable to move near the table, she sat in muted expression watching the pair from the corner of the room.

Chapter 13
Uncertain Fate

Birds were chirping in the distance. The wind was washing over his face as an immense pain came over the side of his body. Charles opened his eyes and blinked. His eyes came into focus as he was looking up at the tree tops above him. He could see the wind blowing and swaying the trees. the birds' chirping was sharp, making him wince with the noise. He went to roll over and pain shot through him like a bolt of lightning. He fell back onto his back, gasping for air. Using his other arm, he reached over to touch where the pain radiated from. "Noo! No, they took my arm, they took my arm!"

Lying there in pain and panic, Charles realised no one was near and no one was coming. He attempted to centre himself, breathing deeply and slowly to attempt to control the pain. Charles looked up at the tree tops. The wind again was moving the trees gently. He watched them sway in the wind while he calmed back down.

"I need to get back to the castle." Charles prepared himself. He yelled as he swung himself into a sitting position. From here Charles managed to stand the ache of his arm and where he had been bitten by the fey radiated through his body. He took in his surroundings and found a path. He looked up but couldn't figure out where the sun was. Looking down, Charles found a path to the left of him and not far from there was a dirt road.

The ache from his shoulder was incredibly blinding. He placed his other arm where his armpit was, slowly moving forward to not jog the wound. Charles made his way onto the dirt road. He realised he was not far from town and looked to have been dumped away from the manor. His stump had been bandaged, which he was grateful for, although the pain was still searing, raw and very blurring for his vision.

Trudging for what seemed to be at least half an hour, he saw the first houses for the edge of the township. Carts drove past, with drivers who stared and whispered to their passengers. Charles kept going, slowly trudging along his energy draining quickly as he tried to concentrate. The trees were slowly clearing the closer he got and they switched to open bare land with jotted houses. Charles made it with a sigh of relief. Stopping for breath, he looked around contemplating his next move.

"Charles!" He heard a familiar voice.

"Charles!" Another familiar voice — it was Oxxy and Ants. They came running towards him.

"Oh Charles, you're alive! We have been so worried." Oxxy checked him over to see if anything else was missing. Once he was successful in his judgement, he had a quick word with Ants, who stayed with Charles whilst Oxxy ran off for a carriage.

"You can't walk like this, Charles. Don't worry, we have your arm. The girls are putting it back together you will be one again in no time." Back together, Charles puzzled over that as the ground around him started to look fuzzy. He relaxed a bit, knowing he would be okay and would make it back to the castle. Charles collapsed, Ants caught him before he hit. the ground. He sat on the floor with Charles' head in his lap. He held the empty shoulder up to not cause any bleeding or strain for Charles.

Oxxy had a fair bit of trouble finding a carriage to carry the one who had defied Lord Caspian. No one wanted to turn their back on a loved man of the town, but a man who in a sense challenged the rule of Lord Caspian was one to steer clear of.

Oxxy had to pay double to hire a carriage to find anything to help Charles, pulling him up and helping Charles on the carriage the three were not far on their way when they picked up Caelan and Alfred.

Charles came to briefly enough to know who was with him. He passed out again shortly after.

At the gates, the sun was coming down. It was dusk when the last two, Fervor and Naga, greeted the carriage with relief, knowing Charles was found and was safe.

As the sun dipped lower, they reached the entranceway where Pollyanna stood with Agatha, still with white eyes, and Variwen. They had waited for the

234

carriage and the returning group. Caelan and Oxxy carried Charles into the kitchen area. They placed him on the table ready for Variwen and Agatha, Pollyanna, reunited with Alfred, stood behind him as watched the two start in the preparations of re-attaching his arm.

Charles was a mess so the group stripped his top half and cleaned him down, careful of his shoulder wound. He was assessed and they found all his bite wounds. There were at least ten of them, a lot to have to clean, sterilize and sort to help Charles heal. They were all worried as fifty percent of the wounds showed dark feathery veins around the outside of the bite mark, a serious confirmation of the infection.

"I'm not sure about this, Variwen. If he has an infection, this arm might not heal. We need to remove the infection first."

Variwen looked over to Oxxy. "A luxury we do not have time for, I'm afraid. If we do not attach his arm, it may not heal and repair either. We will have to work simultaneously, one group on the bite marks cleaning and removing as much infection as possible and the other team reattaching his arm."

They all looked at Agatha. Her eyes were still white and there was no emotion on her face.

"She is coping, leave her be. Agatha has been a great help through this, whether or not she is mentally fully with us."

Caelan moved forward and hugged Agatha who did not return the hug, nor turn and look at him. She was motionless.

"How long has she been like this, Variwen?"

Variwen replied to Caelan with a sullen face. "Not long after you left, she cried herself out, then when she was trying to regain composure, she wiped her emotions. A coping mechanism, it's all I can put it down to."

Caelan tried to hug her again, hoping she would snap out of it. "Do you think she will come out of it?" Caelan now quite worried.

Variwen put her hand on his large clay-like arm. "Caelan, I'm sorry I do not have the answers. She is an unknown for everyone. Being a half blood of an almost extinct breed makes her very unique, but first, we must deal with Charles. I'm hoping once he is dealt with and put back together, she will come out of her trance state. Well, I hope…"

Alfred leaving Pollyanna by the edge of the room came forward and went to put his hand on Charles but Ants held it. "Best leave his chance be for now, eh? We don't want certain parts of the team remaining in a mute state, mate." Ants and Alfred looked to Agatha, standing, waiting for her next instruction.

"Right, Oxxy, Alfred and Fervor, you three are on bite healing duties. Fervor you need to make your bandages much like you did for Agatha's neck. Will you need a helper as well as the other two?" Variwen looked at the three then back to Fervor.

Fervor bowed to Variwen. "I will need one extra to help collect and make up the bandages before the storms come in."

Variwen pointed to Naga. "You go with Fervor, Naga. Let's get this started. Pollyanna, you need to keep the water bowls coming and keep them clean. We need you to be present love! Agatha, Caelan and Ants, you're with me. Caelan, you hold Charles in case he wakes. Get the chloroform. You will need to dose him if he wakes up. Agatha and Ants, I will need one on passing me the tools and the other to hold the arm steady as I reattach it." Ants ran to the kitchen sink and vomited.

"Agatha, go get the arm. You will have to hold it. Ants is on tool-passing duties, last thing I want is someone vomiting on the arm." Variwen glared at Ants.

"Sorry," he says. "It's Charles... he is like family and smelling the sterilization and Ether is horrible knowing what we have to do and what happened to him."

"Pull it together, Ants. I can't have a weak stomach now." Variwen took the arm Agatha held out. It was grey, stiff and very cold. Caelan held Charles in preparation. Agatha positioned herself, holding the arm again as Variwen looked at bone and muscle for the reattachment.

The whole ordeal took many hours. Charles woke up twice through the process, deep belly screams that sent chills down everyone's spines. He didn't last long, though. Caelan put the cloth over his face, it took a few minutes to knock him out again.

The bite marks were also a challenge for the group. Fervor decided it best to cut out the worst of the infection and clean what was left.

Once they were finally finished, Charles was covered in bandages, arms, legs, chest and neck. His face was greyer than usual with dark brown circles under his eyes.

It was late into the night. Variwen had flopped into a chair while Naga took a turn at making cheese sandwiches and tea for dinner. No one could look at meat, considering what they just had to do to save their friend.

One thing that did change, though, was as they were all sitting and waiting for Naga to finish up making everything, sobbing started to come from Agatha. Caelan and Variwen, keeping close to Agatha, immediately helped her, Variwen with a cloth and Caelan babbling on about tea being the best thing for an achy heart.

"Oh Caelan, for goodness sakes! Stop babbling. She needs a hug, give her that."

Caelan relieved on what to do, hugged Agatha and kept holding her while she cried even harder. Charles stirred and moaned from the pain. Agatha pulled herself away from Caelan and went to Charles.

"Hey Aggie," he managed to say. "Don't cry. Don't cry for me, it's my fault." He tried to lift his arm but nothing was working.

"Give it time, Charles, you're still working through the infection from the Fey. Caspian poisoned them."

Variwen was up by Charles, and Agatha was holding his hand, looking him over. He had green-hued bandages all over him from where the Fey had bitten. They were quite large patches as so much had been cut out to deter the spread of infection. The others were all standing back watching Charles.

"I must be popular," he said hoarsely. "I'm sorry, I went to his house." Charles tried to sit up by himself. Caelan put his arm underneath him and helped him into a sitting position. "I wanted to stop him coming for you, Agatha. He is going to find out about who you are sooner or later and use it against you, but I was his trap, it was like he knew I would come."

"He wanted you to, Charles. The Fey were infected with poison. It was intended for you. You are Agatha's interest. The Fey's poison is stopping you from healing." Charles frowned and looked at his arm. He tried to take the bandage off, but Alfred held his good arm from moving the bandages.

"Don't, you know what is under there. I warned you of your immortality leaving. This was Caspian's plan. You're not healing, Charles."

Panic washed over Charles as he feebly pushed Alfred away. He went to move the bandages and this time Agatha stopped him, tears running down her cheeks again.

"Charlie, please, we tried our best."

Charles felt as though his world was closing around him. "Is there anything we can do to fix this? Can we visit Helgam? Will he have something for me?" Charles looked desperately around him at the others. They all hung their heads and Charles knew he was on his last run. A flicker of hope came across his eyes and he turned to Alfred. "What if I walk back through the dimension door…" Alfred, looked confused, and glanced towards Variwen.

Thinking, Variwen moved around the table. "Well, for daemons, it's a way of instantly healing, but you will be thrown back. It could take months, even years, to get back to the gate. Do you even remember the place? How long has it been?"

Charles felt hope for his condition. "Oh, I remember all right. Leaving that place was the best thing I did but I will never forget what it looked like." He turned to Agatha. She was crying silently. "Agatha, you must open the door. I need you to save me."

"I don't know how, Charles. Parts of the book are in another language." Agatha was sobbing as she said this.

"Agatha, it's your duty. Think of it as a practice run for when you send the rest of the dastardly daemons back that are wreaking havoc in this world. This is your heritage." He tried to say it with energy and a smile but only managed a grimace towards Agatha. She nodded and everyone knew her heart was breaking.

"I don't want you to go, Charles."

He smiled sympathetically. He grabbed her hand. "I will never leave you" he put his hand over her heart. "But you must let me go and I will try and get back as soon as I can. Agatha, if I stay, I could die." He cupped her cheek with his hand.

She knew what he meant, but she sucked in a deep breath, giving him a kiss so loving, so heartfelt, her eyes drained to white and Charles' smile dropped. He panicked a little as Agatha walked away leaving the room.

Ants looked at Caelan. "Follow her, Ants, make sure she doesn't get into any trouble." Ants nodded and silently followed her.

"What is that, is she okay?"

Variwen moved over and put her hand on his. "It's how she is dealing with the pain. She functions and is receptive to general commands but anything to do with emotions, she is a blank. She will be fine, she came out of it before. I'm sure she is just using her power to be able to process."

Charles looked at the door where Agatha left, worried. The others had started talking to him although he couldn't hear them his mind was thinking of Agatha.

Ants watched Agatha noiselessly walk down the hallway. He could hear the Fey scurrying around inside the walls like a pack of rats. He watched her climb the stairs. As she got to the top, she turned right, not the usual route to her bedroom. He watched out of curiosity at a safe distance. She stopped and sighed, then looked behind her and her eyes began to glow. Silvery streams of tears ran from them. Slowly the glow ebbed through her whole body like an aura. Walking so lightly you could say she was floating, coming up to a doorway, she opened the door, leaving it open, slightly looking behind her.

Ants hesitated a bit. He went to move forward when someone grabbed him. "Argh!" He yelled and took a swing with a lightning-infused fist.

Ducking, Oxxy laughed. "Shh, far out, Oxxy, what the hell are you doing?" Ants glared at Oxxy.

"What is she doing?" Oxxy looked down the new hallway they hadn't been down before.

"I think she is doing what comforts her. I'm not sure come on let's follow her before we lose her."

Ants lit his fist — being a lightning daemon definitely brought advantages. Oxxy followed him as they walked down the hallway through the doors, towards Agatha and the glow she was emitting. Up and down and around so many corridors they followed her, silently moving and keeping a good distance, every now and again looking at each other but still following. Agatha finally slowed. She came to a wall and started pressing on the wooden detailing. Oxxy and Ants saw her pushing her hands on the wall. Agatha spent ages feeling around to a point where Oxxy and Ants came and helped her. She looked from one to the other, a slight glow about her.

Agatha sighed not finding whatever she was looking for. Sighing, the glow depleted and her eyes returned to normal. "Where are we?" She looked at Oxxy and Ants.

Behind them, a few Fey were crouching in their shadows. The fey hiding in her shadow she could see, it. Shock made her jump and Agatha's eyes turned quickly to white again and she lifted her arm. Oxxy and Ants yelled and ducked as she fired towards the Fey. The three heard the screaming as the Fey were caught and died.

Standing up, Oxxy and Ants looked behind them at the dead Fey on the ground. "Thanks. Next time though, can you yell out so we know you're not trying to kill us? A bit hard when you have your white eye thing going on, we don't know if you're with us or against us." Agatha hesitated then nodded.

Walking back the way they came, hoping to find the hallway back to the staircase, Oxxy and Ants talked with Agatha. "Do you know what you were looking for?"

"I think I was looking for a door. All I had going through my mind was Charles needing to go back through the dimension door. This is what I have been left with. I think I understand now what type of sacrifices my aunt used to tell me about." Agatha kicked a towel strewn on the floor. They were next to a linen cupboard. Agatha looked into the cupboard and found spare candles. Lighting them off Ants; hand of lightening, she passed one to Oxxy and kept one for herself. The hallway they were in was identical to the one they frequented. Scurrying was heard through the walls to their right.

"Let's keep moving, or we might find ourselves facing more than the bunch you finished off back there," Ants stated to Agatha. They moved towards the end of the hallway and found some doors. They carefully opened them and peered through, a dim light could be seen down this hallway.

"I think we are almost there," Oxxy said with a tone of relief in his voice.

"I get it, I do." Oxxy and Ants looked at Agatha as they walked. "I understand I have to become this protector of sorts, I have to be the judge and if I need to be the executioner, for Charles, I have to be that for him. I must find this door, I need to." Agatha drew in a heavy weighted breath.

Ants rubbed her back. "We are here as well, you know. You're not alone."

"I know, Ants, thank you. I don't know what I would do without all of you. It's been so much, you have all done more than I had ever hoped. And the clearance of the place, I would say you have done well, but I swear the place looks worse since you arrived."

Grinning at them, Oxxy rolled his eyes. "Well, if it wasn't for you destroying everything in your tantrums…"

Agatha, smiling, pretended to look shocked. "Oh, a tantrum, hey! Well, I'm rather certain my tantrum, as you so boldly call it, has saved you. As I recall just a few minutes ago, I saved you."

"Pfft," Ants cut in. "That ain't saving — that was child's play. There weren't even very many Fey on that wall. You're just showing off now that you have figured out you're a Choler."

Small gasps were heard in the wall, which stopped the three dead in their tracks. Looking at each other, they motioned to blast the wall and get to the Fey within. They knew if word got out, a whole new type of trouble would be coming for Agatha and the group.

"One-two-now!" Oxxy swirled wind and pushed it, forcing the wall to crack and break. Ants sent shock waves of lightning into the same place and Agatha managed her orb blasts. They successfully got through the wall but whatever was there was now gone.

"I think we need to warn the others." All agreed and started to move quickly towards the doors with the dim light. Reaching them and opening them, it wasn't the hallway they were hoping for, but a massive room with the fireplace lit. Hordes of Fey were huddled within the light of the fire. The three standing at the entrance saw all the Fey look towards them. Four, obviously scouts, raced to the group before the chatter of the Fey began. Agatha slowly spoke. "Run!"

It didn't take much for the three to move backwards, watching the Fey, and shut the door. They ran like mad and found another hallway, racing down. An open doorway came up ahead. Running through, they were relieved to find the landing hallway, not stopping they raced down the steps and into the kitchen where the rest of the group were. Agatha, Ants and Oxxy informed them of the events and the massive group of Fey, the group realised they needed to barricade themselves in for the night. Charles was resting when Agatha returned, although she barely looked at him.

"I know what must be done. We have to find the door."

Caelan looked up. "One thing at a time, Agatha, one thing at a time."

"Caelan, I know my role now. I may not know how to completely handle my new powers but I do know I can protect myself. I must step up and find the hidden rooms, and we need to decipher the rest of the book." Agatha looked serious.

Variwen moved forward. "I'm glad you realise, Agatha, but first we need to sleep. You need to sleep. You have had the longest day and you of all people need to rest. I think Fervor and Alfred are setting up to take watch for the night." Variwen signalled them.

"Yes, of course," Fervor said.

Alfred, on the other hand, said, "Oh great! I suppose I'm to do the dishes while I'm at it! And what about the toilet run too?"

"Enough, Alfred, we all have our roles in this team. We all have things we don't like. Pull your head in."

Caelan flared his nostril as he spoke to Alfred who mumbled, "Sorry."

"Great, now move. I want to sleep as do most of us. We will swap shifts at one. Tomorrow we will assign what needs to be done." Caelan with no more to be said hunkered down. Agatha slept in her cot Variwen had set up for her. Charles was still on the table sleeping, although taking shallow raspy breaths. Naga lay on the blankets in the floor and covered his head with a pillow. Variwen curled up in the comfy chair by the fire, Pollyanna was opposite already in a deep sleep, while the remaining either hunkered down

in their spots or sat whilst on watch.

"Elemental cards?" Fervor showed Alfred. He rolled his eyes and took the cards to shuffle.

Chapter 14
Declaration of War

Agatha woke with a start, Caelan and Naga were making coffee from the smells circulating the room while she was lying in her cot. She looked over to Charles, who was sitting on the table. He was crouched, over obviously in pain. Most of his wounds were seeping through the bandages. A grey colouring was showing through. Whether that was platelets coming through or the infection Agatha was not sure. She scanned the room, the others in the group were asleep or looking into the distance, a way of not taking notice of what was going on around them.

Agatha looked over to the door. A Fey was hovering by the entranceway. Agatha sat up quickly on seeing it. The Fey ducked behind the door again only to slowly look around the corner. Turning her head sideways, Agatha slowly got up and crawled to the doorway, partially to look less aggressive but also to go over and investigate why the Fey was there.

Caelan and the others watched her as she crawls over to the door. "Hey, hey don't go near it, Agatha," Naga yelled, which made the Fey panic and hide behind the door again.

"It obviously has something to say, Naga. Otherwise, why would it still be there and alone?" Conveying her perception on the nature of the Fey, Agatha carried on crawling over to the Fey. It was by itself which she checked by looking down the hallway. Looking back at the Fey, Agatha lowered herself to lying down. She quietly spoke to it. "Hi there little Fey what can I do for you?"

Rubbing its arm, it moved forward. It had no clothing and was obviously cold. "We are many," it said. Nodding, Agatha waited for it to speak again. "We are many but we are alone. We were charged with poisoning your immortal which we have done, and many died doing his bidding. But we have spoken and we feel we want to live. They hurt us, starved us, and kept us in cages, our children were to fight like us and starve like us. Many didn't make it. But you left us, you walked away and didn't kill all of us. So, we ask if we can live."

Agatha was shocked, she felt like they were asking permission. "Fey, I don't know your name. Do you have one?"

This time it was her to be shocked. "Aurelius," she said.

"Thank you, Aurelius. I didn't know how they treated you, I am sorry. But you hurt Charles who is very ill."

"We know we hurt, we hurt on command but he has deserted us, we have been left for dead, but we don't

249

want to die, we want to live." Agatha was perplexed, on one hand they were part in the hurt of Charles, on the other they did not know any better, or so she thought. "I shall let you live, and feed, hunt and whatever you need to do. But I warn you please don't ruin this house or what is inside. Respect us and we will respect you." The Fey began to cry. It clearly hadn't been given options before. "I think a treaty of sorts would work. Would you like that?"

"What is this treaty?" Aurelius said.

Smiling, Agatha explained as simply as she could, Aurelius looked excited and bowed to Agatha. She kept bowing until she ran down the hall.

The groups were waiting inside to see what had happened. "Well?" Caelan asked flaring his nostrils.

"They want to live," Agatha replied.

Caelan was confused but Variwen smiled. "All anything wants is to live, Agatha, well done." Caelan, frustrated in not understanding, slapped his hand on the table where Charles sat.

"Caelan, for goodness sakes," Variwen said.

Agatha placed her hand on Variwen's. "Caelan, they want to live. They have been starved, tortured, played with, and never treated like an equal, they want to live, survive and live a normal life where they have the ability to grow old if they want to."

Caelan was grumpy at first, although he began to calm down. "So, what did you say?"

"I said if they want to live then we need to do a treaty, so that we can coexist."

Caelan scrunched up his face. "Really! You want to have a treaty with those miniature savages."

Variwen stepped in front of Agatha. "You, Caelan, of all people, should understand what difference being given a chance is like. They could help us! They could be the turning point in this coming war."

"War? What war?" Agatha looked panicked at the others, who looked to the floor.

"Agatha." It was Fervor who stepped forward. "Agatha, it has been on the cards for many years and slowly building. Your aunt thought it would happen in her time, although only the mud-slinging persisted."

Agatha sighed. "I don't want to bring them in for a war. They have asked to simply exist. We can't then take it away again. I will offer it to them as a way of fighting for their freedom, but it will be up to them. If they do not want to fight, then the only request will be that they remain out of the way and do not take sides." Caelan contemplated this approach.

"Yalalalala." Everyone turned. It was Aurelius, but she was not alone and she was holding a piece of paper.

"Geez, that was quick!" Naga exclaimed out loud.

Nervous, Aurelius held up the note to Agatha in both her hands. She bowed whilst holding it up. Looking either side of her, Agatha stepped forward. She could see what looked like the entire Fey horde from the room before, waiting in the hall. She collected the note and opened it.

Looking at the others, she was surprised. "We will fight, we want our freedom, we want to be equal, we want land, we want the right to hunt and grow old, we want to have our own choice."

The group contemplated this. Agatha smiled as she could see a handprint at the bottom in ink. She pointed at this to Aurelius. "Is this your leader"

Aurelius nodded and beckoned her leader forward. It was an older Fey with beads of what looked to be coloured paper, buttons and rocks all tied into a very large necklace around her neck. She holds a shiny stick resembling a staff. Aurelius translated for her leader. "We thank you for your offer of a treaty. We wish to keep it for our history as the first item. If you are happy with the terms, we will fight with you when the time comes. We also ask for material for clothing and for our homes. We will stay in the house until our houses are built to keep our children safe."

Agatha smiled as she signed the treaty and handed it back to Aurelius. "Come with me." Agatha took them down to a stock cupboard. She opened it and showed them everything in it. "You are welcome to what you need in here. If you need more, please let me know." Small cheers came from all the Fey. They lined at least a metre of the floor all around Agatha and the cupboard. The front group climbed into the cupboard and heaved the bed linen out, Agatha slowly walked away, tip toeing around the Fey as they surged for the cupboard. As she went, they all bowed to her. Some had mice skulls on their heads, some had mice furs as cloaks, but most were naked. She walked back into the kitchen to the awaiting group.

"I can't believe you just did that." Caelan stamped his feet in protest. "They could turn on us at a moment's notice. They could kill us in our sleep."

"Caelan, enough." Agatha was stern towards him, the first time she had ever been at him. Caelan looked down in frustration. "Caelan, they have never had a life or been worthy of living. Who are you to stop that? They said they will fight for us. I will show them the land and they can choose where they want to live. This place has many miles of land. They might want to live far away from the castle, create their own world. We may never see them again unless we call upon them."

Caelan looked like a somewhat moody child. "I still don't trust them."

Agatha laughed. "And that's completely fine, Caelan, but let them have a life, okay?"

Somewhat depleted, Caelan sat down at the table near Charles. Agatha went over to Charles and, changing the subject, asked, "How are you feeling? Any better?" She looked at him hopefully.

"I'm not in agreement with what you did, Agatha, but understand your sympathy. Let's hope you are right about the Fey."

His unease towards her made her chest ache. She sniffed and stood up straight. Agatha, turning towards Variwen who mustered a serious tone. "Enough about the Fey. We have much more serious matters to attend, like the door, the book and Charles." Agatha turned to Charles, who looked at the floor. "Agatha, the back end of the book shows diagrams of the door but I cannot translate it. We need to decode it or find a translator. Do you remember anyone who would frequent with your aunt who read? I know it is farfetched but maybe, just maybe, we can source a way."

Charles cut in before Variwen finished. "Helgam!" he said with energy.

"Oh, yes! Helgam said he spent many hours reading with my aunt," Agatha returned with a smile, although Charles didn't look her way. She drifted her dropping smile to Variwen, who showed a brilliant wrinkle-free face.

"Well, maybe I should get changed then. It's been ages since I changed my shape."

"Are you getting dressed up for that old warlock?" Ants and Oxxy elbowed each other and chuckled.

"Any excuse to dress up is a good excuse, you two. Now do you think red hair this time? It's been a while since I was a redhead." Grinning, she wriggled about, clearing her throat and flicking her hair. Before it even touched, her shoulders again, it was red, her complexion had changed and Variwen was now a very attractive redhead.

"Well, you will definitely get his attention with that body!" Naga exclaimed, looking her up and down. Her retaliation was a quick smack to the back of his head, providing the others a good laugh.

As the night closed in on another busy day for the group with plotting and planning of their next township venture, Fervor, feeling full and comfortable, said, "Well, it's been a good start to the week, I'd say, a treaty with the Fey, and we know our next step, and who said we were floundering?" Fervor, smiling, patted Charles on the back, forgetting his wounds. Charles yelped as his arm that was stitched back on moved uncomfortably to the side.

"Oh Charles, I'm so sorry, mate." Fervor was bashful and went to help Charles who smacked him away with an angry expression. Fervor, embarrassed, moved away from Charles, who was reeling in pain.

"What shall we do with Charles?" Alfred asked.

"I am right here, you know," Charles gasped as he angrily expressed his emotion at being left out. "I'm not an object and I can't help being like this." He lay back down on the table, obviously exhausted from being a part of the group, albeit temporarily.

"I think we need to bunk down and sort the bodies staying and going in the morning," Caelan stated as he got comfortable.

"Night, everyone" Pollyanna had piped in as she wrestled and moved her bedding near Alfred. Everyone

255

had noted ever since the awkwardness of Variwen's trick potion had worn down, they had become quite close.

The morning came so quickly for all I the kitchen, Agatha woke groggy lying near the table where Charles slept.

She got up and stretched, checking on Charles who slept fitfully.

Variwen had made coffee and her and Caelan were near the fire in hushed tones. Caelan noticed the rustlings of the rest of the group and stood up

"Right, who is staying and who is going?" Caelan rubbed his hands together as the others got ready. Variwen put her hands up in protest.

"Woman, you will not delay this outing. I am so sick of being stuck in this room."

"I for one am looking forward to being in my own bed tonight, but I am doing my protest because no one has eaten and most of all Charles need to be cleaned and fed before we leave."

Charles rolled his eyes. "I don't need someone to clean me, Variwen."

"That's not true, Charles. You can't lift your other arm. Parts need to be cleaned and I am not staying here to do it. Agatha." They all looked at Agatha who was just as shocked as Charles.

"No, no way in hell is Agatha cleaning me!" Charles vented angrily at Variwen.

Agatha looked at the floor. "It's okay, I can do it."

Charles' expression crumbled and he rubbed his sleep deprived exhausted face. "Agatha, it's bad enough you see me like this, but to see me like that, it's too much." Charles' eyes were pleading with Agatha.

Ignoring Charles, Agatha turned to the others. "I need a bath with warm water. Someone to help me get him in and out and another to help in finding some clean clothing for him." Agatha looked at Charles briefly and turned away as Caelan silently picked up Charles; Naga, Pollyanna, and Alfred went out the door closely followed by Caelan holding Charles and coming up behind, Agatha.

Variwen, Oxxy, Ants and Fervor were left in the kitchen. Variwen was busying herself with making porridge and Fervor put the kettle onto the fire to make tea to go with the porridge.

"I think I will do a bit of food shopping while we are in town, Fervor/ We are running low on, well, everything. Can you go to the Fey and ask if they want anything from the town?"

Fervor was shocked as Variwen so casually added in the Fey as a normal part of their life in the castle.

"Variwen, I'm not sure…"

"Oh hush, go find that room they said was at the end of the hallway, on the upstairs level. I'm sure it's not hard to find. Ask if they need anything as our new guests in the castle."

Fervor, usually a peaceful daemon, was struck dumb by Variwen and the fast turn of events regarding the Fey after what they had done to the forest animals and most of all what they had done to Charles.

"I don't care about your thoughts, Fervor. Remember, they were under the control and order of Caspian. This is all new to them, we must make them feel comfortable and not threatened. It will help with our future plans. You must trust me on this, Fervor."

Sighing and understanding her theory, Fervor moved to the door. "If they kill me, Variwen, my blood is on your hands…"

"Yes, yes all right, all right, now get on with it, Fervor, before the pot boils over."

Fervor headed up the staircase. He walked across the landing and towards the end of the hallway to the first doors. Before he touched the handle, a Fey stood in front of him, with its hands up like it wanted to be picked up. It looked young and smaller than the others he had seen before. He bent down then hesitantly put his hand out. The young Fey climbed onto his hand and Fervor slowly stood up. They looked at each other and the miniature child smiled at him. She sat down in his hand and pointed towards the door. Fervor stepped forward and opened the door and walked through. He was shocked to find yards of material lying on the ground with dozens of Fey, cutting the material into sizes for what he presumed to be clothing. As he shut the door, they all stood and bowed at him.

They pulled the material pieces apart and let him walk through. It lined the hallway to the next doors. As he turned the knob, he looked behind him and saw they were still all bowing to him. "Weird," Fervor said under his breath. Opening the next door, he saw candles lighting the floor like a pathway to what he thought was the room they were currently residing in. Slowly walking in, the small Fey still in his hand tugged at his thumb. Fervor looked down and the little Fey pointed through the doors with a smile. Fervor smiled hesitantly back and walked towards the doorway. He was met with light and warmth. He stopped and knocked on the door even though it was open. Every Fey in the room turned Aurelius ran up to Fervor and bowed at him.

"How may we be of service, large one?" she said with utmost respect.

"Fervor, my name is Fervor. We, um, we are going into the town to get supplies. Variwen wanted me to ask if you would like us to get you anything, do you need food, or something?" Using his free hand Fervor rubbed his neck in awkwardness.

Aurelius was not sure how to respond, she bowed and ran towards the fire place. Fervor looked at the little Fey in his hand and smiled. The little Fey stood up. "Fervor," it said and bowed then pulled his finger down.

"I guess you want to be down, little one." Fervor slowly bent down and let the Fey climb off his hand onto the ground. She waved at Fervor, bowed and ran towards one of the small groups to the right of the room.

A Fey whom Fervor guessed was her mother came running forward to greet her child. She turned and bowed at Fervor who was watching them and walked back arm in arm with her daughter. When they get to the group they were in, all the Fey went and started to touch the young Fey. The mother cried and hugged her as more came to touch her in respect.

Fervor frowned at the motion but was distracted by Aurelius coming back from the fireplace. "Thank you, large one, I mean Fervor. My leader wished for food and supplies too. She has asked for a group of us to come with you so we can find what we want. I'm not sure of the translation so would like to come as well to learn words." She bowed at him and waited for his reply.

Fervor was unsure of the others wanting more Fey around but nodded in agreement. "Be down at the entranceway…" he began to say, but Aurelius turned to her people.

"Auri ulah acum." A small group ran forward, one with a mouse skull on his head. Two were naked but had beads of sorts around their necks, holding spears that resembled toothpicks, and the last two looked identical, shaved sides with white spots down their centre. They had string holding mouse fur similar to butt flaps covering their genitalia. They all reached up at Fervor. Realising they were wanting a lift, he looked around the room then decided it best to adhere to their wordless request. Fervor bent down and collecting them all, they climbed up his arms and stopped at his shoulders.

He bowed towards the fire, hoping to be respectful to their leader. He then turned and left the room.

Walking back to the kitchen, the Fey moved about his shoulders with ease. Fervor, on the other hand, was on edge. He made it to the kitchen, not knowing if the others have fallen off on the journey. Fervor, taking a deep breath before heading in, saw it was still only Variwen in the kitchen.

She looked up from the fireplace with a smile. "Ahh, I knew making extra was a good idea." She waved to the Fey on Fervor's shoulders. Fervor stopped by the table, now cleaned and clear of blankets and Charles. It had been freshly laid with bowls and cutlery and other items relevant to breakfast.

Fervor let the Fey off down from his shoulder by sitting and leaning into the table. They jumped down and turned to Variwen who smiled. They didn't recognise her. "Ahh, you remember me as this, don't you?" Variwen changed her appearance for a short while, smiled and then changed back. The Fey were shocked and awed by what she could do. They chattered amongst themselves as Variwen got small serving bowls for the Fey, put a few tablespoons of food in each and pushed them towards the Fey. They looked at each other and stepped forward to smell it, Variwen pointed to her mouth and with a smile and opened it, showing that they should eat it.

She passed teaspoons to them for each bowl which they took. The one with the mouse skull stood back and started spinning the teaspoon, pretending to attack the others with it. Variwen placed his bowl down with the same food only a larger portion. The Fey watched him as he added honey and milk to his porridge then began to eat. They attempted to copy, spilling sugar on the table and splashing milk all around them. Once they had what Fervor had, they tasted the porridge and all their faces lit up with excitement.

"Ahhh, look at that! Isn't that lovely? First time they have had porridge…" Variwen grinned holding a cup of tea whilst leaning against the fireplace.

"Who is eating porridge for the first time?" Charles, looking a lot fresher, walked into the room and went rigid, spying the Fey on the table. He stood up against the wall. The Fey saw this and looked to each other. They stopped eating and bowed low to the surface of the table and remained there apart from Aurelius.

"Mister Charles, Mister Charles." Aurelius continued. "Mister Charles, we are here in peace. We no longer wish to harm you. We are sorry for your wounds. Our Fey that were poisoned in hopes to kill you have all died." Continuing on with, "Please don't harm us," Aurelius bowed down as well and the group chanted, "Please don't harm us," over and over

Charles found this a bit too much. "All right, all right. If you ever step out of line, though, Fey, I will find and kill every one of you. Do you understand? You thank Agatha and Variwen for that. I trust nothing on you."

"Yes, Mister Charles, we will obey, we promise, we will obey," they all said as they bobbed up and down, bowing in time to the repetitions.

"Oh God, why are they here?" Caelan had returned with Charles' dirty clothing. Agatha had followed behind with Pollyanna, Naga who held all the bandages was close behind. Agatha was grey from her task and welcomed the tea placed in her hands from Variwen,

"It is sweet, my dear, give you a bit of life." Variwen winked at Agatha who took a sip of tea turns and smiled at the Fey.

"Have you joined us for breakfast? How lovely!" She sat down near Variwen on the opposite side to Fervor and Charles.

"They are joining us on our trip to town," Fervor added in.

"They bloody well are not, lad!" Caelan was bright red and steam looked like it would come out his ears any second.

"Actually, you great lummox, they are. I offered to buy food and supplies which they accepted and this team will be collecting them and learning the English words for them." Variwen nodded at Aurelius

"Yes, Cae-Caeland, we would like to come to learn. I am most excited to see how you work as you are such a large Chimeon daemon. We know of your history and troubles like us and," they turned to Agatha and bowed, "your Choler here, Agatha…"

The room was shocked into silence. "How do you know that, Fey? How do you know what she is? She is a half-blood Choler. She has control." The Fey bowed to Variwen who had spoken so briskly.

"We can smell it. We knew the day we came here. Most daemons of strength, power give off a scent."

Charles was thinking in the background as he heard the others talking. He pondered on how they can tell the difference. "So… You are telling us that if you came up to a daemon, nine times out of ten, you would be able to tell what type they are just by smell." Charles looked at them waiting for a response.

"Yes, Mister Charles, apart from Variwen. We have never smelt one before whose appearance can change so easily, and there has been one other who evades us."

The group looked at each other then back at the group of Fey. "Who?" was the simultaneous question they all asked.

The Fey looked at each other and gabbled in their language for a moment. "The dark one with the Lord Caspian."

The others slumped. They already knew he was a mystery and didn't know his breed. "Do you know what Lord Caspian is?"

Aurelius thought and then gabbled again with her team. She turned and stepped forward. "Caspian, the lord of the night, calls himself a scientist. He also smells like a mixture of an elemental and a death daemon, not

264

a good mix. Elementals are extinct and death daemons are rare."

"Who's rare? I'm not rare I'm just depressed." Alfred spoke up at this as Aurelius and the other Fey looked at Alfred.

"You are a pure blood, Mister Death."

Alfred raised his eyebrows and looked at the others with a smirk. "Hmm, you can all call me Mister Death from now on." Alfred now felt quite proud of himself; Caelan stepped forward and whacked him at the back of his head.

The group laughed while the Fey looked on with interest. "All right, you lot, sit down before your food gets cold and eat it!" Variwen cut into the conversation.

They all quickly sat and started to eat. Toast had already been toasted, which one of the Fey was trying to take, although this piece looked twice his size. He struggled to get it out the toast holder but manoeuvred it with ease. This Fey was the one with the mouse butt flap. He bit it and chewed and of course, it was dry and now cold. Variwen picked it up off the Fey who was pulling funny faces trying to eat the toast. She buttered it for him and put on jam, then gave it back. The Fey sniffed then licked the toast. A huge grin appeared and he showed it to Aurelius, gabbering away. He picked up the toast in both his arms and took it over to the others, giving them a large piece to chew and handing it around for everyone. The expressions of the Fey with this new food were amazing to watch.

Agatha grinned as she ate and even Caelan and Charles had a semi-wary smile appearing on their faces as they watched the antics of the Fey on the table.

Once all the food was finished, one of the Fey had smeared himself in jam and had dived into the sugar bowl. Another was in the milk jug swimming and drinking at the same time.

"Well, that milk will need to be thrown out now, ha, ha!" Fervor continued on, "Let's put the rest of the breakfast things away before they eat a home into the bread!"

Charles snorted on his tea and Caelan started to laugh at Charles. Variwen picked up the bread as the Fey started to charge the loaf. Stopping mid-charge, they looked up, disappointed until the Jam Fey threw handfuls of sticky sugar at the small group on the table. They looked around ready to charge their fellow Fey when Charles picked up the jam and sugared Fey out of the sugar bowl. He plopped him on the table and the others started to run at him. He ducked and curled up into a ball. The Fey had dived on top of him, pulling clumps of sugary jam off his body. He started to laugh as they scraped their fingers down his body getting all the sugar and jam off him. Variwen picked him up gently and the others stopped staring at the sticky fey in Variwen's hand She walked him over to the sink and dropped him into a shallow bowl of lukewarm water. He stood, soaking wet, looking up.

"Clean yourself, we can't have birds dive-bombing you in town." Aurelius gibbered loudly over to Variwen's area as the Fey looked up and grumbled as he washed off the jam. The others were licking their fingers and parts of each other when Naga scooped up two more and carried them over to the sink. Agatha grabbed the last three and they all went into the sink. It was only a couple of minutes before splashing was going over the sink and onto the floor.

Caelan got up. "Pack of children they are. How long before they destroy this place, hey?" He looked at Agatha.

"First time of freedom, Caelan, what did you do, hey?" Variwen glared at him then looked over to the sink. The Fey had stopped splashing and five little heads could be seen sticking up over the sink. Variwen took over a tea towel. "Here dry yourselves on this, we have a busy day ahead."

She rubbed one of the Feys' heads with the towel to show what it was for, then she passed it to them and walked back to the table. The twins with the mouse butt flaps climbed out next and started to dry themselves. They each pulled this way and that on the tea towel before they yelled and one of the twins jumped on the other and bashed and kicked him for the towel. Aurelius jumped up and gave them both a swift kick and punch all in one flipping movement, leaving them stunned as she told them off. They looked quite sheepishly over at Agatha and Variwen. They bowed and stopped mucking about while the rest dried themselves off in silence. Agatha turned to the rest of the group grinning and the others tried their best to stop laughing.

Naga burst out laughing. "Quite the entertainment they are, hey?"

"Beats listening to Caelan and his stories over and over again, that's for sure!" Ants and Oxxy started to laugh as well and they turned and clapped to the Fey who were standing there not sure how to take the newfound stardom.

They did what they only knew to do — they bowed, causing the twins to bang their heads and end up falling off the sink with one in a headlock and the other trying to grab his legs out from under him.

The group all burst out laughing.

The twin Fey stood up from the floor and you saw their tiny bodies bow to the group. "All right, enough antics, everyone. Dry off and get ready. Alfred, you…"

"Yeah, yeah, do the dishes, I know, Variwen." He stood up and went to the sink. Rolling his eyes, he picked out the remaining Fey and gently put them on the ground. I will help you Alfred" Pollyanna moves to join him as he emptied and wiped down the sink to start doing the dishes. The small band of Fey ran over to the table and climbed up the legs to the top.

Here they collected the plates and stacked them for Alfred. He turned to start tidying the table after filling the sink to find the group rather surprised and the Fey standing next to a tidy pile of dishes and cutlery ready for washing. Everything else Variwen put away, scared they might break the items putting them back.

Alfred remarked at their help, "Why, thank you, little helpers. I'm not sure when the last time it was someone helped me." Pollyanna sniffed disapprovingly. "Do I not count?" Alfred sheepishly turned away from her then he glared at the group before turning again towards the sink.

It turned out to be a warm sunny day outside as the group and the small team of Fey walked outside ready to start their journey to town. Variwen was holding a basket for her shopping and Agatha had another. The Fey were sitting on various members' shoulders yelling and gabbering to each other in their own language. Caelan was getting annoyed quite quickly, which Agatha saw and she took one of the twins off his shoulders. She placed the Fey on her other shoulder as they slowly walked to town.

Charles wanted to join them on the journey to town. He was a stark contrast to his previous look. His hair was now strewn over his face, his lightly coloured grey complexion was now a sickly grey with hollowed eyes, his arms were almost completely covered in bandages and the one reattached was still not really in use and had been placed in a sling. They had to use fresh bandages as the arm was starting to make the bandages smell. Agatha looked over to him, worried.

Charles caught her eye and turned away, still angry that she had bathed him and seen how bad his infections and arm really were. He knew deep down if he didn't start healing soon, he might not come back from this. Catching his own breath and trying to mask his pain, Charles cleared his throat. "At least the walk is warm. I think it will do me some good to be out of the castle."

The others looked over to him, most masking their worried faces with an appreciative smile. Agatha stepped over to Charles. "Charles, it's okay if you want to wait outside for us back at the castle. It may be too far for you…"

"You have pandered to me enough today, Agatha. I would rather you just left me alone." Charles moved closer to Caelan and ignored how hurt Agatha was. Caelan however was in agreement with Agatha. "Charles this journey is not for you mate, you need your rest. Stay here and keep an eye on things." Charles was furious. "I can look after myself Caelan.

"Not like this you can't and I say this with deepest respect." Charles was so angry he didn't know which way to look. The crutch Fervor had fashioned him was thrown to the ground and he sat on the rough broken steps. "Fine I shall wait." Charles said in anguish not liking how the group all thought it best he stayed behind.

The Fey on Agatha's shoulders rubbed her neck. One of the twins hugged her neck, then climbed up on her back. He started yelling at Charles and brandishing his toothpick spear. Agatha smiled at this and reached around her back. "Thank you, Fey, for protecting me. It's okay, he can be mad at me." The Fey twin clambered onto her hand as she brought him back around.

He looked up at her and, hitting his chest, said, "Aril, me Aril."

Agatha smiled down at Aril. "Nice to meet you, Aril. My name is Agatha."

Aril shook his head and pointed at Agatha. "Queen." Then, pointing back at himself. "Aril."

Variwen was looking on at this display and moved towards Agatha. She had the other twin on her shoulders who was holding onto her hair and jumping up and down wanting to join his brother. Variwen reached up and the brother climbed onto her hand. He was holding a shorter version of Aril's toothpick spear. "Aril, Queen," he said with a big grin. He pointed to himself. "Danga."

"Ha, you're danga, all right, or should I say danger, you silly little hmpf." Caelan walked ahead a bit, separating from the others, still upset that the small group of Fey were joining them.

Agatha looked at Danga on Variwen's hand. "Hi Danga, nice to meet you."

"Noce to meeeeett youuuuu." Danga jumped up and down like an excited child, repeating Agatha's words, over and over.

271

"Seems you have the following, Agatha." Variwen stated as she continued to walk next to Agatha.

Oxxy and Fervor had a Fey who was jumping between their shoulders, making them laugh as they tried and moved slightly apart each time. This one had a mouse skull on its head and a toothpick spear. Jumping on Fervor's shoulder, he did a flip and posed with his spear, making the two laugh, even more.

Alfred, on the other hand, was watching Agatha and Variwen's little group while his Fey sat and plaited his hair. Making Pollyanna giggle. It was Aurelius, singing to herself and playing with his hair. Every now and again, she patted his shoulder and pointed to a tree nearby. He moved over to it and she picked a flower or a small leaf and put it in the plaits. It was not long before one side of his head is covered in plaits and plant life. Aurelius moved to his other shoulder and did a simple large plait so it came away from his face. She smiled and hugged his neck when she was done.

"I like you," Alfred said to Aurelius as he put his hand up for her. She climbed on and he held her in front of him. "How do I look?" Alfred said and she smiled and clapped her hands, looking at his hair. She pointed back to his shoulder and he moved his hand up so she could climb back on. Pollyanna sidled up to Alfred. "If I didn't know better, I think you have a fan."

Sitting on his shoulder again, she hugged his neck. "I like you too, Afed."

Alfred replied, "My name is Al-fred," he said it slower which she repeated and corrected herself.

"Well-well-well, looks like Alfred's got a girlfriend." Pollyanna went pink with Caelan's remark. He had come back and joined the group, having got over his upset of the Fey coming with them. "I guess they are okay, but if they kill ya don't say I didn't warn you lot!" Caelan glared at each person one by one, then smiled at the Fey who looked unsure of him. The Fey on Oxxy and Fervor had even stopped jumping about and was staring at Caelan, waiting to see if he would attack or do something. It took a while for the Fey to carry on with their antics, although somewhat reserved this time around.

As the group neared the township coming closer to the shops now, the townsfolk looked on at the crew, with the Fey on their shoulders. They were quiet and whispered as they saw The group nearing the shops

"It's worse than when I first came here," Agatha quietly spoke to Variwen.

"Just keep walking Agatha. Keep looking straight ahead, some of these townsfolk have got a look about them that's not too kind for my liking." Variwen was speaking whilst looking forward the whole time. People had stopped in the street to stare. Even carriages had stopped and were watching as the group past. The unease and tension could be cut with a knife.

They reached the bookstore as a brick was thrown in their direction. It hit Caelan in the back of the head, although it did nothing in the sense of hurting him. He remained still and slowly turned around. He could not see who the culprit could be but held his finger up and looked about. Saying nothing, he pushed the group into the shop and he said, "I'm standing outside."

Agatha looked at him as she walked into the shop. "What are you doing?" she whispered.

"I think I may keep watch, love, I'm not sure on the friendliness of these people and I want to make sure you're all safe." Agatha patted him on the shoulder as she shut the door behind her.

Walking in, Agatha could hear the townsfolk start to yell. "What's with the Fey, Caelan?" said one.

Another voice was also heard as she continued to walk further into the shop. You know Caspian did what he did as penance. You have broken his rules."

Caelan could be heard clear and crisp. "We are not under Caspian's rule here, he is not the actual Lord. Agatha and her family have that right as you well know. She is the one you should be following. You are all a pack of idiots" Agatha reached the counter as Caelan's conversation faded.

"Oh Agatha, you have been the centre of the town's gossip these last few days." It was Helgam with a big smile on his crinkly face. He shook her hand and saw the Fey on her shoulder. "Good grief! Making new friends, I see." Helgam moved his glasses down his nose a bit and shuffled forward to have a closer look at Agatha's Fey. He smiled at Danga and Aril who bowed to Helgam. Chuckling, he held his hand up to the Fey and they scampered on him over his shoulder and onto the counter. They walked around looking at the books piled up. Aurelius pulled Alfred' ear and he lifted his arm up and she walks down it to Alfred's waiting hand.

Helgam looked down towards the entrance of the shop. "I don't think we have much time to chat, Agatha. What can I do you for?" Agatha held up her basket and took out the Ledger. Helgam's face lit up as she passed it to him. "Ahh, I was wondering when I would see this again." He smiled as he took it, running his hands over it.

He saw a flick of red out the corner of his eye. It was Variwen tossing her hair. The colour caught his eye and he stopped looking at the book and shuffled over to Variwen, who was waiting with a big smile on her face.

"If I didn't know any better, I would say it is my lovely Variwen. My, you haven't aged a day, my dear, but then I suppose it's the trick of the trade, am I right?" He winked at her as she stepped closer and kissed him on the cheek.

"And you're still as handsome as ever, Helgam. You always know how to make me feel special." He chuckled again and a bit of pink showed on his wrinkled cheeks. "As much as I would love to catch up with you, Helgam, we are on a tight time frame for deciphering this book. Can you help us?"

Helgam ready to respond to Agatha was cut short as a brick was hurled through the window of the shop.

"I think my time here has ended." Helgam looked at the others. He stood up straight to the shock of the group, removing a wand of sorts and a coin purse. "You mind an extra roommate, Agatha? I will need to time decipher this. Charlie can help where is he?" Variwen seeing the confusion of the missing group member replied in quick succession. "Helgam he is gravely injured and needing your help."

"Why didn't you come to me, I could have given you potions for his relief."

"We can talk more back at the castle I think we should get a move on."

Variwen went to grab her bag, but Helgam held his hand up. "I have tricks too, Variwen."

Helgam looked at the front of the shop as Caelan was heard yelling at the slowly building crowd out the front. The Fey that were on the counter, jumped down onto Variwen's shoulder. Helgam whisked his wand about as books and shelves shrunk into tiny dots and moved into his coin purse. The group started to move about as he collected up all his stacks from around them. He whispered incantations over and over as more and more shelves and books disappeared. One side of the book store began to look very empty and dark. Even the lit candles were swept up in the purse.

Helgam pointed his wand to the back of the store and the curtains along with the tables and everything in the back rooms came flying toward the group. Alfred, Pollyanna, Oxxy, and Fervor, began to duck and dive out the way. Helgam briefly stopped. "Sorry you lot, but we are in a rush. I have a sense that it's going to get ugly outside rather quickly and I need my things."

He started his incantations again and it wasn't long before everything was in his coin purse and the group were standing in a very dark dank-looking room. Moving to the front of the shop, Fervor, Oxxy and Ants stepped forward ready to protect the group behind them. They saw Caelan had brought up a horse and carriage for them.

He saw the others inside and yelled out, "All right, you lot, you took your time, didn't you? I had to buy the beast and cart, no one would rent to us. It costs double to what you would usually get, but at least we have mobility. I think it would be a good idea for you all to come out and we leave in a rather hasty fashion."

Helgam peers over Oxxy's shoulder. "I think Caelan is on the right track, let's move before some more rocks are thrown,"

As the group hastily moved to the entrance they began diving into the carriage and thankful it had a roof, Caelan clambered in the front to steer the horses. The crowd were not willing at first to move out the way, until Caelan got the horse to rear up and kick those in front of him. The carriage moved forward with Caelan apologizing to the fallen. "Ach, you shouldn't have been so stubborn. Why do you have to be such shockers?

Caspian is the wrong leader, follow him if you must, but don't get in our way." He flicked the reigns and the carriage and all its passengers were away and moving quickly through the crowd, getting out into the open, moving away from the centre of town. The houses became fewer to the relief of the cramped passengers.

Variwen sitting next to Helgam kissed him on the cheek again and he blushed profusely.

The Fey were sitting on the windowsills of the carriage, enjoying the ride and seeing the scenery.

"It's a shame we had to leave in such a way," Variwen stated. "I still haven't bought food to stock up. We haven't got anything to take back for the Fey." It was the latter of the two comments that Variwen felt down trodden.

Helgam soon pointed out a farmer's cart coming up. "Perhaps milk and cheese? At least we can get something, and I am partial to some cheese myself." Helgam said as Variwen knocked on the roof of the carriage. Caelan slowed, jumped down and looked in. "All right?"

"Stop the farmer's cart." Variwen pointed to the carriage coming up to them.

He strode forward and called out, "Woah there, are you off to sell in the town?"

"Aye, we have many items to sell, not easy these days, I tell ya."

"Can we save you the trip and buy off you?"

The woman on the cart smiled. "You can buy as much as you want, my dear. It's all for sale."

Caelan looked in. "Ha, brilliant," he exclaimed.

Variwen opened the carriage door and jumped down. She walked over and peered in. Every type of vegetable, bread, milk and cheese were in the carriage. Variwen turned to the cart owner. "Can you drop it to us at the castle?"

"Castle, milady?"

"Yes, the Wilderfort castle, we reside there whilst renovating." Variwen smiled sweetly.

"I guess that's okay, how much were you after?" Variwen walked left and right and moved to the back entrance of the cart looking over everything that was in the cart. "I'd say the lot, how much do you want for it?"

The owner, shocked, didn't know what to say. "I-I'm not even sure how much."

Variwen exclaimed, "Follow us and we can add it up and sort at the castle. When will you do your next delivery?"

The farming woman, still shocked, replied, "Oh every two weeks I'd say," still coming to terms with selling all the produce and items for sale.

"Great you can now deliver everything to us once a fortnight. If you can get hold of meat as well for the next delivery, we'll take it."

The woman looked faint and had to hold onto the cart. "Are you serious, ma'am? I mean, it will feed a lot of people."

Variwen laughed. "You haven't seen what's at the castle yet, or what's in the carriage and there will be more coming too, I'd say, so yes, a fortnight delivery to Wilderfort. Come now, let's not stand in the road all day, we need to sort it all out at the castle." Variwen winked at the woman and turned to re-enter the carriage.

Caelan was still standing there looking at all the food. "Did we just make the best discovery, Variwen?" Caelan turned almost gleeful, climbed on the carriage and steered the horses toward the castle driveway. The farmer's cart comes up behind them. The occupant started to sing a merry tune all the way to the castle.

Charles was waiting on the step, half asleep looking quite sickly. He wakes and manages to stand as the two carriages slow to a stop.

Variwen very happy with her discovery, immediately jumped out in preparation of unloading the farmer's cart. The group exited the carriage and also helped with unloading. Agatha moves towards Charles checking him over as the group moved about excited with all the food, breads, and jams that started to flow into the castle, followed by butter and milk, fruit, vegetables and some yogurt. There was enough to feed a small army, very much to what was waiting in one of the wings of the castle. The Fey.

Variwen added it all up and handed over the cash to the farmer's wife who was almost tearful. "So excuse me, milady, you said bring meat next time yes, and you're happy with all the items here."

"Oh yes, more than happy my dear. If you have any pickles as well, we will take the lot. As I said, we have a lot of mouths to feed." Variwen smiled and the twins showed themselves to the woman,

She screamed a little. "Oh, my goodness, is that Fey?"

Variwen smiled. "Yes, they are and they live here with us, so as much food as you can gather, we would be thankful." The woman was shocked but also very happy with how her day had turned out. "My husband will be so pleased. We live about an hour that way." She pointed in the direction of east. "The road winds around and we are just on the side of the hill over yonder. You are welcome to stop by if you need any top-ups on things."

"Why, thank you. I'm sorry I didn't catch your name."

"Oh, my goodness, milady, I'm so sorry. My name is Eleanor."

"Lovely to meet you, Eleanor." Variwen shook her hand and watched Eleanor climb onto her cart and flick the reins for her horse to move. She smiled and waved as she left, slowly going back down the driveway and turning the way she had pointed.

Variwen turned to the others who had already started eating the fruit. "Okay, guzzle guts." Variwen looked at Caelan who had three apples in his hand as he stuffed a whole one in his mouth like a walnut.

"We need to get this all into the kitchen and divide it up between us and the Fey. Oh Ants, can you find that lady and ask if next time she can bring sewing needles and what not for our guests? That would be wonderful." Ants nodded and sorted the errand.

It took a fair while to get all the groceries into the kitchen. All the toing and froing caused the Fey to start turning up to watch. The ones who went to the township were carrying the smaller items. They called over some more of the Fey that were watching and soon there was a line of them carrying fruit and vegetables onto the table. It was a spectacle that brought smiles on Agatha and the others' faces.

"They look like large ants," Naga commented as he carried a box of pickles into the hallway, trying not to stand on the Fey as they walked in the same direction. He noticed some small Fey had joined although as they collected the fruit, one or two were running in the opposite direction and hiding under the staircase. Naga handed over the box of pickles to Variwen who was sorting and stacking it the kitchen. He walks back around then raced to where the young Fey were running to. An ear-splitting laugh cascaded out of Naga as he came across the young Fey covered in small pieces of fruit. They had been devouring the pieces they had siphoned off the line and burying themselves further into the pile as they ate.

Agatha heard the commotion and came to the same area as Naga. "If only we could have a picture of this."

Naga laughed again. The young Fey were standing in front of the small pile of fruit with their heads hung low. The leader of their group was yelling at them and whacking them with her long staff. The youngest in the group was sitting on the floor with tiny tears rolling down. The leader wasn't yelling at this one so Agatha moving away Charles bent down and put her hand out.

The little Fey sobbing with her hand in her mouth looked up at Agatha. She looked like she had been swimming in fruit pulp the way she was covered. Smiling to encourage her, Agatha watched as the young Fey clambers on her hand, a bit nervous as are the others looking on. "I think you need a bath little one." Agatha said and took the young Fey into a room not far from the hallway. It was more of a storage room with cleaning buckets, cleaning products and shelves with other miscellaneous items the group had been finding throughout the levels of the castle that they had managed to clear for the restoration project. Upon finding a large low bucket, Agatha collected a box of borax and another of soap flakes and started for the kitchen. Her little Fey stood on the side whilst she collected the items and was watching with keen interest. Some of the older Fey had come to investigate, standing by the door and looking in. When they saw what the room held, they clambered into some of the buckets, and gibbered amongst themselves pointing and drawing marks with their fingers on the metal of the buckets. Agatha, leaving. found herself with a group of followers. She made her way to the kitchen with the young Fey sitting in the metal tub. Gathering a boiling kettle and a jug of cold water, Agatha filled the tub with the interest of the Fey around her. Putting in the borax and flakes, it bubbled, making it much like a miniature bubble bath.

This was the first time the Fey had seen this and they were fascinated, gabbling with each other and pointing, Agatha put her hand in which caused an uproar and the Fey jumped around, yelling and shouting. Agatha laughed as she pulled her arm out. "See! It's just water with bubbles." Agatha held her arm out for the Fey to touch and see, smiling as she herself popped a bubble, the young Fey she made the bath for squealed with excitement, clapping her hands together. Agatha smiled and put her other hand out. The young Fey climbed on and Agatha gently brought her over and placed her in the warm water. She giggled in the small tub that looked like a small lake in comparison to her size. The others who were watching also got excited seeing that she was okay. Some of the others jumped in with her.

They laughed and popped the bubbles and swam about in the warm water. Agatha had to stop other Fey from jumping in and overcrowding the tub. "Wait your turn." Agatha said gently.

Looking up, she saw the rest of the inventory from the farmer's cart was in the kitchen. Variwen was sorting and clearing the tables, starting to make a space to commence dinner with Pollyanna. "I think we may as well cook for everyone, and the Fey can either join us or take their food down to that room of theirs." It seemed to sit well with the others. Even Caelan didn't seem to mind.

Chapter 15
The Dimension Door

Variwen with Pollyanna was in the final throes of dinner whilst Agatha was well timed with bathing the last of the Fey. It was her sixth tub of now not-so-bubbly water. "I'm so glad I did this. I swear they have never cleaned themselves. That water is black every time." The last group were wet but grinning in the now black water, Agatha helped out those that needed it and stood them in the not so white towel. Agatha, picked up another clean towel a bunch of very green and white Fey came running in from the hallway.

Looking up, Agatha could see they were gabbering away with the leader who turned to Agatha, yelling, "Aurelius, Aurelius!"

A very green Aurelius came forward, bowing to the leader and Agatha, and speaking her language with the leader. She finished and turned to Agatha. "Queen Agatha," Aurelius bowed. "Some of my family have found a room that moves into another and another. It was where you went with the water man and the lightning man when you were white." Aurelius waited for her response, looking keenly, not wanting to take her eyes off Agatha in case of missing anything.

"I see, can you show us?" Agatha looked at the group as they all now sat at attention around the table. They too had been enjoying the spectacle of the washing of the Fey. Agatha moved for the door. She didn't need to ask the others Variwen instructed Pollyanna to serve up as the rest of the group all followed Agatha.

It didn't take as long to get to the wall as it did last time when she was searching. There was a Fey waiting for them next to the wall. He bowed and looked up at Agatha. He ran back to the wall and a gap she hadn't seen before was apparent as he disappeared. Looking closer, Agatha could see where she might have put her hands before, and realised she was reaching too high. Her aunt had been shorter than her and Agatha remembered her reaching low. Agatha pushed her hands along the skirting board at the bottom of the wall and it wasn't until she reached the edge of the wall detailing that a noise was heard, like scraping. Agatha stood up quickly and glanced back at the others as another loud clunking noise was heard. The wall began to move like an automatic door. And there right in front of them was the entranceway.

Agatha was so excited she looked for Charles, although he was nowhere to be seen. Fervor stepped forward, putting his hand on Agatha. "He needed a rest, Agatha. His wounds are making him weaker." Her excitement dulled as she heard Fervor.

"We had better get a move on then; I can't have him falling apart on us." Agatha bringing forth her orbs of light looked over to Ants. He sighed, lighting his fists, and pointed them into the opening. It was another narrow hallway much like the one found in the fire place in the kitchen. He went to walk in and couldn't. Puzzled, he looked around the entranceway. It was Variwen who pointed upwards.

Along the side of the entranceway was, *"Magia nu intră aici."*

"It's Romanian, although I'm not sure why that language would be in this house." Variwen looked over the rest of the place and ran her hand over the wording. It lit up and had a slight purple hue to it. Variwen tried to move forward more, although she had the same problem as Ants did. Puzzled, Variwen looked back. It had been a while since Helgam had spoken to anyone and she looked for him. He had been watching everything since coming back to the castle.

Helgam stepped forward. "I think, my dear," Helgam looked at Variwen kindly and winked. "This will need a very simple counteraction to sort this out." Helgam pulled out his knife. As far as any one was concerned, he was cutting something.

"Argh Helgam what are you doing?" Agatha saw Helgam cut his finger tip. He placed it on the floor near the spell, then cut through the words on the entranceway with the bloodied knife. The words dimmed in purple light, flickered and then they were all gone. The others were shocked by what Helgam did.

288

Variwen picked up Helgam's fingertip and handed it over. "You are such a drama queen, Helgam. You didn't need to chop off your finger. A simple slice would have sufficed."

Helgam smiled. Rubbing the cut finger, he pushed the tip back onto where it previously was affixed. He rubbed up and down and closed his eyes. It took a couple of seconds and then he squeezed his hand together. "There, see not that bad at all." Helgam smiled as he wriggled his fingers, including the one that was once chopped.

The Fey on the ground were yelling and jumping up and down. They bowed to Helgam and Aurelius was pushed forward. "Ahh Helgam, my name is Aurelius, I am the translator." Aurelius bowed. "You are magic, Helgam, you can fix things together, can you bring people back from the dead, too?"

Helgam looked straight at Variwen, then dropped his eyes to Aurelius. "My dear Aurelius, it is so nice to meet you. My magic, as you call it, is of nature. I am a warlock in a sense. I do not choose to do necromancy."

Aurelius mouthed the word to herself, showing confusion.

"Necromancy, my dear, is that of blood sacrifices to bring people back from the dead or get the dead to do your bidding. Very dark magic, very dangerous and only those who have the will to stay pure so it doesn't stain them can do it, although some have gone to the dark side so to speak." Aurelius still showed the confused look but seemed to process what Helgam was saying.

"Perhaps we can talk more when we don't have more pressing matters at hand." He smiled again and waved his arm towards the entranceway. "Oh, you all may enter now, by the way. The spell has been removed." Ants lit his hand again and walked into the entrance. Moving past the point, he got stuck, he turned around further in and the look of triumph crossed his face.

Following Ants into the dark narrow passage, they went up and down and around corners until the first room opened out the passage. Here they found themselves in a room with holes in the wall, although each hole had a Fey standing and watching them waving at the group.

"Anyone feel like they are in a very vulnerable position?" Caelan looked uncertainly around the room at the mass of Fey. "How did they multiply so quickly?" Caelan nervously looked at them, as he turned around and looked at each wall.

Ants didn't seem satisfied with stopping here and was encouraged to go on further by the same small male Fey who walked into the entranceway. "Hey everyone, come here."

A shout was soon heard and the group didn't waste time in congregating in the new space. It felt lighter in here, the feeling of being anything or become anyone. Variwen grabbed hold of Helgam and kissed him all over his face. Helgam roughly put his hands up and messed up her hair. Caelan laughed, walked up and kisses Variwen on the top of the head. The others stared on in a confused sense, Alfred called for Aurelius, picked her up and kissed her small head. She jumped on his shoulder and hugged his neck.

"Okay, something's fishy in here. I think we need to move on. It smells like magic in here." The Fey were laughing around the group, although a lot of them were doing the same thing. Freaking out. Agatha grabs Variwen and pulled her out of the Caelan and Helgam sandwich. She shoved Variwen towards the next room and the men followed. Ants grabbed Aurelius from Alfred, using her as a lure to get him to follow.

"Okay, I think this room definitely has a different atmosphere, don't you think, Variwen?" Naga was grinning whilst looking at Variwen the first time she showed her embarrassment.

"I'm not sure what came over me."

"Well, obvious, it was some sort of desire room maybe or a spell?" Alfred said as he smiled down at Aurelius who was sitting on the edge of his shoulder. She looks around at him with a pink face. "Pink suits you, Aurelius." Alfred looked down at her and with his index finger brushed her hair off her face. She held his finger and smiled.

"So that's why the Fey were all staring at us." Fervor stepped forward. "They knew what was happening in that room."

"Ha, they must have waited to see what we would do then!" Caelan spoke up.

Helgam was flattening his almost non-existent hair on his almost bald head and Variwen was brushing her hair with her fingers, trying to keep a straight face. Nothing said guilty more than the poor attempt at a straight face. Variwen was also concentrating on the wall. Agatha went to go and speak with her. She walked over but Variwen concentrating put her hand up. "Shh, let me see this. Ants, come here." Ants stepped forward to Variwen's awaiting hands. She held his arm, looked at him and shook it. He lit up his arm and pulling him towards the wall Variwen found it is not a wall at all but another entranceway. This one looked shallow. She turned eagerly to the others.

"We have made it!" she cried with excitement, although stepping forward, a small group of Fey ran ahead and a brilliant blue light flashed in front of them. The group of Fey are no more, although in their stead was a group of mice.

Baffled, they all turned to Helgam, who was cleaning his glasses.

Helgam looked up. "Oh yes, um, okay, let's see now." He put his glasses back on and to the right of him was the coffin of whom they thought to be his daughter. "A fever got her in the end," he stammered although no one else could understand him. Agatha stepped in front of Helgam to protect him and found herself looking at her mother with blonde hair, smiling and floating in magical wind. Agatha smiled although she knew this wasn't real. Helgam understood it too and grabbed her hand. Leading her towards the room, the walls showed photos of each member of the group and a moment from their past. Alfred touched his photo and where he had touched it, the image rippled like water.

"I'm not liking this at all," Caelan stated as they made their way closer towards the next room. In the last room, it was pitch black. The walls, floor and ceiling swallowed any light that was brought into the room. Even Ants and his hand of light made no difference. Agatha fumbled around looking for something that might help them figure the room out. They could hear the mice that used to be Fey walk into the room and shrieks of joy as they turned back to themselves. It was short lived as they walked into the black and it turned silent again.

"Hmm, I'm not sure what to make of this. Can anyone feel a wall or a table anything resembling furniture?" Helgam cleared his throat again as he tried to talk. His voice was raspy as though someone were drying his throat as he spoke.

"I-I think we need to be quick here. I feel like I'm aging in this dark." Agatha strode forward, not caring if she fell but smacking right into what she thought was a wall, pushing her hands around up to as high as she could reach and as low as she could go, wiping her hands this way and that. "Ouuch!" she squeaked.

"Agatha, what have you found?" Caelan's voice was concerned, and the group could hear her fumbling around.

"I'm not sure but I think it may be something." Agatha found the object her hand had smacked into, rubbing her hands around it to get a mental picture. It was a narrow but thick rod, sitting at an angle. Contemplating whether to pull the lever down or not, she said, "Ahh well, better give it a go. What's the worst that can happen?"

"Agatha, what are you up to?" Helgam's voice was heard in the pitch black.

"It's okay, Helgam, I am trying something." The strain in Agatha's voice could be heard as she pulled down on the lever. It slowly released and she found her surroundings slowly taking shape. It was like a fog lifting off the ground. First the feet of everyone could be seen, then up to the waist, then the faces and shortly after that the whole room was clear.

"My, my, my, what an interesting contraption." Helgam walked over to the lever and started poking and prodding around it to see if anything could be opened for further inspection.

Standing right next to Agatha, however, was a short pillar. An orb slowly floated above a book, causing the alluring effect on Agatha to want to touch it.

Variwen smacked her hand down. "Don't ever touch magic you don't know, Agatha," she warned and glared at Agatha before turning herself towards the orb and checking it over. Variwen pinched Agatha's leg and winked at her to show no hard feelings as Agatha moved from the orb.

One of the Fey that had turned into a mouse in the other room was playing around and having a laugh. It was jumping in and out of what looked like a veiled room. Oxxy, who was next to Agatha, was looking around to see if anything was amiss. Agatha glanced at him, puzzled, and looked at the Fey again jumping back and forth.

"Do you think we can follow him?" Oxxy looked at Agatha.

Fervor shoved in front. "Only one way to find out really, and sorry, I wanted to try first this time." Fervor then walked into the wall or what he thought was the wall. He fell flat on his front as Fervor was trying to prepare himself. Agatha put her hand up and pushed it through what seemed to be an illusion. Fervor got up, helped by Agatha, and as he stood, Agatha let go of his arm, making him fall again.

"Hey," Fervor stammered, although looking around as was Agatha. It was a tiny room, with only a skinny stand with a beautifully hand-crafted staff sitting on the stand. Agatha bent down to look closer and saw all the markings swirls, pictures, and so many other designs that all fit perfectly on the staff, much like watching a story unfold. Agatha put her hand out to touch it. She felt warmth emit off the staff and was eager to pick it up, although Variwen was probably the best one to talk to on this matter.

Being very careful, Agatha picked up the staff, turned and slowly walked towards Variwen, who had already turned, watched Agatha slowly glide through the wall. The orb that was floating on the stand had now gone as well as the spell book underneath it. Agatha showed the staff to Variwen. Variwen motioned to pick it up although she tried to touch it and her hand flowed right through it. It was like it was not really there although Agatha was holding it steady.

"I think it wants you to hold on to it, Agatha. We can check it over properly when we are out of these weird rooms." Variwen looked around and she seemed a bit nervous and not quite held together. The Fey that had previously turned into mice were now clambering up Alfred's leg, who through this whole experience seemed not to be fazed by it all.

"You are so calm and collected, Alfred. Have you dealt with this before?" Naga walked over to him and waited for a reply.

"Oh yeah, my mum had a thing about tricking people and doing rooms of 'fate.' It was her way of having a laugh before they passed over."

"Oh, she doesn't sound all that nice, Alfred. I mean, I'm sure in her way she was to you."

Alfred shrugged. "Not really. She used to chuck me into some of the rooms. She said I was too soft and needed to be stronger. These ones are pretty basic to be honest." Alfred shrugged again. "At least these ones don't have traps. That was one thing I hated. She thought it was hilarious, offering a second chance at life, and all she did was torture them, 'Oh, show how pure you can be and pass the test.' She thought it was the funniest thing. I think she was just evil really." Variwen had been silent listening to his past, but once he trailed off into thought she cut his train of thought.

"Come on, I need a coffee at least, after that experiment." Alfred now focused on the present, walked back the way they had come, he did not stop in each room but concentrated on the exit. The group banded together and followed him out with the new belongings.

Hot coffee was brewing on the fireplace as Variwen looked through the spell book. Helgam sat there with the ledger his glasses halfway down his nose and he reached into his pocket and pulled out his fingerless gloves. Pollyanna stoked the fireplace while the others set the table. Hoping that the bread would be sliced for everyone they watched Caelan stab about eight pieces of thick-cut bread with a metal poker. He was toasting them over the fireplace.

Charles had been lying on Agatha's cot bed in the kitchen and was propped up a bit by a cushion and his good elbow. He looked almost green with the infection it caused so much pain it showed on his worn-out gaunt face. One of the Fey who had stayed behind had had a go at plaiting his hair. It had been washed so was very fine and shiny to look at.

"Right." Helgam stood up and stretched. He looked over to Agatha. "Agatha, I think it's time I find a room for myself. An empty one would serve better as I will need to sort through everything in my bag." Helgam looked down at his tiny coin purse.

"Oh Helgam, of course, I am ever so sorry!" Agatha turned and walked right to the door.

From here, looking back the kitchen was so full of life, even if one of them was quite sickly, the people the smiling, Agatha felt like her kitchen was full of family, people who belonged. Even the Fey were ambling around in and out of the kitchen.

Helgam, after sorting somethings out with Variwen, stepped towards Agatha with a smile. "Ready!" he said as they turned and walked into the hallway.

"Well, Helgam, I suppose what is to your preference? We have a fair few rooms to choose from. Would you like the first or second floor"

"Well, I hate to be a pest, dear Agatha, for you have opened your home to so many already, but I truly feel the third floor with those wonderful large windows would be a spectacle, if that is a room. Oh, I hope it's a room." Helgam trailed off into thought.

"Hmmm, well, you see, Helgam, we haven't really gone to the third floor. I'm not overly sure the way to the large windows you talk of." Agatha trailed off, a bit worried. "I sorry, I am not much of a tour guide Helgam."

"It's quite all right, Agatha. A little birdie told me." Giggling could be heard behind them as they walked. It was the Fey following them. Aurelius was amongst the group. She straightened when Agatha saw her and she bowed.

"Why are they giggling, Helgam?"

"Ahh, you see, my dear, your hair… Ahh." Agatha reached up to her hair and patted it to figure out what was wrong. "I don't mean to be rude but it's a tad on the messy side, my dear. I think that is why they are giggling."

Agatha looked back again. "Well, you tidied up Alfred's and Charles' hair, Aurelius, perhaps you could help me with mine?" Agatha looked at Aurelius hopefully.

Aurelius ducked into a moving circle with some other Fey. It wasn't not long before they all looked up and Aurelius said, "Yes, Queen, we would love to plait your hair. We will need many flowers and many strings of beads. We will need to make these for you. It will take many days but we'll make your hair beautiful again. The others will wash your hair and brush your hair until it shines." Aurelius bowed to Agatha, which Agatha looked concerned about.

"Aurelius, we may not have time for…"

Helgam grabbed her arm. "Is this it?"

Agatha stopped mid-sentence and turned to see where they were. They had made it to the third floor and standing in front of them were two very beautiful carved doors. Helgam looked excited at Agatha and tried the doors. They were both locked.

"Of course, they are locked. How typical," he said as he reached into his sleeve and pulled out his wand, a mid-length wooden branch twisted right the way through with the handle end worn into its shape most probably through many years of use with Helgam. He swiped and flicked the wand with a very concentrated face, the door simply gently opened, and the group were able to walk in. The giant windows were on the left side as they walked in. It was a marvellous sight — the stained glass was of beautiful events in history.

Agatha was unsure, although one looked not dissimilar to the castle and it was on fire. Agatha did a double take on the second. "I'm sure that just moved."

Helgam looked at her and smiled. "It may well have, my dear, it very may well have." Agatha returned his smile although in a somewhat puzzled nature.

The Fey were doing cartwheels and dancing around as the room was huge, a wide-open space with chandeliers placed in the centre of the room in two rows of two.

Helgam pulled out his coin purse, placed it on the floor and started to bend and swerve and shift around. Items began unfolding and returning to the full size, moving this way and that as he directed. It was quite a sight! The Fey were ducking and diving with some items and kept getting in the way. Helgam got a book to sweep down and scoop them up. It stayed floating for the rest of the unpacking, making the Fey lean over the edge of the book and watch everything from above. They loved the height and being able to see at a bird's eye view.

Helgam had unpacked his first room of his shop, although this time enlarging the book shelves to accommodate the books that were previously sat in massive mounds on the floor when in the shop.

It was quite an effort and took nearly an hour to unpack and position the books, his bed, the lounging area and of course the potions area. At first, he arranged them like little rooms, separating each off. Helgam felt it was weird so tried again after his first attempt. This second round of moving helped Helgam see the bigger picture and soon they were looking at a massive change around. With aisles of book shelves on one side, the potions area on a corner with a screen to section it off, Helgam had the rest of the room as his living area. Helgam was really excited with the set-up and stood by the windows admiring his work.

The book the Fey were resting on slowly made its way down to the floor.

Agatha watched as they tentatively stepped off the book and looked around at the now full room. Lights that Helgam had left on were still glowing and sitting upon the numerous bookshelves, tables and within the seating area of his living space. The whole room looked cosy and well lived considering it had only just been set up.

Helgam walked around with the Fey following closely behind. After his final check-over, Helgam went and sat down to rest.

Alas, it was short lived because the Fey were trying to ask all sorts of questions.

Helgam put his hand up, asking, "One at a time, or better yet, let's have some tea and we can all chat together." Twisting his wand and moving the chair he was sitting on, Helgam manoeuvred himself around so he was in line with the fireplace. Swishing this way and that and muttering under his breath, he managed to light the fire, get the pot full of water and even brought out the china for the tea.

Variwen had come up to check on the group and to her delight, the business of tea was in play. "Well, I have definitely come at the right time then, haven't I?" She placed the ledger on the table in front of Helgam and Agatha, who was still walking around with the staff, took a seat opposite Helgam.

"Yes, perfect timing, my dear Variwen, please join us!" Helgam offered the chair next to him. Agatha placed the staff across her legs and distracted herself from the conversation by looking over the intricate designs on the woodwork. Brushing her hand across the surface, she could see stories carved into the wood, by whom was uncertain, although the history showed her to be in the part of the gatekeeper her white hair showed on the staff. Turning the staff, Agatha saw a symbol on the top, placed on an enlarged piece of the wood. It was similar to a twisting image or a whirlpool. She saw symbols and letters mixed together which confused her.

"Helgam, this image, where have I seen it before?"

Helgam looked up from his conversation with Variwen. He stood up and walked over to Agatha who pointed to the bulge at the top of the staff. Bending over but not touching it like Variwen had previously told her, Helgam looked over the image, furrowing his brows. He abruptly stood, not saying anything, and went over to the ledger.

Variwen, who was also now standing, moved forward. Also not touching the staff, she bent and took a closer look. Helgam had opened the Ledger and before the introduction of the book was the same image, although none of the letters were present. He handed the book to Variwen and shuffled quickly to his bookshelves. Looking at the books on the shelves, he picked up a couple, read the spine and put them back. Helgam did this for what seems a fair few minutes when he found what he was looking for. He rushed back over to the ladies and placed the books on the table The Fey had joined in looking over the staff and climbing over Agatha to see the images on them.

Helgam pointed to the boiling pot. "Variwen, would you be a dear and finish off the tea making, my

303

wonderful lady? Then I will need you back here quickly to help me."

Nodding, Variwen sorted the tea in quick procession. She brought the ready-made cups to the group and handing smaller versions of tea to the Fey, even though the cups were as big as them and then they still attempted to sip it by sticking their heads over the cups.

None really laughed at their antics of drinking the tea as the Ledger and staff were of the immediate attention. Helgam, scanning through the books they had collected, finished looking through them, stood up and sourced some more. It went like this through the afternoon and well into the night. People came and went, dinner was made and brought up by Oxxy and still Helgam, then Variwen, then Agatha dove into the library hunting for information on the image and translation of the Ledger.

The dark clouds were rolling around the heavy night sky as the rain coursed down. Aurelius and the group that had originally come into the room had fallen asleep all jumbled together on one of the chairs nearer the fireplace. Helgam was straining his eyes, trying to concentrate, rubbing them over and over to keep himself awake. Agatha had all but fallen asleep on a book, although it was Variwen who was in her element. She had five books floating around her as she stood searching each page. She moved and flexed herself to keep awake.

Charles slowly came into the room on his crutch, holding a bag with bread sticking out the top. He was shortly followed by Alfred holding a tray of cheeses and pickles. "Midnight snack, anyone?" Charles managed to say hoarsely. Agatha bolted up right off the book she was asleep on, attempted to straighten her hair that was still a mess as Aurelius and the others hadn't started fixing it for her. She managed to undo the worst of the knots and brushed them with her fingers, tying it back up and making it a bit more presentable.

She wiped her eyes, then helped move some books off the table so Charles could place his bag of bread down.

Alfred placed the tray down and quickly got to work in buttering the bread and arranging the plates.

Caelan strode in. "Okay, I have come to help, I can't take another game of elementals with that idiot any longer. Helgam, give me a book, what am I doing?" He gruffly straightened himself. He sat down and listened to the mumbled instructions from Helgam who was half asleep but still concentrating on his own book.

Oxxy walked in shortly after with Pollyanna, Ants, and Naga. More Fey came into the large room as more books were grabbed to search. "Ahh, well, I'm sure with you all helping in messing up my library in this search we are sure to find what we need," Helgam spurted out, tired and annoyed as the haphazard attempts by the newcomers and their rough approach with the books clearly made him upset. He got up and nervously looked at the newcomers.

Caelan was still standing. "Right, you lot, take a gander at the motif on the staff and the ledger. We think it will help in deciphering the back of the ledger to open the dimension door and save Charles. Very important stuff, okay?" He then walked over to the shelves. "Helgam also said it's a hewey system for these buggers." Caelan had lifted the book up, but at the same time a very grumpy and very tired Helgam stood up.

"Firstly, it's a Dewey system. See, match the codes on the sides of the books to which categories are on the shelves." He shook the book, frowning. The Fey watched this spectacle, including the now awake Aurelius and her small group, jumped up and looked at the numbers. A group of four grabbed a book and wobbled this way and that, marching it round the bookshelves looking for the right place. Helgam, shocked by this, walked around with them and watched. They found the correct place and pushed the book back into order. "Well, I don't think I have been so excited seeing a group of Fey in all my years."

Caelan slapped his knee. "Ha, well, there you have it, Helgam. You now have your librarians to sort your books."

Pleased, Helgam spoke. "Well done, my little librarians. You have done very well indeed." One Fey however took offence and ran and bit him on the leg.

"Ouch!" he yelled, he hopped up and down on one leg while he held the other.

Aurelius, feeling bashful, said, "Um, Helgam, we don't like being called little. We are small, yes, sir, but we are not little like little children, we are strong." She lifted her arms to show muscles. "We are mighty but we are not little… Sir." She added the sir on the end haphazardly.

Helgam, rubbed his leg, stood bent over. "Oh, I am ever so sorry, Fey. I'm not sure what else to call you, but I won't say little any more."

The one who had bitten him stepped forward when Helgam said little again. He raised his fist and garbled something in his language, shaking his fist. Helgam held his hands together, bowed down to the grumpy Fey. "My apologies, I am so sorry." The Fey stepped back, glaring at Helgam, it joined the rest of his group as they carried on to pick up another book and return it to its rightful place in the library. Helgam turned towards the others who all looked like they were waiting for something to explode. Helgam shrugged his shoulders and the group burst out laughing. Even Variwen was having a good laugh at Helgam.

Helgam returned to his seat, a touch more pink on the cheeks than before, and continued to scan his book for the symbol or any information regarding the staff.

Chapter 16
The Final Feat

It was early hours of the morning when Charles called out. "Helgam! Helgam, this is it!" Charles stood up as everyone jumped awake at the sudden loud voice. Helgam, blinking bleary-eyed, rubbed his face.

"Bring it here Ch... Oh, sorry, I'm coming." Helgam had momentarily forgotten about Charles and his state. Even though Charles looked grey with a thin film of sweat on his face and neck, the excitement of finding something had put some colour into his cheeks. Helgam moved towards Charles and bent over to look at the book.

Frowning, Helgam picked it up and looked at the cover. "Mysteries and myths of the Personalul și lumina de dincolo," Helgam read out the book title. "Who would have thought..." Helgam read the page Charles was on. He turned the page and scanned that and the next and the next. Putting it down, he ran for the Ledger.

"Agatha, Agatha! Come here with the staff. Of all the places it would be!" Helgam looked through the ledger, He found a common verse he raced back and grabbed the book he sorted through the pages and using the staff as a starting point for the letters matching to the symbols, Helgam stopped. He stood, rubbing both his hands through his hair, looking from one book to the other, then resting his eyes on the staff in Agatha's hands. "Ha, ha, ha, hi, ho, and away we go!"

Helgam started dancing around like an idiot jumping about. One would have thought he was in his twenties with the way he was moving about.

Agatha excitedly said. "You did it! Oh Charles, you found it!" Agatha grabbed Charles and kissed him. She was so excited she had forgotten where she was and stopped, looking at the floor. "Well done, Charles." Agatha had become bashful, knowing the others had seen them.

Helgam was still dancing about, as were the Fey on the ground; it was a spectacle indeed!

The rest of the group, all awake now, were resting in their chairs, tired but enjoying their moment with the discovery in silence. They were quite happy to be watching Agatha going red in the face and Helgam with his arm in the air dancing like a lunatic.

"All right, all right, Helgam, as much as we love to see you dancing, what's next?" Caelan asked.

"Ha, ho, he, ahh, well." Helgam slowed down and calmed himself. "Right, well, we need to get to the dimension door and start the preparations." Helgam grabbed some paper and a pen and started to write what they needed, He looked from one book to the other and wrote down with an excited buzz around him. He handed the list to Caelan and picked up the books.

"Come, Agatha, we must get to the door. Variwen, you, too, my dear. Caelan, we need everything on the list as quick as you can." Charles went to turn as the orders were being spouted out by Helgam. He reached out for the table to hold on as he moved but missed and crashed to the ground. He wasn't moving.

Everyone stopped their commotion and rushed towards him, Helgam being right next to him, as was Agatha. Both checked for his pulse in different areas. They checked his bites and his arm. Everything was infected. The light sheen of sweat was now a serious covering of perspiration. He had obviously been hiding how bad he was, even though everyone knew he was pretty ill with infection.

Variwen came closer and placed her hands on Charles. She looked at Alfred, who didn't want to look at Charles. He had his head down. "You knew, didn't you, Alfred? You knew and you didn't say anything."

Agatha's, anguish over Charles's collapse spilled over. She went towards Alfred as her eyes burned white. The ground shook as she moved closer to him, but Alfred just held one arm in the other and looked at the floor.

"Agatha, we all already knew he was dying. It's still hazy if he does or not. I get flickers but that's it." Alfred was still looking at the ground.

Agatha replied with venom in her voice, "You knew, Alfred, Death Daemon, and you did nothing but watch." Her voice echoed within the room. The Fey ran towards the exit and they were all gone in a flash. Alfred was stepping back hesitantly and Agatha slowly moved forward some more.

"How would you like to feel his pain, Alfred? Shall I put his pain onto you?"

"Enough!" Caelan stood up. "Agatha!" he shouted. "Enough. Alfred is young and is still learning the ropes of his trade. Do not go after him for something that is beyond his control."

Agatha hesitated and faltered. Her emotions were washing over her and from the group's perspective, it was like a lightening wave washing around a bubble with Agatha inside. She breathed out loudly in a vain attempt to calm herself. The waves slowed and came closer to her skin then disappeared altogether.

"I hate this. I hate that he is dying. I hate that everything is a struggle and I can't stand my outbursts — they are so dramatic." Agatha's face was hot and red with her outburst. Hot tears ran down her cheeks as she turned back to Charles still lying on the ground. Helgam and Variwen were working their magic in a way to help ease the pain and help arouse Charles from his collapse.

"Agatha, we must get him to the door." Helgam lifted his head to Caelan who was still standing there. "Get the items, Caelan, we have almost run out of time."

Caelan summoned Naga, Oxxy, Fervor and Ants to him. "You four pick items that are known to you."

The Fey that had run off out of the room with Agatha's outburst slowly returned, holding the edge of the door and peering round. Aurelius was pushed out front of them. She tried to run back behind the door although the group pushed her out again. Caelan looked over to her. "Want to help us?" She nodded at his request. "Group off with Naga, Fervor, Ants, Oxxy or myself and let's find these items. Charles needs us!" Aurelius nodded. Shouting to the other Fey, she ran over to Caelan and climbed up his trouser leg and torso to check the list, yelling out the items to the Fey. Naga, Fervor, Oxxy and Ants put their hands up to the corresponding items in the list they had stated they would be collecting.

The groups were all sorted in quick succession and the teams quickly set off, leaving Alfred, Pollyanna, Variwen, Agatha and Helgam behind with the unconscious Charles.

Using the bread bag, Helgam put the two books in. Turning to Agatha and the others, he said, "We need to put him somewhere safe. Can we put him back into the bedroom until we need him?" Agatha nodded and started moving the chairs out of the way, creating a path to the doorway. Alfred grabbed Charles' feet while Helgam went for the arms. For an older male, he was surprisingly strong. Variwen, taking the bag from Helgam, followed them out with Agatha and Pollyanna trailing behind.

Agatha grabbed her staff, took a final look at the room and shut the door.

It was a short journey to the bedroom. Thankfully the fire was still alight with embers. Variwen stoked the fire and placed some more logs on whilst Helgam and Alfred made Charles comfortable. He was still unconscious but breathing steadily. Variwen stood up and walked to Charles as Agatha and Pollyanna entered the room.

"I will stay here with Pollyanna she can help me. Alfred, check on me when you can. You two, find the door. Let's get him back through, otherwise he isn't going to survive much longer." Agatha was straight-faced although tears streamed down her cheeks.

Helgam hugged her. "Come on, Agatha, one final push. It will save him." She nodded and wiped her teary eyes. Standing up straight, Agatha took a deep breath and straightened her shirt and trousers and followed the others out, taking a quick glance at Charles lying in bed with Pollyanna moving towards him with a basin of water, Agatha pulled the door to.

The three made their way down to the main level. Helgam turned to Agatha. "Right missy, lead the way."

Agatha faltered. "I-I thought you knew where the entrance was…"

Alfred moved towards the back of the stairs, not saying a word. He opened a hidden doorway on the side of the stairs and waited for the others to come towards him. "Well, come on. I thought we needed to be hasty," Alfred remarked as the other two sped up towards him.

Down flights upon flights of stairs in an area that was surprisingly damp, dank and very musty smelling, the three went down at least three levels. On each level, there was no door, only the doorway big enough for the oak doors at the entrance to fit into nicely.

They found high-ceilinged hallways and so many doors that came off them on either side of the staircase going down into darkness on either end. On the third and final level, this one showed a different finish to the area.

With the high ceilings much like the above floors, this one, however, had weight-bearing pillars that arced across the ceilings as far as the eye could see. "How far does it go?" Agatha asked Helgam.

"To be honest, my dear, I have no idea. Alfred, do you know?"

Alfred shrugged. "I never asked, sorry." He skulked by one of the pillars and looked at the other two. They looked around the darkened area, not sure where to go next.

Helgam sidled up to Alfred. "So, Mr Sulky pants, can you show us the way to the vault?" Alfred, who began to say something but then cut himself short and rolled his eyes. He huffed as he moved and walked south for a while.

An unusual glow slowly started to grow the closer they got towards the vault doors. It emanated in front of them. The detailing of a massive row of identical vault doors, very old, very ominous, but only one with the unusual glow became apparent, almost as if the edge of the door had a grey sheen about it, although it was more like a grey shining outward.

As they came to a halt, Alfred lifted his arm up. "Enter if you dare!" he said in a spooky manner with his head drooped. "Kidding, just be careful, all right? Some things are not what they seem in that room. When I came through the door, I thought my mother was standing and waiting for me here, scared me half to death, although come to think of it, I'm already death so… Well… oh, I think you know what I mean." Alfred turned to the others as he spoke. His confusion put a smile on their faces which they hold fixed in case they started laughing. Knowing full well if they did, he would become the upset sulky boy he was thankfully, becoming less of. All would rather he kept reducing it.

Rolling his eyes at them again, Alfred then moved forward and opened the door for them.

The grey matter of the dimension door looked sealed, and with the table in front, made Helgam only guessed it was for the preparation of what was needed to be done.

To either open or close the door.

Placing the books on the table, Alfred stepped back and resumed leaning against the nearest pillar, checking over his fingernails as Agatha, with her staff, and Helgam with his bag of books, moved forward and began to translate the summoning for the opening. The deciphering with the key previously found in the Myths

315

and Legends book, along with the image on Agatha's staff which Helgam wrote down, only took minutes.

Alfred stood up again to say, "I better check on Charles. Are you two okay here, or do you want to come back with me?"

Helgam looked up from closing the books. "Oh, we will go back up with you, Alfred. I need a few utensils for this and I'm feeling quite peckish. We may need to refuel the old tanks before heading into this." Helgam rubbed his stomach in a distracted manner. Agatha thought to herself it could be more than just hungry. Maybe Helgam was comfort eating, knowing what they all were about to do was incredibly dangerous.

Alfred rolled his eyes and started to walk back towards the way they had come. Helgam pushed the vault shut, smiling a grim smile at Agatha, as they walked back together.

It took a while to get up to the main floor again, although they were greeted by Caelan racing into the castle along with Naga, Fervor and Ants. There were a fair few less of the Fey with them as the smaller group climbed down off their partners and huddled together.

"We got ambushed," Caelan panted. "They took Oxxy and a bunch of Fey, they just threw them into a cage like they were rubbish, the twins, that young one was in the group — we have to get them, we have to get Oxxy back!"

Variwen, having heard the panic, rushed down the stairs to join them. "What's happened? Caelan, who got taken? Calm down and stop yelling. I can't understand anything you are telling me." Variwen looked sternly at Caelan, who was really upset and out of breath.

It was Ants who slowly moved forward. He put his hand on Caelan and began to explain the story. "We all left together to go down the road and gather everything you asked us to. Oxxy was having a great ole time with the twins and the others who went with him. We were to meet back at the entrance of the gates to make sure everything had been collected. It was here that the footman and some daemons for hire, I'd say, were knocking Oxxy out and throwing him into their carriage. The Fey that were with him, like Caelan said, were stuffed into a small cage. We didn't manage to get close enough to help and the carriage rushed off once the Fey cage was thrown into the carriage. They took your young one, Agatha. I'm so sorry. And Danga and his twin, Aril. We think they took four Fey. As soon as it happened, we raced back here. What do we do?"

Ants Caelan and the rest of the group were watching Agatha's response. Panicked, she looked shocked. They were expecting an answer from her. "Well… We need to get them back. You say you saw the footman Hesiss, is that right?" Agatha looked between Caelan and Ants, waiting for an answer.

Caelan stood at full height. Breathing in deeply, he clenched his fists. "We can't go after them. It will endanger the rest of us. We will have to wait and hope they come back. We have come too far gathering everything to have to barter with Caspian and his crowd for the return of the others. I think we should finish what we started with Charles as we are so close." Before he could start talking again, the uproar from the Fey was clearly heard. Caelan even got stabbed in the foot a few times. He held his hands up, looking at them all. "Let me finish, will ya? I said let — me — finish!" Caelan was calm but his voice was deadly. He glared at the Fey, who were silent, immediately.

Caelan knelt down in front of them. He put his hand on the floor, trying to get lower and be level with them, not an easy feat for Chimeon daemon sized at eight feet tall. "I know what I began to say sounded harsh." Caelan held his hand up as some of the Fey became noisy again, waiting for them to stop which only occurred when their leader sidled through and whacked the noisiest one on the head with her staff.

"I know it sounded harsh, but what I was trying to say was, let's get Charles out of the way, get him through and finish it with him. Then we can move to save Oxxy and your kin."

He looks at them all as they mulled it over. Aurelius is shoved forward next to the leader who spoke as Aurelius translated. "We hope that no blood is spilt because of the delay, Caelan. We want our people to be safe. We don't want any more harm bestowed upon us because of you landies." Aurelius looked at Caelan, waiting on his reply so she could translate for her leader, although Caelan looked confused.

"What's landies?"

Aurelius looked up and pointed at him. "A landie is you, Caelan. You're so big to us you could be an island, so we call you all landies."

Caelan, distracted briefly, smiled at this then replied to her comment. "I hope no blood is spilt either, Aurelius. Our Oxxy is with your folk too and, well, he holds a lot more blood than one of you Fey, that's for darn sure." Caelan moved to get up and looked at the group of 'landies'. "Okay, well, we have our plan, yes?"

The group looked at one another. Agatha nodded in agreement.

"All right then, did we get all the items on the list? Helgam, come and check everything." Helgam stepped forward as Aurelius spoke to the remaining Fey from the foraging party. They all began to place their items next to each other. One of them had thankfully grabbed Oxxy and his group's collection. Helgam walked through and checked the list off.

"I think I will go check on Charles, he is going to need his energy, Oxxy, I mean, um…" Knowing her mistake, Variwen was crestfallen as she wouldn't be able to rely on Oxxy. His absence fell greatly on her mind. "Fervor and Alfred, can you please make a simple soup for Charles? Better yet, make a big pot. That way we can all eat and have the energy for what is next." Variwen, still crestfallen at her mistake, slowly walked up the stairs, Fervor and Alfred looked to each other and started to make their way down to the kitchen,

Aurelius went to follow when Agatha called out, "Aurelius, we are going to need you with us. Can you ask your Fey if they can follow Helgam down to the vault with all the ingredients, and we can begin making what is required."

Helgam, however, put his hand up. "No, no, I need a bowl, a spoon, a knife and a pestle and mortar firstly."

Agatha replied, "It's okay, I can get those. Let them help you take everything down, Helgam. Variwen has gone to check on Charles. We need to finish this. We can't have Oxxy and the others out there somewhere being tortured or even killed. I won't have it; I can't let it seep into my mind. These are hard enough as it is, Helgam, please just… One thing at a time, okay?"

Helgam nodded and motioned for the Fey to follow him. They picked the items up and slowly made their way to the door and the awaiting Helgam. Agatha made her way down to the kitchen where Alfred and Fervor were busy making a big pot of soup, using almost everything they could get their hands on. Alfred and Fervor were frantically chopping veggies and getting them in the big pot over the fire.

Agatha collected the items she needed, but before leaving, turned to Fervor. "Am I okay to take these? Do you need them?" Fervor stopped and looked at Agatha.

He stopped chopping and moved to Agatha. He held her shoulders and said, "Agatha, we are here at your service. If you need those for the door, take them. We have plenty here to keep us going. Concentrate on you and Charles and don't forget to have some time with him before he goes through. None of us will know what he will be like when he comes back."

Naga added in, "Yes, when he comes back and what his mind is like when he does is the next big question." Fervor hit him over the back of the head as Agatha showed panic and worry.

"What do you mean? What he will be like when he comes back? How long will it take, what will he come back as?"

Fervor turned to her again with a sympathetic smile. "Agatha, one thing at a time. Take these to Helgam and spend time with Charles. If he is awake, ask him yourself." With that, Fervor rubbed her arm then turned back to his work.

Agatha haphazardly left the kitchen. So many questions were flying through her mind. *What does he mean when he comes back, and what he will be when he does? Why is this making me so nervous?* She was so engrossed in her thoughts she accidentally kicked one of the Fey who had come flying around the corner. He fell backwards, yelling and shaking his fist.

"Oh, I am so sorry!" Agatha, holding all the items, went to bend down when the knife fell out of her hand and narrowly missed the Fey on the ground. More yelling and shaking of his fist were done while Agatha placed the items down on the floor. She removed the knife from its standing position as it fell tip first and stabbed into the flooring. Then she put her hand out for him. He had the grumpiest look, but takes her finger and pulled himself up, rubbing his belly.

"Are you going to be okay? I'm ever so sorry." The Fey rolled his eyes but bowed to her and pointed in the other direction. "I'm not sure what you are meaning." Agatha, confused, waited for another attempt from the Fey. He then pointed to the pile of items and the knife, then at her, then pointed to the floor. "You want me to go down with all the items. Oh right, Helgam sent you!" he nodded. Agatha, picking up all the items again, put her hand out for the Fey who ran up her arm and sat on her shoulder. He grumbled the whole way to the vault room, giving Agatha a brief but welcome distraction as the ever-changing events had many obstacles and things that needed to be overcome.

Helgam collected the items from Agatha. He mumbled a thank you while he stayed focus on the Ledger and the book. "Right, Agatha, when we are ready to go, you will need to stand at the entrance and say the incantation to open the gate. Once the gate is open, we will need to be quick in getting Charles across. It will take him a few seconds to get right the way through, so that will mean we will have to be prepared for anything trying to come out." Helgam turned the page and flipped it back again in quick succession.

"Does it have to be me that opens the gate with the staff?" Agatha looked worried and unsure of herself.

Helgam focused on Agatha now and turned his body towards her. "My dear, you are the gate keeper.

This is your role. I'm sorry, but it has to be you. We will all be right here for you, though, and will protect you as best as we can. Have you seen Charles yet? Is he awake?"

Agatha replied, "I'm about to go there now. Does he need to do anything before heading through?"

"No, no, just make sure he is awake. He needs to eat soon as once I am ready, we will send him through. You understand what happens after, don't you? I mean, once he is there. Have the others told you yet?" Helgam with a concerned look waited for her reply.

As she hesitated and fiddled with her white hair. "They said to ask Charles."

Helgam stepped forward away from the table. He hugged Agatha. "It's probably best it comes from him, my dear." He turned back to the books and was engrossed again in what he was doing, leaving Agatha with mixed emotions hesitant to make a move upstairs.

It was Naga who broke the reverie in Agatha. "Hey, everyone, soup's ready. Charles is awake, and on his way down. He wants to eat with us."

As they all made their way back upstairs, Agatha had a dread growing inside her. It felt like she was walking to a funeral. Her throat was tight, her chest felt heavy and tears were so close to falling she could barely see herself taking one step at a time.

As Agatha reached the top, Charles was waiting by the door. Her heart raced as she saw him. "You're clean!" she exclaimed with a teary smile.

Charles smiled back. Although he was still looking very grey, his bandages were fresh and he looked relatively tidy considering the amount of pain he was in. "Before we go for dinner, Agatha, can we talk?" Agatha nodded as she was unable to speak. Her heart felt like it was breaking into a hundred pieces. Was this the last time she would see Charles?

The rest of the group made their way down to the kitchen, leaving Agatha and Charles slowly making their way to the seating in the entranceway. He eased himself into the seating and put his hand down next to him, motioning for Agatha to do the same. She sat down, briefly looked at him, then turned her face down to her hands.

"I know this is bad," she said with a slight hiccup. "The others keep saying to talk to you and say goodbye. Am I never going to see you again, Charles?" Tears started to fall down her cheeks and onto her hands. Charles put down his crutch and wiped her eyes with his fingers. He cupped her cheek and pulled her face to look at him.

"Variwen gave me a potion to help with the pain to make it easier for me to cross over." Tears were rolling down her face; she looked so broken Charles bent in and kissed her mouth. "I won't be gone forever, Agatha. I will get back to you as soon as I can."

"How will you get back if I'm closing the dimension door? Why are the others telling me to talk to you, why are they saying we need to talk about what you will be like when you get back? How long will it take, Charles? I can't do this without you here." She sobbed even more. Charles brought up his arm and put it around her.

"You are a strong capable woman, Agatha. You don't need me, you never needed me, not like that. I will miss you terribly, my love." He looked her in the eyes as he said the words.

She stared back. "I love you too, Charles. I hate that you're leaving me."

Charles put his hand on her face again. "I'm not leaving you, Agatha. I will never leave you, but I do need to go back for a small while. I need to heal and the only way to do that now is in the other realm."

Agatha stood up. "I know that's what you need to do, Charles. We have no option but to do that. How long will it take?" She looked at him as he patted the seat next to him again. She sat down much like a moody child.

Charles picked up her hand and rubbed his thumb over her knuckles. "Where I am going, my love, is a place that will on one side only take minutes but the other will take months. What could be five minutes in the daemon realm could be a month here. You need to be prepared to be without me by your side for at least six months."

Agatha gasped at the time frame. More tears spilled down her cheeks. "With regards to what the others are saying about my temperament upon my return is that whenever a daemon returns to the human world from the daemon realm, it's like a small strip of their soul is taken, making them a bit meaner when they first come back. The horrors that you see there... It's a wonder anyone comes back sane. But I have a secret. I have a new power I'm going back with." Charles was smiling although Agatha's confusion was obvious. He chuckled bent in and kissed her. "You! You are what will give me the power and the strength to come back. You are my homing beacon, Agatha. I will always want to be where you are."

Agatha sighed and bent her body in towards Charles. "I'm going to miss you so much, Charles. I love you!"

Charles slowly pulled back from her. "See, that's the first time you have said that to me, Aggie, and that is what will carry me through." His smile wanned as noise made them turn towards the archway.

The oak doors had not as yet been repaired. Coming down the driveway at hurtling speed was none other than Caspian's carriage.

"Of course you would turn up, wouldn't you?" Charles mumbled. Agatha heard him and squeezed his hand with hers.

She stood up and walked towards the arch, breathing deep breaths, ready to fight, ready to tear apart the one who had caused so much damage in such a small amount of time in her life. The ground around her began to vibrate as loose rubble and stones began to float up around her. She concentrated on the carriage, waiting for it to slow down, but the closer it got, she noticed the speed did not reduce. Stepping further out into the once pillared verandah area, Agatha had a cold wash over her. The stones dropped around her and it felt as if someone had zapped all her powers from her. The carriage was still maintaining its speed as it started to round the driveway. The carriage door swung open and a box was thrown towards Agatha, who was distracted by the box. The carriage continued making a full circle of the driveway and hurtled back down and out of the property. It was so quick Agatha barely had time to recover from the drain of her powers. Fumbling for the box, Agatha screamed as blood covered her hands. She ripped the box open and screamed again. For inside the package was a jar and inside that jar was blood. Some had seeped out when it was thrown but it wasn't cracked. It was packaged with care.

Charles managed to get to her before the others who were in the kitchen and had heard the commotion. He sat down and with one hand managed to open the box further and pull the jar out.

He vomited all over himself, holding the jar away from him and looking away. The jar now in full sight made Agatha scream a bloodcurdling scream. Caelan was first on scene running towards Charles and the jar. Fervor and Naga ran outside and checked the area for any who might not be welcome.

"Oh God." Caelan placed the jar behind the box so it was not in immediate sight. The Fey were crowding around the archway on full alert. It was Variwen who marched forward to check the jar. As soon as she realised what it was, she turned and walked towards the Fey leader and Aurelius.

"I'm so sorry, my dear, dear, friends. Your Fey that were captured did not make it." The leader ran out with her staff towards the jar. Caelan put his foot in front of it to block the full extent of what was in it.

Aurelius yelled, "We demand to see them."

"Aurelius, not like this, you don't want to see them like this." Caelan was almost grey, an unlikely feat for someone who was orange.

"Then tell us, how have they come?" Aurelius stood next to her leader.

Caelan went on to say, "Friends, what has happened here is a tragedy, it is not something that should be seen but should be buried and time should be taken to grieve. Your Fey that were taken are dead. They have died in a gruesome manner that no one should witness. I beg you, please do not look. It has already made Charles sick, I'm not far off. I think we should put it back into the box and bury what is left of them." Agatha began to cry again, Charles was also crying, and the Fey behind them were angry, confused or crying.

It was not a good sight.

Taking a deep breath, Caelan sat on the ground and put his hand out for Aurelius and the Fey leader. he spoke in a softer tone explaining the situation. "The Fey that were returned looked as though they had been blended up and returned in a jar. There were body parts floating in what looked to be blood and a clear syrup, an obviously dramatic way of displaying what had been done."

Naga looked to Caelan. "What do you think has happened to Oxxy?" His worried face moved from what could be seen of the jar and Caelan's face. Caelan remained blank with his expression. "We need to sort Charles first. Get him to return, then we can plan whatever needs to be done."

The Leader still on Caelan's hand was yelling and jumping up and down. Aurelius, wincing at the response, waited for her to finish. Aurelius looked at Caelan and calmly stated, "Our fearless leader wants the head of the thing that did this to our kind. We want recompense; we want revenge and most of all we want the same to happen to them as they have done to us."

Agatha sat down next to Caelan's hand. "I will help you however we can. We need to plan this properly or more will die. I don't want any more of us to die. Can you help us?" Agatha did it in a way that made the Fey want what she wanted. They bowed to her, including their leader.

"What has happened can never be undone," Aurelius states. "We must sort your lover, then move to strike!" Aurelius hit her fist into her palm and the uproar of the Fey behind them was loud and clear. The adrenaline from this catastrophe flowed through all that are present.

Helgam moved to Charles. "Do you still want to refuel before we send you back, Charles? It takes a lot out of you going through the door."

"Yes, I remember it well, my friend," Charles replied. He put his good arm out and Helgam helped him stand.

Passing the crutch to him, Helgam responded, "Can you eat, my boy? You need all the energy you can get."

Charles held his hand up. "With what we have just witnessed, I don't think I could look at soup and enjoy it."

Helgam rubbed his back. "Well then, I guess we had best not waste any more time then."

Caelan called for the others. "Fey, for those that know Charles, you are more than welcome to say your goodbyes. Whilst we head down to the vault, we will need everyone to stand guard in case something tries to come through." Caelan put the leader on the floor along with Aurelius, who translated Caelan's information.

Some Fey stepped forward and bowed to Charles. He smiled. "I won't be gone forever. I will be back before you know it." He looked at Agatha, who was crestfallen, Agatha wanted more than anything for more time with him. But their time had run out. It needed to be now.

As he made his way back to the archway, Charles beckoned Agatha to walk with him. Agatha placed her hand on his back. She leaned in and kissed him as they walked. "The time will fly, my love. You are my strength. Be my strength and show me and everyone here how amazing you can be. They know you are the one who literally holds the staff. You are meant to be the Lady of this town, you are the Gatekeeper. What else do you need to be? I will count down every minute I'm away."

Agatha turned to Charles, shocked. "How will you be able to come back if the door isn't open?"

He stopped for a moment and thought. "Helgam, Helgam!" Charles called as they entered the entranceway of the castle.

Helgam rushed over to Charles. "Are you okay?"

"Yes, yes, I'm okay, Helgam, but how will I be able to make it back if you close the door?"

Helgam stopped and furrowed his brow. "Well, if I work out roughly when six months is, I can open the door then."

"What if I don't make it back then?"

"Well, we will have to open the gate every six months until you return, how's that?" Helgam moved forward again, yelling a bunch of commands to the Fey, and to Naga he called out, "Naga, I need more paper downstairs. I need to make some calculations before this can work." Naga rushed off towards Helgam's room to gather more paper. "He can meet us downstairs. I guess we had better finish the setup, hey? No time for soup now. I don't think I could eat it after that delivery."

Helgam sniffed. "It's a shame. It smells delicious too."
Looking around, Helgam noticed all the people
watching him for the next step.

"Well, why are you staring? We have work to do
and you all need to be ready for what might come
through. Charles, be careful on those steps." Helgam
watched Charles move towards the doorway. The Fey
all raced to the door. They went fast past Charles, being
careful of where he puts his crutches as he made his way
down the staircase. Agatha followed close behind while
the others slowly overtook Charles.

It wasn't long before it was just Charles and Agatha
left on the staircase making their way down. Charles
was panting as they reached the first level and Agatha
made him stop for a breath. "Are you sure you don't
want to eat anything before you go across?"

Charles looked and smiled. The effort to get to this
level had completely wiped him out. He felt his arm
throbbing and aching. With each movement, the bite
marks pulled he felt it tearing his skin further. "It's
okay, I'm okay, the potion is wearing off. They don't
last long, unfortunately." Charles smiled a waxen smile;
he put his hand up to Agatha's face and nearly
overbalanced. Agatha speedily stepped forward and
caught him teetering on the edge of a step. Charles
yelped in pain as the place where she had grabbed him
was right on a bite mark. Moving to balance himself
again, he gently pulled her hand away from his side. The
pain slowly ebbed away.

Agatha was tearful again. "Shouldn't I come with you? What if you don't heal and you die, Charles? I will never know. What if you get worse or something happens to you?" Agatha sobbed as Charles put his arm around her.

"My love, you are my strength. Be strong for me so I can be strong for you. Let's get downstairs. The sooner I leave, the sooner I can find my way back to you." He smiled as she nodded and helped him slowly down the staircase.

Everyone was waiting for them. The table was all set up, and the Fey were all standing at attention. Variwen was next to Helgam, both full of concentration while Caelan and Alfred were trying not to look. Fervor stood at attention, nodding his head slightly to Charles as he slowly got closer to the gateway. Charles put himself into place and waited for the others. Agatha collected her staff and with one more look at Charles, who nodded at her to begin, she started the incantations Helgam had set up for her to use. Variwen moved forward and whilst Agatha spoke, she opened the bolted doors enclosing the dimension door. The grey matter was eerily silent as the glow crept further into the room.

Charles began to cough uncontrollably. He grabbed his stomach. Agatha hesitated as the noise, once so silent and calming, became a loud and intense whooshing noise, cracking like lightning streaks through the room. the grey matter sent out sparks to match the noise, almost like a delayed visual effect. A separate booming noise was heard above great crashes and cracks in the ceiling.

Variwen coaxed Agatha to keep going, yelling, "No matter what, don't stop!"

Helgam placed the ingredients around Charles and the door at a certain point in the incantations Agatha was repeating. A flash of grey matter hit Charles, who was wheezing, holding a fist to his chest. The once calm but worn-out Charles from just before was now a panicked, exhausted and almost scared an immortal, facing what not many of his kind faced — death.

Alfred went to move forward to Charles but was held back by Caelan, who shook his head. "We need to check upstairs Alfred. Something's happening and we need to stand guard." Alfred nodded and Caelan motioned to Helgam that they were going up. Some of the Fey noticed also and a group paired off with the two to check the commotion.

Wind swirled around Charles, blasting his damp wet hair this way and that. He shivered as a crack of lightning hit him in the chest that came out of the door. Bending over in immense pain, he turned his head to Variwen who nodded her head, motioning for him to move forward. Shuffling forward, Charles took a last look at Agatha. The pain was coursing through his body as another strike of grey lightning hit him.

It shoved him backwards and he yelled in pain. The noise of his yell was eaten up by the winds. Agatha covered her eyes, carrying on saying the incantation, tears rolling down her face. The anger and frustration of the situation created an overwhelming impulse, making lights throb through Agatha's body as she pushed on.

Agatha could see Charles was hurt and screamed as she held her staff up. The pressure and weight of the staff became overwhelming as the opening of the door began to show. She stepped back and pushed the staff back up again. A connection between the staff and the door appeared as the door opens further. Agatha, blinded by the wind rushing towards her, screamed the last of the incantation. Her shoes were slipping on the concrete as the power and pressure from the staff pushed her even further. She was now squashed against the table, thankful that she was still able to hold her position as the door slowly opened even further.

She briefly looked behind her to a scene that shocked her. Something had chased Caelan and Alfred back down the stairs and a battle was ensuing right behind her. A giant behemoth-type monster was swinging its arms this way and that as Fey climbed and covered it with their little bodies as they attacked. Helgam and Variwen were throwing potions and many other magical items towards it to fend it off. The whirl and swirl of winds made the Fey not properly attached to the Behemoth fly further away from the group, only to crawl their way back and attach themselves to it again. Caelan was throwing red hot clay and melting and pulling apart pillars to throw at the monster. It was absolutely chaos but the chaos gave Agatha new strength. She pushed the staff back towards the door as the hole slowly grew even further. Taking one step at a time, she made herself even with Charles, who was crouched near the ground holding onto part of the uneven flooring. His crutch had flown away and from her brief glance at the Behemoth, was being used to wipe away the Fey off his body.

Charles looked up at Agatha as she looks down to him. A small hole in the floor was inches away from Agatha and she used her ebbing strength to push the staff into the hole. It was amazing that the staff fit. The relief on her face was visible even to Charles who, with one eye open, watched Agatha and her pulsing light going through her, like waves on the sea. The speed of the light began to speed up as she pushed the staff in a vertical position in front of the door.

After what seemed an eternity, the door finally finished opening. The winds slowed right down and the noise was replaced by the battle behind them.

Charles scrabbled to a standing position as a flying boulder headed their way. Looking back, they were both shocked as it hurtled towards Charles. It was the size of a carriage wheel and the last Agatha saw was his look of shock at her as the boulder crashed into Charles. Agatha screamed as the boulder and Charles were hurled through the dimension door and Agatha was left stunned and alone in the room with the door. "He's gone!" Agatha mumbled in a trance.

Turning from the opening, the battle was shown now in front of her. Helgam was scrabbling towards her, ducking and weaving to miss all the rubble and bodies being thrown this way and that.

"Shut the door!" he yelled at Agatha.

She couldn't hear him as she slowly walked towards the basement level out of the vault room. Helgam yelled again as he reached her. "Agatha, shut the bloody door!" Helgam shook her awake from her trance but her eyes were still white and with one flick of the staff, Agatha's motionless face provided the conclusion to the madness. The door shut in an instant, the Behemoth stopped fighting, and the Fey that had been climbing over it were thrown off. It rose up into the air along with the Fey weightless, it struggled and swung it's arms trying to get back to the ground.

All looked towards Agatha as she continued to walk towards the stairway, her body flickered in and out of vision, with each step. The Behemoth tried to move again and a sudden snap back into reality made Agatha beam completely whiteness out from her body. The whole basement was encased in blinding, white light. No one could see anything. The Behemoths' grotesque yell caught Agatha as she started to floated upwards, holding the staff next to her, she uttered in a quiet tone, "Be gone" and the Behemoth managed a strangled cry a before it dissolved into nothing.

The echoes of screams as he dissolved in front of everyone's eyes came from Agatha as the room went back to the dank, dark way it previously had been.

The Fey held in mid-air held in place by Agatha's power were released from her grip and dropped to the floor, they brushed themselves down, picked up their weapons and watched Agatha for any instructions, but none came.

The basement was in ruins from the fight, load bearing columns were crumbling but no one paid attention. It was Agatha who made everyone hold their breath, they didn't know if she was finished, they didn't know if she would kill them next.

She was, still a stark white, Agatha floated silently to the stairway, as all looked on. She left the battle and glided up and away from the basement. The group were left in stunned silence.

Oxxy was missing, the Fey that had been captured were dead and waiting to be buried and Charles was gone, sent hurtling into the daemon realm, by a boulder. Wilderfort Castle and its occupants were left in utter confusion. And Agatha the half Choler, no one knew how to care for her or help, she was alone and that feeling swamped every particle of her being.

The end.